Haven

Dria Andersen

Dedication

To my husband who was my sounding board, my cheerleader, my critique partner, and all the things I needed to finish this project. I appreciate every hour, every word of input and most of all, your unwavering support.

To my family who had to deal with mommy being on in another world for hours at a time. Thank you for your patience.

To my sister Tina, who reads everything I write and gives me honest feedback and encouragement, thank you mucho mucho. I appreciate your continued support and cheerleading!

Thank you to every fan who continues to stick with me while I tell the stories playing in my head. I appreciate each and every one of you.

Preface

It has taken me a few years to work on this book. I researched gods and goddesses from all over Africa to bring my story to life. Some of the names have been used as they appear in their legends, and some have been changed to fit into the world and mythos I've built. It has been done with the utmost respect for the culture, and I hope you enjoy it.

Contents

Chapter 1

BLACK BOOTS, check.

Short, tight black skirt, check.

Liliana adjusted her corset for maximum cleavage and took a deep breath. She pulled the heavy cross on the end of her chain up to her painted lips for a kiss, praying she could pull this off, her sister's life depended on it.

The black building loomed, and trepidation skittered down her spine. This was the last club on her list, the last link to her sister. Four years, and countless clubs later, Liliana was exhausted. One way or the other she had to get answers. She didn't think she could keep up the charade any longer. Hunters dogged her heels in every city she'd stopped. She'd barely escaped New York. Hopefully, though, she was hours ahead of them and would have the time she needed.

She took a deep breath and forced the tension from her body. Loose and limber, that was the only way to get through this last stop. Fluffing out her short curls, she began her sashay toward the club known as Haven.

Getting into this one had proved the hardest yet. As it well should, it was the Amanda's headquarters, security was tight. She'd managed to wheedle a guest pass from a guy who owed her a favor. He made it clear when he gave her the guest pass that he didn't know her if something went down tonight.

Liliana blew out a disgusted breath. "Coward," she muttered.

It wasn't a big surprise, Sergio's main motivation was money. He held no loyalty to her, or any of his other customers. If the situation turned to shit he would've been useless to her in a fight anyway. It didn't matter. She could take care of herself, had been doing a fine job of it for years. Though, the years were catching up to her.

Her heels crunched loudly on the gravel in the makeshift parking lot. It had taken her an hour to drive outside of the city of Atlanta to reach this Haven. It looked like an abandoned factory, and were it not for the number of cars in the parking lot, she'd have thought Sergio had set her up. A small line formed outside of the club, which didn't surprise her. It was the same at every other Haven she'd visited. There were no lights, no music, nothing to betray the building for what it was, yet a line of eager people waited to get in. Liliana ignored the wolfish stares and catcalls as she walked to the back of the line.

The bouncer at the door was a huge linebacker of a man, tall and wide. His dark brown skin was smooth, his muscular shoulders and arms gleaming in the moonlight. The sleeveless shirt he wore did nothing to hide his built chest and flat abs, nor did it disguise the power pouring from him. Liliana shivered as she received the brunt of his gaze. His eyes were hazel with a circle of glowing green ringing the irises. He checked IDs of the guests as they passed, but his gaze kept straying to her. By the time she reached the front of the line, her hands were shaking. No matter how many times she went through this, fear of discovery dried her mouth.

"ID." His voice was deep, a rumble of thunder on the clear summer night.

Liliana fumbled with her small clutch pulling out her pass. The bouncer eyed the pass, and then eyed her, his chiseled features serious. He spared a cursory glance at her bare arms then back up to her face. She fought not to squirm under his scrutiny. Finally, after several tense moments, he handed her the pass.

"You got trouble written all over you, shorty," he told her. "I ain't in the mood for trouble, ya' hear?"

With a sharp nod, she moved quickly into the building. She shuffled behind a group of giggling females down a dark hallway. The music was dim, but it shook the building. A door opened and her eyes widened. Music filled up space in the hallway rattling her chest. She went through the door and stopped in shock. Liliana's skin tightened, tingled, and an odd hum moved across her nerve endings. Lust was the setting for tonight and if her body was any indication, it was ripe in the air. It was the magic of Haven at play, but damn if she could stop her body from responding.

The place was cavernous, not at all what she was expecting from its appearance on the outside. Though the door she'd come in was street level, where she stood was at least one or two hundred yards above the dance floor. The metal grate of the floor allowed her to see the dancers. The spotlights surrounding them were various shades of red, brushing over the crowd, painting the half-naked bodies in its rosy shades.

She walked over to the railing and stared down at the crush of bodies undulating and swaying to the heavy bass line of the rap music blaring from the speakers. She looked up and spied railing that indicated at least three more levels above the main floor. Goosebumps chased up her arm as she thought of what went on in those upper levels. It seemed this Haven spared no expense. From the smooth hardwood floors to the silk damask covering the booths surrounding the dance floors, opulence was the name of the game.

She walked over to the bar that lined the wall, her hips swaying to music, that on a normal day she would never listen to. Hungry stares followed her movements as she climbed onto a barstool and crossed her legs. A shiver worked down her spine at the friction the motion caused between her legs.

She panicked at the lack of control over her body and quickly erected mental shields she'd spent her life perfecting. But try as she might, the magic beat against her tired body, battering her shields.

Fighting proved to be useless.

Every sweep of eyes across her body was a caress, pushing her purpose further to the back of her mind. If she didn't get a hold of herself it would be near impossible to carry out her plan in here tonight.

She leaned over the bar, motioning for the bartender. Her lips kicked up into a seductive smile before she could catch herself. The bartender was fine. Shirtless, his brown skin gleamed under the light.

He swaggered over to her and flashed straight white teeth. "What can I get you?"

"Rum and coke." The alcohol probably wasn't a good idea, but she couldn't muster up enough alarm to change her order.

Whatever magic was in the air was powerful. Sexual energy pulsed through her body, every beat of the music throbbed against her skin. The other Havens she visited were nothing like this one. Liliana reached for her drink gratefully, and tossed a twenty on the bar, waving away the change. The bartender gave her a smile that promised he would be back and went to serve the next customer.

Liliana rolled the cold glass against her chest to cool off. She brought it to her lips and gulped down half the glass's contents.

Big mistake.

Heat bloomed in her chest, burning a path down to her stomach. A pleasant buzz suffused her mind and she relaxed. It had been months, maybe even years since the last time she'd felt able to do so. Downing the rest of her drink, a side of Liliana she'd kept dormant for years awakened.

Awakened and decided that tonight was a night for impulses.

Thoughts of her sister surfaced, guilt niggled, but another wave of magic washed through her and swept worries about Kita away. Liliana closed her eyes, and breathed deeply, valiantly making the effort to fight the magic. The tangy scent of sex, the mixture of perfumes, musk, and sweat assaulted her senses.

Her nature rose, the power she'd purposely dampened surfaced. The urge to do something reckless rose and took over.

"You look amazing."

Liliana turned to face the voice shouting to be heard over the music and smiled. Wearing a pair of tight leather pants, and tight black t-shirt, he was certainly great to look at. When was the last time she'd fed? Months, at least. Surely once she had, her senses would return, the shields righting themselves.

She cocked her head to the side… he'd do. "Let's dance."

***

LEO SLAMMED THE DOOR to his brother's office thoroughly lectured and two kinds of pissed. He'd just spent the last thirty minutes having his ass chewed by his brother Xavier, same subject as always: Leo took too many risks, he never checked in, and on and on. His brother was a champion worrier and an even better nag. His long legs quickly put distance between the two of them.

"Damn it. Why you gotta be so hard-headed? The shit you do is unnecessary, Leo." Xavier shouted down the hall after him. Work in the dimly lit caverns halted and the banging in the kitchen next to them stopped as the employees paused to stare at the spectacle that was sure to come. Fighting between him and his brothers was nothing new.

He stopped and took a deep breath, wrestling his already shredded patience. He turned and faced his older brother. "As long as the job is done, the how shouldn't matter. I've been hunting Demis on Earth for over a century."

"That's not the point." The sharp planes of Xavier's face were illuminated in the hallway sconce above his office door. It highlighted the furious expression darkening his eyes.

"What is the point, bro? I don't need a lecture every time I take a risk, it's my job. You wanna take it from me?" It was an empty threat. No one could do Leo's job and they both knew it. He was Death's Messenger, responsible for hunting down and taking Demis sentenced to death to Azrael, their Hell. The things he saw and did…No. No one could do his job. Not and stay sane.

A small stab of guilt hit him at the hurt that flickered in Xavier's eyes.

"You know what, Leo. Fuck you. Do what you do." The door slammed behind his brother.

Leo shook his head and headed back down the hallway spoiling for a fight. He growled at one of the bartenders backing out of the supply closet taking pleasure in the fear that leaped into the servant's eyes. He snatched a bottle of liquor from him and opened it with his teeth. He took a long drag, thankful for the potent heat.

"No, you know what, Leo? I'm not done." Xavier barked from behind him.

Leo kept walking, refusing to face his brother. He lifted his middle finger instead. Xavier cursed, and the employees in the hallway snickered. Again, same old fight, different day. Haven's employees were used to the screaming matches, and they found a great amount of amusement in it.

Leo gave them a dark look that had them scrambling. Yeah, they were amused, but they still had a healthy fear for Death's Messenger. Glasses clinked as the busboys rushed out of his path.

He knew flipping his brother off would have Xavier in a rabid state of mind. He needed to get lost, and he knew the perfect place. His brother refused to come out during club hours, so the dance floor would be a safe enough place to hide. It was Saturday, Sensual Saturday to be exact, he could lose himself in a beautiful woman and by the time he got home, his brother would be over it.

He stomped down the corridor and rounded the corner. He took the stairs two at a time to reach the entertainment level. He nodded to the bouncer at the door separating the back rooms from the rest of the club. Opening the gilded door, lust immediately swamped him. He drew the energy in with a deep breath, taking it and feeding it through his body. Instantly he thrummed with power. His vision became sharper, every shadow dissipated as his gaze swept the dance floor. He knew his normal gray eyes would be silver warning others a predator was at large.

Leo smiled as hands brushed his body, women on either side drawn to the danger, as he sauntered through the crowd. He laughed outright as one bold woman reached over and cupped his crotch. He grabbed her hand and twirled her around. Dipping her low, he kissed her deeply, drinking in the lust she fed him. He pulled back a moment later and moved her to the side. He wanted a willing female, but it was in his nature to hunt.

He so enjoyed the chase.

The woman pouted prettily, dismissing Leo as easily as he had her. There would be many takers for what she offered tonight.

He bopped through the dance floor letting the music enter his head and drive out the B.S. of the day. A woman backed into him, her hips grinding into his and Leo threw up his hands to give access. Her pants were skin-tight, the rest of her covered by an intricate web of string, barely hiding the good bits. Leo grabbed her waist and started dancing. Sensual Saturday was in full swing at Haven, and he would enjoy the lust that filled the air.

A fine mist sprayed from the ceiling as electronica blasted over the speakers. To the left and right of him, both women and men were shedding their tops on the crowded dance floor. Leo felt the power spike in the club, the lust doubling. It swept away inhibitions while those who could, fed off the energy. He looked up at the mirrored windows of the private rooms lining the third floor. Behind nearly all of them stood powerful beings taking the energy in, and pushing out just enough magic to sustain the sexual haze the humans reveled in. Judging by the crowd, the Demis would be well fed this night. And the humans…

The majority of them would get lucky. High off the lust and magic, they would leave the club and have the best night of their lives. It was how they kept the club packed, people clamored to get into Haven hoping to recreate that night over and over again.

Leo removed his wet shirt and tossed it into the crowd. The Roots song 'Rising Up' came on and he let the music and magic sweep him away.

" " *I got something you been waiting for* " " Chrisette Michelle sang, her voice echoing through his mind right as a vision with short-cropped black curls snagged his attention.

Curvy hips moved and swayed captivating Leo. Her short skirt and tank top displayed brown skin the color of fine whiskey and twice as potent. He hardened instantly, his erection swelling, pushing against his leather pants. Her eyes lifted and Leo was trapped in their depths. Tilted up at the corner, her eyes held just the right amount of mischief, of daring. It was a siren's call and one Leo knew he had to answer.

She lowered her eyes and turned her back to him, hips working, tempting him closer. A coy peek from over her shoulder tightened his dick, and dried his mouth. She ran her fingers through her short hair, her full lips lifted in a smile.

Yeah, she knew he was feeling her.

He moved closer, shoving humans aside as he made a beeline to her. She turned around colliding with his chest. Her hand lifted, touched, tracing the thin trail of black hair leading down his abs.

No words were exchanged, their eyes met, burned, heightening the awareness between them. Heat pooled in his abdomen as his hands skimmed the smooth skin of her narrow waist, a light caress that aroused him further. Her skin was silk, warming under his touch. Her mouth opened on a sigh and he took full advantage, stealing her lips in a kiss.

Ask him how they got to the hotel, he didn't know.

How they got a room? Hell if he could remember.

When their clothes came off? Damned if he cared.

Oh, but the feel of her when he slid in. Oh Gods, he could write a book about it. The way the walls of her sex clenched around him, pulling him deeper. The greedy nips of her teeth on his shoulders.

Yeah, he remembered that.

Little puffs of airbrushed his ear as her whispered cries urged him on. Ahh, the silky skin of her thighs as they slid against his. Long legs wrapped around his waist, heels digging into his back as she met his thrust, he remembered that too. Memories of the way her back arched, her breasts lifted in the air, her lush mouth parted in ecstasy would be burned into his brain.

He would never forget her scent as long as he lived. Peony and moonlight, he'd never look at nighttime the same way again. Leo clenched his teeth, squeezed his eyes shut as he fought to keep his human skin. His hands tightened on her hips as his beast fought for dominance.

Did they exchange words at all? They had to have spoken, right? None of that mattered when her nails scraped the back of his neck. Nothing but the heat engulfing his shaft, the fire rushing down his spine. He was lost, his mind gone, sensations, smells, sounds, his only focus. Sweat dripped into his eyes, down his back as he picked up speed, desperate thrusts into her eager body. Magic from Haven flowed between them. Light painted the walls, the ceiling. Color swirled between them and for a moment their minds touched. He took in that energy and strength flooded his body, adding to his high.

Her eyes opened and he drowned. The green orbs pulled him under. He sipped her gasp of surprise, licked her bottom lip before sucking on it. His tongue explored her mouth, learning every crevice. Her pleasure was there in her mind, an open book to him as the spell pulsed, heightened, opening her further to his exploration. He drew the magic into his body and used it to feed the erotic images in her mind.

Her thighs tightened, the slick heat of her sex squeezed him and her orgasm tore through them both. He drove in deep one last stroke before his world exploded. His heart stopped, his body flew apart as pleasure he'd never experienced washed through him. He collapsed.

"My God." She whispered.

He grunted, rolling her over before he crushed her under his weight. His hands roamed her back, he burrowed his head into her neck and he inhaled, pulling her scent into his lungs.

"Name," he whispered hoarsely. "What's your name?" He had to have her again. His beast was sated, well-fed from their magic, but the man…the man wanted her still. She was a drug in his system, a heady combination that pushed caution and good sense to the back of his brain.

She wiggled her hips and his stomach tightened, his erection springing back to life, just that fast.

She moaned, her lips trailing a path across his collar bone. She bit his ear, pulling the lobe into her mouth. "Destiny."

He guided her hips until her wet center was positioned over his throbbing shaft. He entered her in a single stroke.

Destiny.

Yeah, he would remember Destiny. He was sure of it.

Chapter 2

HE WATCHED HER SILENTLY FOR HOURS, her face alternating from frustration to finally, triumph. She'd found his gift to her. A dangerous gift, one he would surely pay for if discovered but made worthwhile by the look on her face. Her dark eyes were lit with victory and the wind around him in her orchard picked up its speed in response to her excitement. There were so few gifts one could give a goddess, if he had to pay for this one, so be it. Especially since Oya guarded the souls he needed.

Melodrama aside, the future of the Earth depended on him getting those souls. He'd noticed blank spots forming around the Earth and its many realms. Blocking the sight of his many responsibilities. There was only one being he knew that left a trail of voids in its wake. He squelched the shaft of fear skittering down his back. If Ofeere was stirring…

The wind died as suddenly as it'd started and she swung around to face him. Her beauty was renowned and not lost on him. Her long, oval face glowed with her power, her large brown eyes displaying her conflicting emotions. Her full lips firmed, straightened into a taut line as her expression closed down. She gathered herself to her full height of six feet.

"Rugaba, you did this?" she pointed to the well she used as a window into the world.

He leaned casually on the tree next to him. "You know I cannot get involved, rewa." It was as close to a lie as he could come. Any word from his mouth became truth and he had worked too hard for that gift to see it wiped away by a lie.

She tipped her head to the side, her long black hair trailing her shoulder, she saw through his omission easily. "You cannot become involved, yet you harbor those abominations." Her eyes were hard, mouth set in an angry line.

"I only police them, mi okan, it has kept your warriors safe these last few centuries." It was an argument they had frequently.

Reigning in the Ajo was the only thing he could give her after his betrayal. Yet she didn't see it that way. The Ajo were stealing power from her temple, she wanted them wiped from the Earth. She'd never understood that the Ajo were the price for her interference on Adro. The primal source always demanded balance. The balance was why he'd come today, why he'd risked his gift to her.

"They have broken their treaty with you, yet I am bound by careless words I said in anger." The wind around them picked up, bending the trees in her anger. Her normally covered hair whipped around her body in a sensual dance. They stared at each other, trees lining the worn path on either side of them sending leaves dancing between them. Always a showdown between them.

Rugaba straightened, unfazed, her anger nothing new to him. She turned away from him, his first point in this round.

"You are a goddess, Oya, yet even you must answer to a higher power." He kept his voice calm. He couldn't afford to anger her further, not when he'd come to ask a favor. It was time to release the Kokoro souls, and only she had the power to do it.

She turned to him, her expression sly as she walked closer to him.

"I have all three women in position, and thanks to someone's help, the amulet is in play. Are you here to stop me?" Only an inch separated them, her scent wrapped around him, tempting him to close the inch between them.

He stepped back, his body burning for her. "As you have said, they broke the treaty. The Amanda won't stand in the way of your hunters."

She nodded, a smile blooming on her face. "Then I will release the souls you need."

His relief was immediate. He didn't bother trying to figure out how she knew what he'd come for. The souls would be reborn, that was all that mattered. "Thank you, rewa."

Her eyes softened, and for a moment and like every time he saw her, regret was a weight on his chest.

"In truth, Rue, I released the souls centuries ago, you didn't have to risk you and yours for this boon you have given me." She said softly as he turned to leave.

Rugaba fought down the triumph that moved through him at her words. He didn't trust her expression. "You released the souls already?" he wanted to be sure.

"They needed to be mature for your purpose. No matter what is between us, I could not risk Earth in this coming war. The voids are already spreading."

"Then it will be soon?" His mind spun with details. There was much he needed to do. She was right about the voids, and having the souls already mature was a huge boon.

"I want no part of this war."

Rugaba chuckled. "But you are so good at war, mi okan." She was after all a war goddess.

Her lips turned up slightly. "I fight to protect what is mine."

"Then prepare yours for what is to come." Right now the blank spots on the Earth were small, but history dictated that the voids would grow bigger, the more Ofeere escaped his prison.

Her face sobered instantly. Rue's hand reached out instinctively to comfort her, but she stepped back quickly, her face as torn as he felt.

"Rewa," he whispered. His betrayal stood as a wall between them. One her anger would not allow him to scale. The time for should've could've had passed though, and now they were stuck in this dance.

"Careless whispers," she said sadly.

Rue nodded and turned to leave, he accomplished what he came to do, there were no other words needed. He quickly transported himself from Alafia to Earth. He had work to do, and according to Oya, not much time to prepare. His first trip would be to the Mina, he needed to know who the souls were. It would be too much for Oya to give him, the fact that they had already been reborn was gift enough. As soon as he found out who they were, he would send the Amanda to protect them. The Earth could not survive another war.

***

Five days after her disastrous attempt to investigate Haven, frustrated and dusty, Liliana was shoved into a plush office and met with a suspicious, near hostile glare.

"Look what I found snooping around outside," her captor announced.

She pulled her arm from his hand and adjusted her t-shirt and jeans. Instinct told her trying to break into Haven was a bad idea, but she'd felt guilty from her failed attempt the other night.

Caught trying to pick one of the locks at the back door, the bouncer let it be known with a shake of his head that he didn't want to hear anything she had to say.

He'd silently led her through the club that had been transformed. Gone was the dance floor from a week ago. Large, comfortable-looking sofas and chairs were scattered across the floor, and the place looked for all intents and purposes like the private club it claimed to be. The loud rap music was replaced by the quiet murmurs of conversation and soft jazz. The bouncer led her down three flights of stairs, through a dark hallway, and into this large office. Her sneakers were soundless on the gleaming wood floor as she was led and shoved into a leather wing chair. She took in the pale gray walls covered with bold landscapes and looked for an exit. She pinned her eyes to the painting of what looked like the coast of Chiuta, the Cagyn realm. It was a deserted beach scene that captured that perfect moment right before sunrise. The ocean met the edge of the black sand, some of the grains sparkling as they caught the growing light. She wished she was there, watching the sky change from purple to blue as the sun rose. She'd been to Chiuta once when she was a child, too young to appreciate its beauty. Now after years on Adro, she longed for a glimpse of the Demi realm. Any glimpse, even if it wasn't of her native Legba.

"Close the door Fallon, so we can talk to our guest uninterrupted."

Liliana watched the man behind the desk warily. His eyes were hard, icy hazel ringed with green, startling in his dark brown face. His sharp cheekbones and squared chin made him impossibly handsome. The snub nose softened his features enough to make him semi-approachable. The power emanating from him was intimidating, but not threatening. He sat back in his chair and stared at Liliana, regarding her curiously. The silk shirt he wore was open at the neck and rumpled, she guessed he'd either slept in it or had not yet fallen asleep.

"What's your name?" he asked her.

The door closed with an ominous click and she flinched. The one called Fallon walked around her and sat on the edge of the large teak desk, a smirk on his face. She recognized him as the bouncer from the other night.

"I knew you were trouble, shorty." He shook his head.

"Name, lady," the man behind the desk demanded.

"Destiny." The lie was automatic, one she used often.

Fallon snorted. "Apt."

"Let's try this again, I'm Xavier and you are?" Xavier leaned back in his chair, tucking his hands behind his head. It brought attention to the muscles bunched underneath his shirt. He was a sexy man.

Those damn Cagyns.

Her research told her the head of the Amanda was one of the creatures. Sex on a stick, the whole lot of them. The corner of his mouth lifted in a small smirk as he caught her looking at him.

Liliana opened her mouth, another lie at the tip of her tongue. A growl from behind the desk closed her mouth with a snap.

"Please don't let another lie slip past your lips, Trouble." Fallon crossed his arms over his chest, amusement dancing in his eyes.

"Look, clearly I made a mistake. If you let me go-"

"Whoa, whoa, with all that extra, lady. Let's get your name first, then I'll decide if you can go." Xavier's eyes speared hers.

Her mind worked furiously, trying to figure a way out of this mess. Could she tell him why she came? Why not? The worse he could do was, tell her to get lost. No, the worst he could do was send her home. She shuddered.

No.

She'd kept ahead of hunters for over three years, no way would she give up now. She couldn't afford to be sent home yet.

Before she could make up a story, two hard raps sounded from the door. Liliana's stomach dropped, then clenched in hard lust. Her body betrayed her as another knock sounded.

Crap!

He was here.

Her five-day respite was over. She knew who was on the other side of that door. She didn't have to see him, she could feel him. Feel his energy behind the door, calling to her, pulling responses from her body she desperately tried to deny. Fallon's eyebrow rose in question, a moment before the door was opened.

He walked into the office, though walk didn't accurately describe the swagger he had. It was more like predatory stalking. His muscular body moved with a sensual and dangerous grace. She suppressed a moan as her body heated, tuning itself to him, reaching for him even as her head screamed in denial. His eyes narrowed as he spied her.

"Not now, Leo," Xavier told him.

So that was his name. Leo. She whispered his name, tasting it on her tongue. She didn't bother asking the other night, and in her mad dash to leave the room, waking him to find out was out of the question.

"Now is probably a good time, Xavier," Fallon said simply.

She looked between the males, curious at their byplay. Their faces held small similarities that defined them as family. Where Xavier and Fallon's faces were all sharp and hard edges, Leo's face was slightly rounded, softening his slashing cheekbones. His broad nose and squared chin were a little different, but they all had those full sensuous lips. She remembered the feel of Leo's on her body and shuddered in need. Leo's eyes traced her face, his gaze a caress. She sighed as fire raced through her blood and pooled in her abdomen. His thick eyebrows bunched and his tongue darted out to wet his lips. The moisture on his bottom lip sent shivers down her spine. She adjusted in the chair, crossing her legs to still the burning.

"How long has she been here?" Leo asked Fallon.

"I just caught her trying to break in," Fallon supplied.

"Do you know her?" Xavier's gaze narrowed on him.

Leo shrugged. "Last time I saw this broad, she was sneaking out of my hotel room, leaving nasty notes."

A flush crept under her skin. "It was one note, and it was not nasty."

Xavier sat back up, looking between the two of them. "So you came here looking for him?"

"Yes." She seized on to the excuse.

Xavier pushed himself up from his desk and marched around to face her. He snatched her backpack from her shoulder and pulled out the wallet with all of her illegally obtained identification. She sighed, this was going to hell faster than she'd anticipated.

"You seem incapable of telling the truth," Xavier growled.

Fallon smiled. "Tell me about this note."

"Fuck you, Fallon." Leo snarled. His jaw bunched, fists clenched at his sides.

"It was not a nasty note." She stood, embarrassment and guilt stained her cheeks.

"'Gotta go, don't bother looking me up, not interested,'" Leo recited her hastily penned note.

Fallon choked to hide his laugh. "You're right, bro. That was nasty."

She cringed and lowered her head. "Sounds bad when you say it out loud."

"Liliana Thomas." Xavier read aloud, putting an end to that conversation. He typed the name into the computer on his desk.

"You told me your name was Destiny." Leo pinned her with a stare that sent a shiver of foreboding down her spine.

"Oh, the irony." Fallon laughed outright.

Liliana's heart dropped. Fallon was right. The irony of her fake name hit her along with the wave of fury emanating from Leo. They'd marked each other, partially mated even.

She was his destiny.

She looked to the door for escape. Xavier was angry, this she knew, but the look on Leo's face was pure, banked fury. He moved a step closer to her, and she shifted one more step to the side. They moved in this dance until she was backed into a wall. The slate scraped along her back.

"Now, baby, why would you go and lie about your name?" His derisive tone cut through her. His large body dwarfed her own five-nine frame stealing her air and her personal space.

Liliana's heart pounded at his nearness, her breath coming in heated gasps. Her breasts swelled with arousal.

"Everyone lies about his or her name." Her tone was crisp, clipped, as her accent threatened to push through in her panic. She pushed against the brick wall of his chest, for all the good it did. He was entirely too close for her comfort.

She struggled to put distance between them. "It was supposed to be a one night stand. You can't possibly think I would give you my real name." Her voice was shaky, her argument weak. She knew absolutely nothing about one-night stands, let alone any etiquette that went along with it. But he didn't know that, so she infused as much confidence in her tone as she could muster.

"So let me get this straight." Leo leaned over a breath from her face. He braced his arms on either side of her head. "You would let a total stranger into your body, but giving him your real name is preposterous?" His voice was low, dangerous, sending thrills straight to her womb.

Liliana should've been running for the door, instead, her nipples beaded and her body arched into his. "That's how a one night stand works."

Goddess his nearness stole good sense. Now that she knew Xavier was his brother, she wondered if the heat was from their mating, or the natural pheromones Cagyns were said to produce. She prayed it was the latter. The former would put her in way too much trouble. The way her stomach tightened, cramped with arousal, she could barely think straight.

His lips turned up into an arrogant smile, dismissing her false bravado. "I'm hurt."

Damn him. Her chest expanded with the effort to draw in air.

"There are things I did to this body that I wouldn't normally do to a one night stand." His large hand traced the column of her throat, squeezing slightly then released.

She should've been scared, anything but so damn turned on. Even as she chastised herself, her breath hitched. His dominance touched every erogenous zone in her body.

"Manners, Leo," Fallon called from behind them.

Leo stared at her for long moments, ignoring the command.

"Back up, Leo," Xavier said from his desk.

Liliana drew in a shaky breath, thankful when Leo took a step back.

"If you weren't looking for me, what were you doing here?" His face dared her to lie again.

"Looking around." It was at least half true. She cleared her throat, still feeling his hand there. "Everyone knows this Haven is the best. I was curious." Yeah. Leave it at that.

"You know, I have a real problem with liars, Ms. Thomas." Leo's face was hard, his eyes, warm days ago, now chipped ice.

Liliana felt a punch of guilt but shoved it aside. She did what she had to do. She raised her chin, meeting his eyes. "I didn't come to cause trouble."

"The first truth you've told today. Who are you really?" Anger smoldered in Xavier's eyes.

"You have my ID, you know who I am." Liliana pushed a hand through her hair, she'd paid a good chunk of money for that ID, and it had better pass a routine check. This situation was entirely out of control. She would just have to find some other way to get the information.

"You're hiding something," Leo declared.

"You don't know me well enough to say that." Liliana protested.

"Honey, I have been all up in your head, your body-"

"Leo," Fallon barked.

Leo shrugged. "There's not much you can hide from me."

Liliana scoffed, anger and panic drowning out restraint. "Anything you saw in my head, I put there for you to find."

She regretted the words the instant they left her lips. She'd blame it on her exhaustion. She would've never made such a slip otherwise. The running was finally catching up with her. Every occupant of the room had grown still. Power saturated the room, nearly stealing her breath.

"Explain yourself, now." Xavier's tone sliced through the air. His voice did not rise, but Liliana felt the order, the power in his tone.

"You're not human?" Leo asked.

"I'm Demi…Eshu." Liliana announced.

"Ah hell, Trouble, now you done gone and done it." Fallon shook his head and sighed.

Her stomach dropped and fear dried her mouth. Yeah, she'd done it now. It was only a matter of time before they sent her home.

Chapter 3

LEO BACKED AWAY AS THOUGH STRUCK. She was not human, she was Demi. Not just Demi, but Eshu. Messengers for all realms, the Eshu were one of the most trusted races among the Demis. And the one race he vowed he'd have nothing to do with.

He'd locked himself in his room for nearly a week brooding, alternating between disgust and anger. Anger, because after only three hundred and fifty years of existence he'd been marked. The disgust came with the fact that the female who marked him, wanted nothing to do with him.

Last night anger won out, and he'd spent the night in the club pounding on other Demis there for fight night, venting his anger. Today, he came to tell his brothers he'd been marked, mated, a fate worse than death, at least as far as he was concerned. He barely trusted the women he considered friends, now he was tied to one he knew nothing about, and to top it all off she was Eshu.

His past crowded him, threatened to swamp him. He hated her for that. Leo saw the looks his brothers gave him from the corner of his eye. He refused to meet their eyes. The last thing he wanted was to see the pity in their gazes.

He should've been more careful.

"How long have you been on Adro?" Xavier asked sharply.

Leo took an involuntarily step forward, the mating bond urging him to shield Liliana's body from the anger in Xavier's voice.

"I don't have to answer to you. I've broken no council rules."

"No, you've only broken our most sacred and important rule." Leo snapped.

Damn her for the emotions threatening to drown him. The memories he'd worked hard to bury clawed through the barriers he'd put up around his heart and mind and nearly undid him.

"You entered Earth's realm without registering at Haven. Only someone with something to hide bypasses Haven." Fallon's voice was soft, curious.

Liliana remained silent, refusing to answer their question or even meet Leo's eyes. She hid something. Her defensive posture said it all.

"I registered at a Haven up north."

Xavier growled. Fear leaped into her eyes and Leo dug his nails into his palm to keep from pulling her into his arms, hating that he couldn't deny the need to do so.

"Tell me another lie, female, and it will be your last," Xavier warned.

Leo growled low in his throat, not liking his brother's tone.

Xavier pointed at Leo, his face tight with anger. "Don't growl at me, especially since you saw fit to hide the fact you were mated." He turned his icy eyes to Liliana. "Show us your true form."

Leo backed up from her again, not wanting to be near her when it happened. To take her true form in front of him would snap his control like nothing else. Jealousy rose already, sharp, stabbing into his chest as he thought of his brothers gazing onto her body in her true form, especially since he'd not had the pleasure himself.

"You can bite it." Her tone was angry, panic and fear rose off her like steam, tangling with the lust pouring from her body.

"Nice talk for the sainted Eshu." Leo couldn't keep the bitterness from his voice.

Her angry eyes bore into his.

"How were you able to mask yourself from me the other night or Leo for that matter?" Fallon asked.

Liliana scoffed. "The Amanda are so arrogant, you think you're the only ones able to wield magic easily."

Xavier's hand slammed against his desk, his control snapped. "Enough! Why are you here, instead of on Legba where you belong?"

"Why do you care?" she asked stubbornly.

Xavier's hazel eyes turned copper, encompassing his pupils, and his voice lowered to a growl. "It is my responsibility to know who's roaming around Adro, especially an unprotected female posing as human."

Liliana swallowed, and sweat beaded her forehead. She took a cautious step towards the door. Her need to escape raked at him, and he wrestled the beast in him fighting to get out and help her. Xavier's temper was legendary, and moments from raining down on her, he took a deep breath to calm himself.

"Reveal your true form, Liliana," Leo ordered. He kept his voice quiet in an effort to keep his magic at bay.

"I'm leaving." She turned to the door.

Leo ordered her again, this time in the ancient language, putting as much power in his voice as he dared. Words said in the ancient language became a spell. It was the way most Eshu kept their mates obedient. A practice he found barbaric but very useful to him in this moment.

Her skin rippled as a wave of magic engulfed her body, shedding the human skin, or rather the small changes she'd made to her true form. The Eshu were the most human of all races. Only their hair and eyes set them apart from the humans who inhabited the Earth realm they referred to as Adro. They were often confused for the human legend of fairies.

She kept her back to them, still, the air left his lungs as he took in her true form. Her hair was a waterfall reaching the bottom of her hips, almost to her knees in a riot of red, yellow and orange hues, silky and straight. The brilliant shades of color made his fingers itch to feel its silky strands. So much of her was covered under the heavy mass of hair. Leo was grateful for the length. Naked as the day she was born her toffee-colored skin glowed under his command.

His skin tingled as she used magic to cover her body in the Eshu traditional gown. The dress was yellow, tied around the neck. It covered her breasts, wrapped around to cover her bottom and hung to the floor. It left her back bare, had she been in Legba her hair would've been held up in intricate braids tied so her back would be displayed proudly. Leo ached to see the markings on her back. His teeth lengthened, the need to taste her, a throbbing pain.

"Move your hair," he ordered in the ancient language, his voice husky, filled with the burning need moving through his body. He moved closer to shield her from his brothers' eyes.

Her hands shook as she grabbed the curtain of hair and moved it to the side. Leo moaned, she was beautiful, more than he could've ever expected to have in a mate. On her back were orange, red and blue lines forming a beautiful outline of wings from her shoulders to the top of her hips. Every Eshu had them, proclaiming them the winged messengers of the gods. Liliana's wings were still light, placing her age only past one or two hundred years. The older she was the darker the lines would become. Even as he was turned on, Leo felt betrayed, though she had no idea his family history. She turned to face him, her narrow face was defiant, her pointed chin lifted, the fine and dainty eyebrows arched in a challenge. The glowing green of her exotic eyes called to him. Leo stomped to her, grabbed her and pulled her into a branding kiss.

Liliana's arms wrapped around his neck, and she opened her mouth. Leo deepened their kiss, his tongue driving into her mouth as passion engulfed them, threatening to burn them to a cinder.

She moaned as he cupped her ass, dragging her closer to him. Gods, the heat moving through him drove all thought from his mind until there was nothing but her. He pushed her back into the door and hissed in satisfaction. It had been five days since they were separated, and though they hadn't completed the mating, his body craved hers. The mating frenzy had started and wouldn't abate until their souls were sealed.

"Back off, Leo." Fallon's irritated voice penetrated the fog over his mind. "Bro, you got an audience."

Leo jerked back from Liliana's mouth.

"Oh gods," she whispered, covering her mouth.

Leo's stiffened, the anger returning twofold, yet he couldn't pry his body from hers.

"What family do you belong to?" Xavier sounded weary.

"Ours." Leo declared.

Her previous family didn't matter. She was his and he would not give her up. Directly below her palm, in dark ink, was her family's name, and below that was Leo's, the dark symbols glowing, signaling the mating ritual had not yet been completed. The glow and the mark would fade if they didn't complete the ceremony by the new moon. Of course, the punishment for not completing the mating would last for much, much longer.

"Welcome to the effing family." Fallon's voice was thick with sarcasm, "But that's not what he's asking and you know it, Leo. We need to contact her family formally."

Liliana raised her head. Leo gave her props for her strength. She stood up to him and his brothers in a way few would dare. He and his brothers were a part of the Amanda, a military-like force, charged with protecting the Demis, and policing them. They had a reputation for being no-nonsense and ruthless, it'd been a long time since someone dared speak to them the way she had. That this delicate woman did, set fire to his already throbbing erection and made him want her with an all-consuming madness.

"I still can't believe you didn't tell us you were mated," Xavier accused Leo. "She's already marked?"

"I thought she was human, Xavier. It's not like I could go out and claim her. I was in my room, trying to figure out how to even find her." His gaze traveled her body while he fought his own.

His chest rose with his harsh breaths, he leaned into her neck, inhaling her scent. The hard pebbles of her nipples pressed into his chest and Leo knew if he didn't back up, he would take her here, in his brother's office, with them watching. With a growl of frustration, he moved away.

She was not happy, but neither of them could stop their bodies from reacting. Even now, when he wanted to feel hatred, the urge to rub his body along hers nearly overwhelmed him.

"I hate liars," he growled.

"I never lied to you."

"Did you intentionally target me or was I the only available body to fuck that night?" Anger rode him as hard as passion did.

"Where did you learn to talk to women?" She sputtered, offended.

"From my mother," Leo spit out. "She was what some would impolitely call, a ho."

Liliana flinched "I'm sorry."

"Don't be, I never liked her." The acrid taste of hate turned his stomach as did the thought of his mother.

"Filter, bro. She could be a noble, show some respect." Fallon barked.

"She's the one slumming. She can't call foul when one of the peasants says something she doesn't like." Lashing out at her was unfair, but anger was the only outlet he had. That, or take her against the wall. Somehow he thought that was out of the question.

"Enough!" Xavier's tone cut through the room, silencing them. "Liliana sit."

"You can't hold me here, I haven't done anything," she protested.

"The Amanda can't hold you here, but as your mate, you can't go anywhere without my consent."

Realization dawned in her eyes and fear clouded her face. Leo crossed his arms over his chest. Oh yeah, his little mate was screwed, just as soon as he could get her alone.

Chapter 4

LILIANA FOUGHT TO KEEP PANIC AT BAY. They couldn't hold her here, despite what Leo thought. Her eyes narrowed. "We're not in Legba, and I've been too long among the women here in Adro to take any crap from you."

His sinister growl traveled along her spine and her body tightened in anticipation. She swallowed to ease her dry throat. There was no way she would win against him if it came down to it. Between her body's demands and the power he held, resistance was a joke. She would just have to find another way out of this mess. She sighed and sat in the chair facing Xavier's desk.

"I want to know why you've been skulking around my club, but first my question still stands, what family do you belong to?" Xavier stared at her intently, his eyes broking no argument.

Her heart slammed against her chest. "Marcolev." She flinched at the ripe curses that came from their mouths.

"Not the Marcolev daughter the queen has been screaming down my ass for us to find?" Xavier's face went harder if possible. "The very same Marcolev chick that I've had my hunters looking for, for nearly four years?"

Liliana looked to Leo but his face was inscrutable. No help from that quarter.

"Please tell me you're not that Marcolev." Xavier leaned forward, his eyes changing, his voice deepened to a growl. "You don't want to be that girl."

Oh Gods, she'd heard about Xavier, the leader of the Amanda, but nothing prepared her for the sight of his anger. It was well known among the Demis that he didn't suffer fools lightly. It was said gaining his attention ended in pain, or banishment. It was the reason she'd saved this Haven for last. Fear and sharp panic stabbed through her.

"There is only one Marcolev daughter left, and she wouldn't be allowed to roam Adro without an escort." Fallon raised an eyebrow. "You didn't strike me as dumb enough to defy Queen Kaylin, Trouble." Unlike his brothers, Fallon was calm, his gaze steady as he waited on her answer.

She shuddered as she thought of the hunters she'd barely escaped throughout the years she'd searched for her sister. Her eyes burned, a lump forming in her throat as she thought of Kita. "I came to the Earth realm not long after my sister went missing. My father refused to do anything about her disappearance, I decided to try and find her on my own."

"Kita went missing over four years ago," Fallon said incredulously. "The Queen has been hunting for you for at least three of those years. You've been on Adro this whole time?"

"Do you know my sister?" She restrained the urge to jump in excitement. She knew sneaking in here would give her a lead.

"Shorty, you're swimming in waters way too deep for you," Fallon said in answer.

"If you know my sister, you can help me." A spurt of hope rose.

"What we know, is that you're supposed to be promised to Kedric of the Eshu royal family." Leo's speculative look made her nervous. "You, little Eshu, are in a whole heap of trouble."

Liliana lowered her head. She refused to feel guilty. Damn it, but she felt so guilty. "Kedric was promised to Kita. If I can just find her..."

"It doesn't work like that." Xavier leaned back in his chair. "Do you have any idea the little shit storm you've just tossed into my lap?"

Obviously, she was in over her head, but really she'd not been given a choice. Mating was never up to the individual, it was always up to Fate. Or rather the Eminzu. The ancestors had the final say on who mated whom. It's not as though either she or Kedric wanted the mating. Couple that with the fact the prince was…

No. She wasn't going there.

Nope, not letting those thoughts escape her iron control.

"Liliana, why come to Adro yourself, why not go the Eminzu with your grievance? That's the purpose of the council of ancestors, to settle family grievances." Fallon's eyes were compassionate.

Her skin warmed and started to glow in her anger. She pushed down on her power, praying for patience. It was harder than normal to control her magic since she'd fed a few days ago, but she wrestled it down. "It's your job as the Amanda to protect the Demis. This isn't just some family grievance. My sister is missing! She could be…" She couldn't say it, couldn't put that into the atmosphere.

"It's our job as the Amanda to protect the world. Not individual families. No one individual is put above the fate of the world." Xavier corrected.

"Don't talk to me like I'm some dumb girl. I survived this fucking realm for four years by myself, I'm not going to go away because someone pats me on my head."

"And how far did that get you?" Xavier sat up and braced his forearms on his heavy desk, taunting her.

"I tried to go to the Eminzu they refused my query. Wouldn't even see me. What the hell was I supposed to do?" Liliana dashed tears from her eyes, pissed at the injustice. No one would help her, her parents included.

"I'm sorry about that, Liliana." Fallon placed a comforting hand on her shoulder.

Leo snarled and moved closer to her, shooting his brother a deadly look. Fallon lifted his hand.

"Come on now with the tears, shorty. I don't wanna deal with that." Xavier growled, but compassion tempered his tone.

"Why come here, Liliana? Why this Haven specifically?" Fallon handed her a tissue from the desk.

"I was given information that Kita was last seen at a haven. I've checked all of them. This was my last one. My last chance to find her." She shook her head, pushing aside her exhaustion. She wouldn't give up searching for Kita. Not while the alternative hung over her head.

Xavier sighed. "And once you broke into my Haven, what exactly was your plan?"

"I didn't have a plan per se." Her cheeks burned with embarrassment. She had a plan, but she didn't think telling the head of the Amanda that she planned to seduce someone in his security room to look through footage would be prudent.

"My gods, Trouble, do you not know who you are? You can't be traipsing around Adro as though you aren't a noble." Fallon stared at her like she was crazy.

"Do you have any idea how many times your father has been in this office pacing the floor? How many times the Queen has been in here chewing on my ass? And you're walking around playing Veronica fucking Mars." Xavier leaned back in his chair with a look that sent a shaft of mind-numbing fear through her.

"You don't understand." She swallowed down the rest of her tears. They couldn't possibly understand what she had on the line. There was no way she could've returned without Kita. She flinched as she remembered the night she left Legba. She still carried scars from that night.

She would do anything to find her sister.

"You have to go back."

Liliana jerked. Xavier's words landed like a blow. She shook her head. "I can't" the words came out barely a whisper.

"It's not negotiable. You go home, to the Queen." Xavier slid her wallet across his desk to her. "Leo, take your mate to your room. Don't let her out of your sight until we can figure out how to transport her without a royal stink. And for goddess's sake, make sure no one sees her."

"I can't. I won't." Her throat closed as panic seized her. She whipped her head around to Leo. "You can't make me stay here."

Leo grabbed her arm. She jerked her arm fighting his grip.

"Give it a rest, Liliana. As you can tell, no one's happy about this little clusterfuck you have us in." Leo led her from the room.

Liliana desperately tried to keep track of their route, but soon gave up, as one hallway ran into the next, becoming a blur until they came to a pair of steel doors.

Leo entered the security code and pushed her into his suite. The spacious room was airy. Daylights gave the room a soft morning glow, despite the fact that the room was underground. The living area was large, the plush sofas surrounding a large T.V. in the middle of the room. They skirted the large entertainment center that cordoned the room off from the foyer and headed to the dining area to the left. Liliana whipped around and stared at him, anger, fear, and frustration burning her chest. Neither of them spoke but continued to stare at the other.

"I don't know why you're so mad, it's not like you're the one being held hostage here." Her chest heaved as she battled to control her temper and fight the tide of fear.

Leo scoffed. "This band around my wrist says otherwise." He held up his arm showing her the dark red band that encircled his wrist with her name etched in the middle.

"What's your problem?" She threw up her hands. "You're not the one being mated with a Cagyn, the least faithful race of all the Demis. "

Of all races, the reputation of the Cagyns as rogues and rakes was the most talked about. Females whispered about it to their friends with lusty sighs, and males kept tight locks on their wives and daughters. The look he gave her froze the air in her lungs. She took a step back.

"Don't presume to know anything about me or my race. Hell, you don't even know what I am."

"I know what Xavier is and he's your brother. I hear the stories, Cagyns change their appearance to suit their lovers, hopping from one bed to the next, unleashing pheromones on unsuspecting innocents, seducing them to get their way." She sneered. "You said as much about your mother. You obviously know it to be true."

Leo's smile did nothing to comfort her. "Then I suggest you keep your mate satisfied, and you won't have that problem."

"I'm leaving." She tried to push past him. Gods, how did everything go so wrong? It should've been simple: sneak into Haven, and find out if someone here had seen her sister and leave. Now she was locked up downstairs with a jerk her ancestors had seen fit to tie her to. And worst, she was headed back to Legba where her punishment for leaving would make banishment seem like a vacation.

"You're not leaving, Liliana." Leo pulled her back to face him. "You rushed headlong into this situation and now you're stuck."

She attempted one last appeal. She'd heard of how males spoiled their mates, perhaps if she softened her tone. "Look, I can't stay here. The queen's hunters will find me, and I'm not leaving until I find my sister." Gods, please help her find Kita.

"You mean to tell me, that after you were told your sister disappeared from here, you thought it was a good idea to follow in her footsteps? Did it occur to you that something could've happened to you?"

"You can't possibly understand." Her shoulders slumped in defeat. "I need to find Kita." Her knees weakened, exhaustion finally caught up with her.

"Damn it." Leo ran a hand over his face. "Why Liliana? Why risk your life for this?"

"She's my sister. What would you if one of your brothers were missing?"

He flinched, but the anger left his face. He stared at her for a moment. "Arguing will get us nowhere. Are you hungry?"

The abrupt change of subject threw her off, but she understood the olive branch he'd extended. At her nod, he went to the phone and ordered them a late lunch. When it arrived they ate in silence, neither of them sure what to say to the other. Once they were done, Leo cleaned the table and set the dishes into his sink.

"Don't even think about trying to leave. You would get lost in the catacombs and having to look for you would piss me off." He left the threat in the air and went to take a shower.

So much for their truce.

Liliana's heart lurched in fear as she finally realized what kind of trouble she had gotten herself into. She wandered into his living area and took off her sneakers. The cherry wood floor was surprisingly warm beneath her feet. Plush microfiber was soft as she ran her hand across the arm. She sat and stretched out on the sofa at a loss. How in the name of the Gods was she going to get out of this? She closed her eyes for just a moment, she told herself.

Chapter 5

COOL AIR WHIPPED AROUND HIM, moist and carrying the scent of forest life. Tendrils of sunlight fought to reach the bottom of the lush canopy of trees. Rugaba strode through the thick vegetation, his footsteps silent. Movement in his peripheral confirmed the natives knew he walked through their land. He paused at the center of the forest, a centuries-old tree, the largest one in the forest loomed, its power intimidating. He watched dispassionately with only a trace of impatience as two knots on the tree bark opened and blinked at him. Brown eyes, ringed with the barest trace of gray stared at him warily before mist from the ground gathered and surrounded the tree. Moments later a form separated from the tree, joining the mist.

"Rugaba, my lord, how may I serve you?" The thin, musical voice floated to him.

"Take your form, Aleah, I need to confer with you." Rugaba's gaze flickered to the trees surrounding them.

The forest held its breath, the Mina inhabiting the trees hoping to catch a bit of gossip. For a race of people able to foresee the future, they were obsessive about gossip in the here and now. They constantly sought validation of their visions, observing others as lab rats. Rugaba narrowed his eyes and shook his head as the leaves rustled and shifted with their curiosity.

The mist that was Aleah firmed into a rail-thin body, translucent and pale. Her brown eyes dominated her thin face, surrounded by thick lashes, blinking lazily. Hair the color of a stormy day floated around her body, its tendrils sweeping the forest floor. Her tapered fingers moved nervously through the air, her thin pink lips moving silently in a spell. Fallen leaves gathered, circled her body at her command, until they formed a strapless gown, covering her naked form. The corset-like top hugged her slender waist and small breasts, while the rest of the gown flared around her hips, falling to her ankles.

"If you'll follow me, my lord."

Rugaba inclined his head in agreement and followed the Mina deeper into the forest. The foliage became dense, the trees closer together, the gnarled branches lower as they walked. Almost as if the forest tried to stop their movement. He ducked through hanging moss and pushed aside wide leaves until they came to a clearing. The log cabin where she led them was the only structure in the entire realm. Used as a meeting place, it kept prying eyes and ears from observing their conversation.

A quick flick of her wrist opened the door and released the stale air of the cabin into the forest.

"How may I serve you, Rugaba?" Aleah's voice firmed along with her body, gleaming brown skin covering her translucent form. She sat at a scarred wooden table and waved him into one of the hardback chairs.

"War is coming." He settled into the narrow chair, eyes scanning the room. The bare walls and floor made him feel as though they were in a cardboard box. He noticed how the inside stretched to fit his tall stature.

Aleah shuddered. "The elders have seen it and confirmed it with Oya. What do you need from me?"

Rugaba sat silent a moment. There were many things he needed to know, but this small female could not answer all. Though she occupied the centuries-old tree, the position of seer had just passed to her some decades ago. He worried she would be too young to give him the information he needed. But there were few options.

"Oya has released the Kokoro souls. Have you seen them?"

Aleah pushed her hands through her hair. "I have seen them."

Rugaba swallowed his frustrated sigh. The Mina would only answer the question he asked, no elaboration. Patience was needed in spades when dealing with them. "Are they active?"

"No."

Rugaba growled.

Aleah blinked, her owlish expression not wavering.

He stood and paced the room. As a sun god, he could create life, he ruled the skies, but he could only see the future, as he affected it, not before. Even the smallest action from him could alter the natural course of someone's fate, so he'd stepped back from the Demis, gave them over to his councils. The Amanda and the Eminzu policed them, advised them, and in most cases punished them. He only interacted when there were problems that affected the world in its entirety. And war, certainly qualified. Someone was trying to unleash the ultimate evil and though he couldn't interfere, he'd make sure the scales were balanced.

"Who…" he stopped. She wouldn't give him a name. That he had to find himself. "How soon before one is active?"

"Soon."

"What exactly does that mean?" He ran his hand over his head in frustration. What was soon to immortal creatures? Soon could be anywhere from a day to a decade.

"The one prophesied to change the tide of war has found the one which will influence that decision. Soon they will mate and shortly after the Kokoro soul will activate."

"Aleah, I need more to go on. I cannot help with these half-assed answers." He stood and paced the room, rotating his shoulders to push way the trapped feeling.

"My Lord, I can only answer your questions. I can't interfere any more than you can. We've given you, and anyone else seeking, the prophecy. It's all we can do." She was right. The Minas were the closest to the gods, they were bound by the same rules.

Wait…

Rugaba stopped mid-stride. "Someone else has asked for the prophecy?"

Her shoulders slumped in relief. "There have been two who've come to us for the prophecy."

He frowned at her answer. No longer succinct, it sounded like a warning. Her eyes beseeched him to understand what she could not use words to say. He lowered his mental shields, probing her aura for impressions, information. "Who?"

"I can't give you a name." Aleah held up her hand to halt his anger. "It's because I do not know, my lord. They didn't come to me." Frustration played across her face and tickled the edge of his senses. The admission was rare, as puzzling and troubling to her as it was him.

"Who did they see?"

"It's shrouded." Her form wavered, her anxiousness evident. She wiped her brow with shaking hands. "Much about this war is shrouded. We were given the prophecy, but anything to do with Ofeeree is…"

Rugaba nodded. Hidden. It was how Ofeeree worked. Those who followed him kept his secrets. "Are those of the Kokoro protected?"

"All three will be protected, my Lord."

"By who?"

"Their mates."

Rugaba frowned. "Mates? They are female?"

"They are female."

"All three?"

A small smile tilted Aleah's thin mouth. "Yes, my lord."

"This amuses you?" Females. It explained the smug expression on Oya's face as she told him of their release. Protecting them would be a nightmare.

"Your confusion is amusing."

"Females are vulnerable, would you rest the fate of the world on their dainty shoulders?"

"Females are the reason this world is worth fighting for, my lord. I would rest much on our capable dainty shoulders."

He smiled ruefully. This new seer was a feminist. Who would've thought? "Now that I've been put in my place, I'll leave." He ducked under the cabin door and strode back through the clearing.

For the moment, the souls of the Kokoro were safe. He'd warn Xavier, and have the Amanda protect the women as soon as he found out their identities. That was paramount. He glanced back at the log cabin, an odd sense of unease trickling down his spine. His head started a dull throb as a vision flashed before his eyes.

He hissed in impotent anger and rushed back into the cabin.

It was too late, the Mina's form wavered as her life force diminished.

"Demis… helping…searching for his corporal…" The Mina died, her form fading away and blowing from the cabin on an unseen wind.

"Damn it." The cabin was empty, with no signs of her killer or how she died. He opened his senses but felt nothing. There should have been some trace of the energy left behind. Great pains were taken to hide the killer's trail. He knew only one group capable of hiding their magic. He said a quick prayer for the Mina's soul, sending it to Alafia, and left. Earth's war had started and earned its first casualty.

***

LEO WRAPPED A TOWEL AROUND his waist and pulled another out of the closet for his hair. In his natural form, the midnight black strands reached the middle of his back and were a pain to dry. He stopped, his apartment was quiet, alarmingly so. He rushed from the bathroom and his bedroom to find her stretched out on his sectional, sleep, and completely oblivious to the world. Her beautiful hair wrapped around her waist like a blanket. Her lush lips were slack, her face relaxed as she slept.

His heart melted… just a little. She was gorgeous. He allowed himself a moment to feel pride in the fact that he'd been given such a beautiful mate, and strong too. He changed back into his human form and gathered her in his arms. He could imagine the weight she'd been holding on her shoulders. The search for her sister couldn't have been easy, especially for a noble who was surely coddled her entire life. Earth was a rough world with its occupants selfish and unforgiving of anything different. Most Demis only stayed for as long as was needed to replenish their life force and then they headed back to their own realm. This Haven was located in Atlanta, the metropolis made it easier for the Demis to blend in with the humans, but the city had its rough days. He marveled at the strength it would've taken Liliana to survive alone and unprotected. How she escaped the hunters his brother and the queen sent after her, was beyond him. It filled him with a sense of pride.

He settled her onto his bed and crawled in behind her. His body was protesting its lack of sleep. He'd had maybe four hours of sleep in the last two days, and soon, the proverbial shit would hit the fan. It would be good to catch a few hours of sleep before that happened.

He'd barely closed his eyes when she moved. His body reacted immediately, burning, a fire of need centering on his groin, pressing into her back. Liliana wiggled, a drowsy moan left her lips and he tightened his arm around her waist.

"Unless you are inviting me inside that hot body of yours, I suggest you quit squirming." Exhaustion had roughened his voice making it a deep rumble.

Her body tensed. Fully awake, she kicked her legs, trying to scramble from the bed.

"Rest." He dragged her struggling body back into his, spooning her. "I haven't slept well in a week and since I doubt you're waking for entertainment, I'd much rather go to sleep."

"Yes, well we don't have to sleep in the same bed."

"Ah, but I don't trust you, Destiny, so sleep in the same bed we shall."

He laughed at her frustrated growl, grabbed her hair and draped it over his body, luxuriating in its silky texture. He burrowed his face into her neck and inhaled. She was intoxicating. Goosebumps ghosted down his arms as he laid a small kiss to her neck. Her sigh of pleasure slid past his defenses, and for once the craving he had was not for sex, but for this small intimate moment. He kissed her neck again, pleased when her hand lifted to caress his face.

"Stop that." A weak protest, especially given the way her hips arched into his.

He traced the shell of her ear with his tongue. He'd heard it could be this way with mates, but nothing prepared him for the way his body strained to be in hers. Tender feelings assaulted him, confused him. Only hours ago he was pissed about being mated and now…he had no idea. He nipped the base of her neck, loosening the clasp of the gown, pulling a ragged moan from her. Her cheeks heated, her embarrassment at her reaction evident. A blush traveled the length of her body, her skin heating under the rush of blood as he moved the gown down her body. As tempted as he was, he would leave her alone, didn't mean he would allow her to cover her body from him though.

"Sleep, darlin'." He covered them with a sheet and tucked her head under his chin.

***

Hours later, he woke again, this time he found her draped across his body. He opened his eyes in slits as she lightly ran a hand across his chest. She thought herself unobserved as she explored his body. Her finger trailed his stomach, moving lower. He lay there, riveted, her touch shy but no less effective. He grit his teeth and fought to keep his body still under her ministrations. She looked up and he was speared by the lust in her eyes. His hand tangled in her hair and brought her lips up to his for a kiss that sent fire through his blood.

The mating frenzy was upon them.

Leo was lost. He couldn't think of anything sexier than waking up and feeling a woman's touch running along his body. Control was out the window as her moans spurred him on. His mind may not be sold completely on mating, but his body was one hundred percent invested. He deepened their kiss, turning to place her body under his. Liliana's eyes were dark with lust, the green color deeper than an emerald. She wrapped her legs around his waist and lifted her hips, urging Leo to take what he wanted.

Oh Gods, did he want.

She was pliant beneath him, her breasts moving with her deep breaths. Unable to resist Leo leaned down and suckled, rolling the hard pebble around his tongue. It was the sweetest taste and he was greedy. His hands moved between them, testing her readiness, she was wet, tight, and hot enough to singe his fingers. He'd be lost if he didn't slow down, he knew that, but somehow couldn't get his body to cooperate. Liliana arched into his hand.

"Just a taste, a small taste." Whether the promise was to himself or her, he didn't know. Control was elusive. His teeth scraped against her breast, nature demanding, beating at him.

"Do it, Leo," she demanded hoarsely.

Leo nipped her skin lightly, his teeth elongated, crowding his mouth. He moved his mouth over her neck. He cursed as a hard knock sounded at his front door.

"Stay, right where you are," he growled. His voice was deep, fury and lust battling as he moved from Liliana's warm body. He rolled from the bed. "Don't move," he ordered again as he conjured a pair of jogging pants and slid them up his legs. He turned and she sighed, arching her back, her breasts an offering to him.

"I'll be right here." Her voice was sultry, taunting him.

His thoughts flashed to the other night, to the memory of the way she gripped his body and he cursed. His vision sharpened as his eyes changed. Lust momentarily beat out fury.

Leo knelt on the edge of the bed and crawled back to her. The kiss he took was raw, possessive, stealing his mind as their tongues dueled.

"Leo?" a husky voice called.

He stiffened at the voice in the living room.

Liliana slapped at his shoulders. "Who is that?"

"Fuck!" Leo scrambled from the bed and raced to the living room.

He cursed the Dziva's timing as well as the fact that she was in his apartment. He'd never given her the code to his room. Sneaky fucking Dzivas. He wondered who'd given up the codes to his room. The Dzivas were nothing if not resourceful, they manipulated and controlled those around them with the flick of their hair or a twist of their hips. Any being with common sense knew to avoid them. The dumb male probably never saw it coming. Still, wouldn't stop Leo from kicking his ass when he found out who it was.

Verity stood in his living room her body posed, a sensual pout on her full lips. Tall and slender, the purple iridescent scales covering her body caught the light, dazzling the eye as they were designed to do. Of course, the short dress her boobs were near tumbling out of, could've accomplished that on its own. Her hair was long and the palest the color could get and still be called lavender, reaching her hips, some of the strands lit, twinkling beautifully. Her hair like everything else on the Dziva's body served the purpose of distracting their prey. By the time a Dziva's victim got past the outside beauty, they were either dead or screwed out of everything they owned.

Leo sighed. He didn't have time for this. "What do you want, Verity?"

The Dziva smiled, shaking her hair, the movement mesmerizing and catching his eye. "I only want to talk, Leo. I don't like the way things ended." She walked around his glass coffee table and skirted his leather armchair to stand in front of him before he could regain his senses. She placed a hand on his shoulder.

The lust he felt moments ago for his mate dissipated at her touch, leaving only fury in its wake. "Well, I didn't like you screwing other males."

Verity pouted, wrapping her arms around his neck. "Don't be that way. It meant nothing. He had information, I needed it, and I did what I had to do to get it."

Ah, the logic of a faithless bitch. Was it any wonder he didn't trust women? The danger and excitement of screwing around with a Dziva had worn off the moment he caught her in bed, or should he say office desk with another male.

He didn't share…anything. "I told you when I broke it off, I don't share." He saw movement from the corner of his eye.

Liliana crept into the room her anger palpable, power making her hair glow. Lust returned twofold, pushing Verity far from his mind. His robe swallowed Liliana's small frame, slipping down her shoulder in a way utterly provocative because she was so unaware of it.

"You can move your hands from around my mate, Dziva." Her haughty voice sounded every inch the Eshu noble.

He scrambled for a way to diffuse the rage swimming in Liliana's eyes. Verity hissed, her pale gold eyes narrowing in instant dislike. Liliana crossed her arms over her chest, refusing to back down from the stare.

The Dziva lifted Leo's wrist, shoving it back down as she saw the markings. "It's your loss. Call me when you get bored with your frigid noble."

Liliana charged, slamming into Leo's chest as he moved into her path.

"Don't, Liliana." Leo didn't release her until the front door closed.

Liliana shoved back from his chest. "Although I don't want to be, we're mated. You will not disrespect me."

Leo watched the magic playing across her skin, lighting her hair and damned if it didn't make his dick hard. He watched the way her chest moved with her angry breaths, and he imagined all that passion focused on him. His own anger at her words rose, fueling the fury he already felt at being interrupted from their earlier play.

"Is that right?" he taunted her, crossing his arms over his chest.

"I won't tolerate you having other women." Liliana raised her chin in defiance, her eyes full of fire.

"I guess that means you'll need to keep your mate satisfied. If you want, I can call Verity back to give you lessons. Dzivas are known for their technique." It was nasty he knew it, but he couldn't stop the words.

She gasped, her eyes widening a moment before her hand snaked out and slapped his cheek. He smiled, the small lift of his lips bearing his teeth. Liliana met his stare head-on, cocking her hips sideways in a challenge. Oh, yeah, they would tangle now.

"See, Xavier. They're getting along great." Fallon's voice broke through the tense silence.

Chapter 6

LILIANA PALED, withdrawing her magic immediately. Gods, she'd never lost her temper enough to strike someone. He damn well deserved it, but she hated that there were witnesses. Lust clouded her judgment from the moment she woke up sprawled on top of the infuriating male. Memories of their night the week prior, combined with the feel of his steely body under her was her undoing. How was she supposed to resist him? But wasn't that the purpose of the mating frenzy? It kept the couple from outright rejecting the mating, without at least giving it a chance.

Xavier and Fallon stepped into the apartment, closing the door behind them.

Leo rounded on his brothers. "What?"

Xavier shook his head and walked into the room. "I just passed a pissed off Dziva murmuring about Eshu nobles on this side of the portal?" His voice made it a question.

Liliana raised her chin. "He's impossible." And sexy, with magic hands that made her body shudder. Gods, her emotions were all over the place.

"I've noticed that myself." Xavier made himself comfortable on Leo's sofa. "You were supposed to be lying low."

"I'm not staying here a moment longer." Liliana clutched the robe to her chest. She turned to leave the room, but not before giving Leo another nasty look.

"On that, we can agree. I've just informed the portal station at Legba of your impending arrival." Xavier announced as she reached the bedroom door.

She whirled around, her lips pinched, panic draining the blood from her face. He couldn't mean what she thought he did. He wouldn't send her home this soon. "What are you talking about?" Her eyes darted between them.

"You're betrothed to the prince, Liliana, you thought you could run away days before your mating ceremony and no one would notice?" Fallon asked.

"I'm not going back." Anger took panic's place.

Xavier's power flooded the room. "You will go back and you'll deal with the crap you created when you ran away. As it is, I'm stalling a cadre of the queen's soldiers asking to speak with me."

Liliana refused to back down. She couldn't go home, not yet. Not without what she came for. "Can't we do the ceremony here? I'm not going back until I find out what happened to my sister."

"If what you say is true and your sister was last seen here, then I will look into it."

Elation rushed to fill the places previously occupied by lust and anger. She barely restrained herself from shouting in victory.

Finally! Someone would help her search for her sister.

He raised his hand to stall the torrent of gratitude on the tip on her tongue. "I'm done dealing with Queen Kaylin, so no, the ceremony will not be held here. You'll be mated, traditionally, so my brother is not further disrespected by this foolishness." The light glinted off of Xavier's copper eyes, no mistaking his anger.

Liliana took a deep breath, joy leaving, replaced by confusion. She looked up and tried to see past Leo's stony expression to find out if Xavier was telling the truth. "Do you feel disrespected?"

His eyes betrayed him for only a second before the wall went back up. She saw the spark of hurt and was deeply ashamed. Her mother said she was selfish, but never before had she felt that way until now. Her only thought upon waking had been escaping a mating with the prince. She'd not once thought of how that would make Leo feel.

"You were promised to another. The longer we put off telling your parents, the shadier it will seem. As you've pointed out, the Cagyns are not exactly trusted. You mentioned pheromones and unsuspecting…how did you say? Innocents?"

She flushed in embarrassment. Her earlier words to him about his culture put a bad taste in her mouth. "I'll be ready after I shower."

She used the time in the shower to think. She stood under the overhead showering panel allowing the deluge of water to paste her hair to her back. The hot water steamed the glass doors and enclosed the stall in fog. She sat on the warm tiles, her back against the marble and went through her options. It made sense for them to finish the ritual in Legba, the royal family would fight the mating otherwise. She would not embarrass her family, least of all Kedric. She shuddered. No, she couldn't embarrass Prince Kedric, the punishment for that… It didn't bear thinking about.

Besides, Cagyns by nature were possessive, competitive. She didn't want to think about what Leo would do if his claim were challenged. Though he obviously didn't want a mate, she imagined he would make an example out of the first person to oppose their mating. It would be a nightmare. The gossip would be unbearable. As it was, her returning would stir up a hornets' nest of chatter. Her stomach churned.

She could well imagine the mess she'd made when she left. Had her parents survived the fallout with their social status intact? She didn't even want to think about it, let alone face it. Gods, she could barely think with the frenzy riding her. She stood and rinsed off, her mind in chaos, her body throbbing in need. After five days, she was near insane with want. It would only get worse as they waited to complete the ritual.

She stepped out of the shower and grabbed a towel. She was wrapping it around her body when she registered his presence.

His eyes devoured her. "It's a shame we were so rudely interrupted." He swallowed her gasp of surprise driving his tongue into her mouth.

She tasted his fury, felt the evidence of his need brushing against the apex of her thighs as he lifted her onto the double sink. He dropped her towel and lowered his head to her neck. Her head fell back and his fangs scraped along her skin. Lust poured off him in waves, dragging her under.

"Do it. Bind us." Desperation drove her.

Leo stared at her, his eyes burning a hole through her, turning her blood to lava. Liliana's breasts swelled, her stomach clenched with lust, her body painfully aroused. She wanted him with a ferocity that bordered on insanity. He pulled her legs around his waist burrowing his thick length tenting his pants against her center. Whimpering, she closed her eyes as his teeth nipped at her skin. He trailed kisses to her ear and a shudder racked her body.

"We will be bonded the traditional way or not at all." He growled.

Her eyes opened. She was panting with lust, her thoughts scattered. "Why?"

His eyes hardened. "I don't want to hear any shit about the Cagyn bespelling you into anything."

She nodded in understanding, knowing of the tales told about Cagyns. She wrestled her body back under control. Leo leaned over and wrapped her hair around his hands, tilting her head back. Tension stiffened his shoulders, and his eyes broadcasted his own battle with their passion. He kissed his way down her throat, she whispered his name and arched her body forward. His teeth raked against the side of her breast, and she thought she would explode.

"Please, Leo, do something."

Madness, that's the only thing that could describe the lust tearing through her. Power moved along her bronze skin, and her hair glowed, painting prisms on the wall as her body prepared itself for its mate. They should stop, they really should, but judging by Leo's harsh pants, he too was having a hard time remembering why.

He kissed his way back up her neck and rested his head on her forehead. "Gods, I want nothing more than to bury myself in your body, but not until we speak with your father. I'll not have one person saying I seduced you into this." He stole one last kiss before backing away from her completely.

He walked out of the bathroom leaving her shrouded in steam, seconds from orgasm. Liliana slid to the floor, her body burning, the now cold tile doing nothing to help. Would she survive the heat before they were completely mated? She blew out an impatient breath. It wouldn't be so bad if she had not already tasted him or known firsthand how well his body moved within her. Liliana touched her lips with trembling hands.

"Liliana?" Leo called from the next room.

"I'll be right out." She stood, grabbing the towel from the floor. She dried and dressed in the traditional gown. Twenty minutes later, satisfied with the intricate braids she'd conjured she left the safety of the bathroom.

She was a little self-conscious as she walked into Leo's bedroom. Her heart stopped, then slammed into a hard, fast rhythm as she spotted him in his uniform. The black shirt fit tight across his chest, showing off muscles she'd touched and ached to touch more. Rugaba, their God's, symbol was on the chest and sleeve. The bright red patches had a gold sun in the middle surrounded by thorns. Black cargo pants were tucked into black boots giving him a dangerous air that made her body melt. He looked up from buttoning his sleeves and caught her staring. A wave of fierce pride moved through her.

Pride that she'd been chosen to bond with someone as powerful and gorgeous as him. Her earlier misgivings about being mated to him raced through her mind, but she pushed it aside. She would be tied to Leo for eternity, it would do her well to get to know him with no preconceived notions.

"I'm sorry if you felt disrespected," she blurted the words before she even realized what she would say "It was never my intention."

He looked taken aback. His eyebrows rose in question. They stared at each other for a moment and he sighed. Leo held out his hand and understanding the unspoken, she grabbed it relishing his touch as he pulled her into his chest. The patches on his uniform were scratchy against her face. Strange how she found that sensation comforting.

"I don't trust females as a rule." His voice was gruff, a deep rumble against her cheek. "I don't know what to do with a mate."

Liliana looked up into his eyes, the gray depths pulling emotions from her she was not ready to have. "What do you say we start over?"

Leo nodded and dropped a kiss to the tip of her nose. "I apologize for the Dziva interrupting us." He looked a little sheepish as he lifted her chin. "She's never been in the apartment before today. There has never been a woman in the place where my mate would rest."

Her heart melted, surprised and touched.

He cleared his throat. "We need to go." He kept a hold on her hand and led her through the confusing catacombs.

Liliana's stomach gave a nervous lurch as they approached the portal room. The cavernous place resembled an airport, with people bustling through the area. The murmur of conversations in the different languages floated in the air as Demis waited in line to be checked in. Leo and she moved through the line, not bothering to check in with the soldier guarding the entrance to the main portal. He led her into the dark hallway away from the bustle of the cavern. She saw soldiers of the Amanda striding purposefully down the hall, only slowing to salute Leo. In awe of the deference Leo received from the other soldiers, Liliana scrambled to keep up with his long strides. They reached the end of the hallway, stopping at a blank wall. The smooth stone held no trace of the portal that would carry them to her realm.

Leo reached out his palm, touched the wall and immediately a spell was activated, ancient symbols glowing in a grid. Leo's hand moved quickly through the grid, weaving the symbols together until the symbols for Legba glowed bright red. The grid disappeared moments later and the wall shimmered until Liliana could smell the sweet air of her homeland.

They stepped through the shimmering wall and for a moment there was nothing but bright white light. She closed her eyes and shook her head to shake out the fogginess traveling through the portal gave her.

"You okay?" His concerned eyes searched her face.

Liliana nodded. A small thrill at finally being home again filled her body. It had been four years. The portal room in Legba was bright. The glass walls let in the blue skies and light from their sun. Built off the ground, everything in Legba was high enough where the green of the forest could not interfere with the beautiful sights of the sky. Their wings were useless, so their stories say the Eshu built Legba in the air to give them the feeling of flying.

Liliana was surprised when Leo did not head straight for the door leading to the transports. Trade capital for the Demis, Legba's portal building was bustling. They pushed through the crowds, passing a line of people waiting at the check-in station. The guard working stood and saluted. Leo pressed his hand to a glowing crystal, standing still for the retinal scan. The guard nodded when it changed color to purple in acceptance. They both stared at Liliana and nervously, she pressed her shaking hand on the stone, blinking as the bright laser scanned her eyes. The crystal warmed beneath her palm and turned red. Her heart stopped.

The guard looked down at his screen. Her name glowed, instructions underneath. He cleared his throat. "Mistress Marcolev, you are to be escorted immediately to the royal house."

Gods, Xavier was sending her straight to the Queen. No! Not yet, she couldn't face him.

"I will escort her to her father's house. You can log it." Leo ordered.

The soldier looked agitated, unsure of what he should do.

"Just log it." Leo pulled Liliana behind him to the exit.

She fought to keep the relief off her face, and her breathing normal. She didn't know how long her respite would be, but she would take it. She'd come back a failure and soon as the prince received word, he would hunt her down.

Chapter 7

LEO LOOKED DOWN at Liliana. Her hands were shaking in his grip, fine tremors moving through her body. She'd been that way since they had checked in at the portal. It tugged at protective instincts he'd long suppressed. He could understand her reluctance, he himself dreaded this trip. He hadn't been in Legba since his mother dragged him here at the age of seventeen. Almost three centuries ago, the memory burned and he fought to push down on his fury.

He looked around the sky lift station and sighed, he hated having to check-in, but it was necessary. One: he wanted the royal family to know they had arrived. He was not skulking and sneaking onto their realm. And two: never let it be said that he was afraid of the royal family or what they could do to him. Xavier's instructions to him were clear. While his brother held no fear of the Queen, the inconvenience of pissing her off was not something Xavier wanted to deal with. Seeing the way Liliana paled at the portal officer's instruction, he couldn't do it. His brother would be pissed, probably accuse him of once again doing things the hard way. He'd take the dressing down from his brother in order to spare his mate the fear wafting from her.

Stepping into the sky lift, he watched as Liliana punched in the code for her parent's home. Her mounting fear pulled him from his unsettling thoughts, the need to comfort her a compulsion. His hand reached automatically to rub her back. The contact with her skin tingled. She sighed and moved closer, settling her head onto his shoulder. Leo leaned down and laid a small kiss to her hair, inhaling her scent and allowing it to push away his anxiety at being back in this realm.

They rode in tense silence. The portal station was situated in the metropolitan area of the realm. It needed to have close access to the market square, which was central to Legba. They sped through the realm's business districts, and the bigger buildings gave way to small neighborhoods. The Eshu neighborhoods were large floating pods, on which multiple houses were built. Each pod was usually occupied by a family from immediate to second and sometimes third generations. Sometimes the wealthier families had individual pods for each family's home, and a central pod on which they gathered and the children played. As the air lift continued, the groupings of houses were more sporadic, the space in between the pods where the Eshu lived wider. Leo tipped his head in curiosity, wondering how far outside of the city they would travel.

His eyebrows winged high on his forehead when the lift came to a stop. Leo took his first look at the home where Liliana grew up. The large oval structure was white with large windows from the roof to the ground. Their yard was lush, native shrubbery lining the iridescent tiles that cut a path from their front door to the air lift pad. Their house stood well apart from the others in the neighborhood, floating on its own pod. It spoke of her family's wealth, that they were not connected to any others. It gave the family privacy and exclusivity. No one could simply 'walk' or stroll onto their land, they would need permission or would plunge thousands of feet in the attempt. Their nearest neighbor was barely visible on the horizon.

"You're awfully far from your neighbors." He kept his voice casual as he held out his hand to help her from the lift.

She grimaced. "Yeah. My father's an only child, and he and my mother's family don't get along. The family pod is the one we passed a moment ago." She pointed to the neighborhood to the east of them. If my father could be further from them, I'm sure he would be. He wanted to live in the city, closer to his investments. My mother wanted to live close to her family. This is their compromise."

"A mansion…near the edge of the realm no one can access."

She smiled at his dry tone. "Did I mention my father could be petty?"

"Oh Gods, Lily. We are saved." Her mother's cry interrupted them. She descended the front steps, her stride unrushed.

In a simple long sheath of gold, Liliana's mother was elegant. Her aqua tresses were pinned atop her head in a series of tiny braids. Gold bangles jingled on her wrist as she glided to them. Her eyes, large and tilted at the corners, glowed from her caramel face. With the push of a few buttons on the control pad in the yard, the tiles on their walkway extended, connecting the airlift pad to the front yard and bringing her the rest of the way. She grasped her daughter's hands and kissed Liliana's cheeks.

"Do you have any idea how worried we have been?" She examined his mate, her expression anxious, and relief plain on her beautiful face.

Something was off, but he couldn't put his finger on it. Her mother made all the correct motions, said all the right words, but an air of falseness surrounded the woman. Leo wondered what she hid.

"I'm sorry, mother," Liliana whispered, tears streaming.

The sight pulled at Leo and he stepped closer to her. He slid an arm around her shoulder. Her mother stepped back and eyed him from toe to head, disdain curling her lips. Could be his human skin or the fact he was touching her daughter, the Eshu were strict about propriety. Openly touching her daughter in public was frowned upon. Only his uniform kept her from saying the nasty words glowing in her eyes.

Leo smirked. The fireworks would fly when she realized he was her daughter's mate. Suddenly the trip was looking up. Yeah, he was petty, but anything that took his mind off of where he was, he'd take.

Her mother bent her legs in a small dip he assumed was supposed to be a curtsy. "Thank you for bringing my daughter home. If you will come in, my mate will be home soon to thank you properly."

Liliana's eyes met his entreating him not to say anything. He nodded and her mother escorted them both into the two-story glass structure. A large painting of who he recognized as the lost daughter dominated the wall directly across from the front door, he gave a surreptitious look around for one of Liliana. Finding none, he made a mental note to ask Liliana about the clear preference her parents had of Kita. It could explain the falseness he felt around her mother.

The place was well kept. The Eshu nobles were known for their exquisite taste…and the tendency to show off. He could hardly see the paint on the walls through all their 'good taste'. Expensive artwork littered the table surfaces and covered the walls. Leo sat in the plush leather armchair and controlled his urge to roll his eyes at the trappings of wealth.

"Would you like some tea?" Her politeness was forced, her hands white-knuckled in fists at her side. Evidently, Liliana's mother didn't think much of him either. But then he imagined no noble would like feeling beholden to an Amanda soldier. Though they ranked high in status in most realms, the Eshu regarded anyone in service as lower.

Leo nodded and the woman turned to leave but turned back quickly to hug her daughter once again. They were left alone and an awkward silence descended. Liliana looked at him. He could almost read the thoughts crossing her face. Doubt and fear were the clear winners as she worried her bottom lip with her teeth. She opened her mouth to speak when the door crashed open.

"Arian, is it true?" Her father rounded the corner of the room and came to a halt. "Lily, my darling." Her father crushed her into a tight hug. "You've had us worried to death. The prince and his family will be over soon to greet you."

Leo cleared his throat.

Emerald eyes the same as Liliana's stared at him from over her shoulder. An older version of her, Liliana's father had hair the same colors but muted with age. His hair pulled back into a neat queue, revealed his narrow face and stubborn chin, the twin of his daughter's. His skin was a darker brown, its pallor dull. Worry had taken its toll on her father. Compassion welled unbidden.

"I cannot thank the Amanda enough for finding my daughter." He held out his hand.

Leo shook it, giving Liliana a pointed look.

"Sit, baba, I have news." She grabbed her father's shoulders and guided him into a chair.

Her mother rounded the corner with the tea service. "I've ordered the maid to bring in tea cakes once they're ready."

"I'm mated." Liliana blurted.

The teakettle crashed against the tile floor, sending shards of ceramic skittering under the table and chairs. Tea splashed on the surface of a table, the leaves landing scattered in a pattern like an ominous warning.

Her mother looked down and saw the glowing Sanskrit on Liliana's wrist. "No. You would not be so reckless." Arian turned to her husband. "Evan, this can't be true. The Eminzu approved the bonding to Prince Kedric."

Evan's shoulders slumped. The resigned look on his face emphasized the wrinkles around his mouth. "Lily, even for you, this is too much."

"Baba, I didn't do this on purpose."

Leo cringed at her statement. Maybe she hadn't done it on purpose, but the fact was, had she followed Eshu customs and remained celibate until mated, she wouldn't be in this predicament.

Leo's eyes darted between mother and daughter. Both held a stricken expression, Arian's hair and body lit in her fury, a blue halo surrounding her body. He wondered if he would need to step in.

Arian straightened her back, rigid with anger. "I think you did exactly that. Goddess, the shame. Why can't you do anything without embarrassing this family?" She paced the room muttering under her breath. She stopped and turned to Evan. "The Eminzu promised we would be joined with the royal family. I'll protest the mating straightaway."

Ah, he began to see the real problem. "That won't be necessary."

"Is that right? What would you know about the situation? As a matter of fact, you've done your job and escorted my daughter home. You may leave." Frost dripped from Arian's tone.

A small smiled tilted his lips. "As your daughter's mate, it's best I stay."

"Excuse you?" Arian stopped pacing. The look she gave him could cut through steel.

Leo squelched the urge to check his chest for stab marks. "Your daughter and I are mated."

Silence descended and lasted exactly three seconds before the situation exploded.

***

Her parent's shouts drowned out her apologies. She couldn't get a word in edgewise as they took turns screaming their displeasure. Oh gods, this was bad.

"You are responsible for this, Evan. You spoiled her entirely too much." Arian shouted into her mate's face. Their magic blended, blue and yellow halos merged, battled and green sparks crackled in the air between them.

Her father brushed past her mother, pushing her aside. "Lily, do you have any idea what you've done?"

Arian slumped into a chair, her magic withdrawing. "Oh gods, we'll never be able to show our faces in public again."

"You." Evan faced Leo. "Show me your true form now."

Liliana held her breath, praying he didn't go off on her father. Leo shrugged seemingly unconcerned and shed his human skin with a simple spell.

Her heartbeat spiked, and heat flooded her body. He stood before them shirtless in the flowing Eshu lounging pants. His chiseled chest and rock hard abs made her sigh in longing. His skin was beautiful mahogany, marbled as with most Cagyns, with hints of bronze lines flowing through his skin. Black hair flowed to the middle of his back. Every shade of black from a shade slightly darker than gray, to color so black it was blue. The light loved his hair, playing in the midnight strands, highlighting them.

Her body heated, melted, as a fierce craving moved through her. Liliana put a hand to her stomach. Why did her chest hurt? Oh, yeah, she'd forgotten to breathe. Power tingled down her fingertips as she fought to keep her composure in front of her parents. She stepped closer to Leo, an involuntary step, her body demanding his nearness.

"The Eminzu have given you what you asked for. Your family will join with the Eshu royal house." He turned his back to them.

Her hands shook as she pushed his hair to the side. The soft downy strands flowed through her fingers and she fought the urge to wrap the length around her body. Wings covered his back, black and bronze, very dark lines from his shoulders to hips. Oh gods, he was half Eshu. Sitting between his shoulder blades, a crown, the mark of the royal family glowed. His mixed heritage showed in his hair color and the copper-colored lines that flowed throughout his skin. Cagyns, as a rule, were ebony-skinned with jet black hair.

"Gods above, he's half Cagyn, how do we know he didn't—"

"Arian, stop it." Evan sliced a hand in the air to cut off her mother. "They are marked. Pheromones or not, the Eminzu wouldn't have marked them if they were not meant to be together."

She licked her lips, tuning out her parents' arguing. "Why... why didn't you tell me?" Her voice trembled, confusion and shock taking turns with the butterflies in her stomach.

"You're not the only one running from family duty." His voice carried no further than her.

"Oh gods."

Her mother's hoarse whisper spun her around. Her father stood with his mouth open. He wiped a hand across his face. Guilt stabbed Liliana. She'd put those worry lines on her father's face. Would he forgive her for this?

Evan cleared his throat. "I'll contact the royal family. The *di êjê* must take place immediately, the new moon is barely three weeks away."

"What has happened?" Arian sat on the edge of the sofa, her eyes dull with shock.

Her father started to leave, but turned back, with a weary sigh. "Who are you? I don't know you, or your family name." He closed his eyes. "My baby is to be bonded to a man I know nothing about."

His weary tone ripped her apart. How did everything go so wrong?

"I am Leonalph Tegan."

Her heart stuttered, and she reached blindly for a chair. She plunked down as her knees gave out. Oh gods. She didn't think… she'd forgotten about the king's illegitimate son. Foolishly when she saw the crown, she'd thought of a cousin, but never…

Her family was done. There would be no living this down.

Arian gasped. Her eyes speared Evan, her finger shaking, pointing in accusation. "Liliana is your daughter. You allowed her too much freedom and this is the result. We'll be ostracized."

"Arian, hush and go make plans for a *di êjê* befitting our station. My wealth assures we will not be put out of society." Her father was one of the richest merchants on Legba, which guaranteed the ceremony would have to be a large affair. There'd be no brushing this under the rug. She lowered her head, how she wished Leo had bound them at Haven.

With one last look at Liliana, Arian did as bid, leaving the room with a ruffle of skirts.

"Baba," she whispered, aching to find a way to fix this.

Her father ignored her, instead, his attention wholly on Leo. "You are Leonalph, Death's Messenger, and the king's bastard?"

She flinched at her father's callous question. Leo's sharp nod was his only answer.

"And your brother, Xavier is the leader of the Amanda?"

"He is." Pride straightened his shoulders and Liliana's heart contracted, squeezing painfully as a rush of longing pervaded her body.

She didn't think it possible for her to be more attracted to him as he stood before her father unapologetic for who he was.

"Then my daughter is in good hands. We will not shame you with the *di êjê*." He turned to her. "And you…" Evan shook his head, a heavy sigh moving his shoulders. "For once act appropriately and show your mate to the sleeping quarters he'll be using until you're mated. Though, it seems that ship has sailed."

Liliana blinked. Her father's words stung. He'd never in her life raised his voice or said a harsh word to her. His disappointment shamed her. It was no less than she deserved though. Because of her recklessness, her family would be cast out of the society her mother relished. Embarrassment, anger, and heat burned her cheeks.

She motioned for Leo to follow her and walked stiffly down the hallway she'd romped through as a child. This was really happening. She would be mated, and for all intents and purposes, she knew nothing about Leo. He was Death's Messenger, one of the most powerful hunters in all seven realms. Gods, just the thought of it made her faint. How could she not put that together when she saw him in the office with his brother? How could she keep up with him? He would run her life. She'd be no better off with him, than with the prince. And her family's money would give her no leverage with him. His family ran the Amanda and had done so for as long as written history dictated. Their wealth far outweighed her father's.

The guest room was across the hall from her room and she hesitated at the door. Her parents' room was two doors down, nothing would happen. It didn't matter. His nearness would play hell on her sleep tonight. She opened the door and blinked at the brightness. Windows from floor to ceiling covered two walls. The entire ceiling, made of glass, made the room appear as though floating. A large bed covered in soft, supple, blue sheets her mother probably paid a fortune for, took up the middle of the room… and all of her focus.

Gods, get a grip!

She cleared her throat. "This panel dims the windows." She indicated the crystal panel next to the door. She pulled down on a small lever and the windows frosted, dimming the room to a low intimate glow. Nerves made her hands shake as she continued to explain the control panel to him.

"The bathroom is, is hidden. This button will open the d-door. There is a closet inside the bathroom where you'll… find anything you need." She stuttered through the demonstration.

"I know how the panel works, darlin'." Leo tipped her chin up, pulling her gaze from the panel. "You're angry."

Liliana snatched her chin from his hand. "No, not really. More angry with myself. I'm mated to a male I don't know at all. I just realized the price for my impulsiveness."

"Do you think I would hurt you, Liliana?" Leo looked into her eyes. "Or is it because I'm illegitimate?"

"I don't know what you would do, Leo. You hated me not even two hours ago. I don't care that you're the king's basta—" A single tear escaped. Damn it. Everything was catching up with her, sending her emotions reeling. "I'm sorry, I didn't mean that."

Leo smiled. "I didn't hate you, Liliana. I admit I didn't want to be mated, but that doesn't mean I'll treat you badly. There's a lot I have to give up to mate, I was angry at that."

"My selfishness has caused you and my parents to give up a lot." She ducked her head, swiping at her damp cheeks.

And yes, selfishly she knew she too would have to give up a lot. Her four years of freedom flashed before her. Like a daydream it scattered, taking her hope with it. She would never get that freedom back.

He raised her chin again and kissed her deeply. "I don't like the situation we're in. I thought to avoid Legba for as long as I was alive. I'm sorry if I took out my family issues on you." He said softly against her lips.

"I'll try and be a good mate for you, Leo, I swear it."

"No more nasty notes?" he joked.

Liliana laughed and swatted his chest. "And no women, Leo, I won't allow you to stray." She thought of the Dziva.

Leo stiffened and backed from her. "Despite the circumstances of my birth, I don't cheat, and I won't tolerate a mate that does." His eyes were hard, the green ring around the iris glowed.

Liliana shuddered at the intensity. "Well. At least that's one thing we have in common." She turned for the door. "I'll leave you to get settled."

"Liliana," his voice stopped her at the door. "We'll get to know each other. I don't want to be stuck in a miserable mating any more than you do."

She nodded and stepped into the hallway. She had to get her riotous emotions under control. She headed for the kitchen intending to go out the back door. When she rounded the corner, the smells assaulted her. Fresh teacakes, baked by the woman she ran to when her childhood problems were overwhelming. Her mother's maid arranged teacakes on a china server, her movements brisk and efficient. Her marbled cocoa skin had onyx lines gleaming in the morning sun from the large windows. A petite woman, her jet-black hair was pulled back tightly in the bun she'd always worn. Her simple dress pressed within an inch of its life, clean despite the work she did.

"Bea." She whispered.

"Oh, my Lily." Bea raised her head, tears pooling in her dark eyes.

Liliana rushed into her outstretched arms. "Gods, I've missed you."

Bea pulled back and held her at arm's length. "Let me look at you."

"There is nothing different to see. I promise."

"Sit, then, and tell me about everything." Bea grabbed small plates and served them both the small confections she'd made. She fixed them a glass of cool juice and sat across from Liliana. "You've surely stirred up things around here, but then, that's not unusual for you."

She blew out an exasperated breath. "I've made such a mess of things, Bea."

Bea snorted. "Child, from the day you could walk you were making a mess of things."

Liliana smiled. "Well, I'm not so sure you can fix it this time."

"My Gods, Lily, mated. I've never seen your mother so mad. If you had a death wish, it may have been easier to just deliver yourself to Death's Messenger and have it done with."

Liliana's eyes widened and she choked on her juice.

Bea looked at her sharply. "Liliana Arias Marcolev."

She laid her head on the table.

"So 'tis true? I just called my under maid a liar. In the name of all that's holy." Bea laughed. "I told your father you had more guts than brains."

Liliana winced. Gossip flowed faster than the breeze in Legba. "There is nothing funny about the situation, Bea."

"Sweetling this is just too hilarious." She continued to laugh, holding her stomach.

"Do you have any idea how much trouble I'm in?"

Bea held up a hand, tears of laughter trailing her face.

Liliana watched for a moment before the contagious laughter shook her shoulders. A smile crept and a chuckle escaped before she pinched her lips to trap it. "It's not funny."

"Do you know?" Bea took a deep breath and wiped her face. "Do you know, when you were about ten I told your father you had enough guts to kiss death on the mouth and escape unharmed?" She broke off in another peal of laughter. "Even for you, Lily. This is over the top."

"I didn't do it on purpose."

Bea shook her head. "Of course not, dear. These things just happen to you." A fresh peal of laughter erupted. "My gods, mated to Death's messenger. Only you, Lily."

Liliana crossed her arms over her chest. "No need to be so amused about it." Her lips twitched and she gave up, once again joining in Bea's laughter.

Bea sighed. "I have missed you. Life has been downright dull without you getting into trouble."

"I was not that bad."

"When you were five you decided to take the sky lifts all on your own. We found you at the portal room in the Amanda's office chatting to the officers on duty."

"I was curious."

"You scared twenty years off my life. When you were fourteen we caught you on top of the palace parapets trying to fly."

"Hey! That wasn't my fault. Kedric and Kita dared me."

"You have a streak of mischievousness in you a mile wide, Liliana."

She smiled. "What can I say?"

"What have you been doing these past years?" Bea sobered.

"I've lived on Adro for all four of them."

"More guts than brains," she muttered.

"I was careful, Bea."

"What did you do on Adro?"

"I wandered around."

Liliana told Bea about the things she saw on Adro, careful to avoid the real reason she went.

An hour or so later, Bea crossed her chest and sent up a quick prayer. "You are too much, Liliana." She stood and gathered their dishes.

"That's what I hear." She sighed, and then added, "I also looked for Kita."

The plates dropped with a hard clang. "Lily."

She held up a hand. "I know, Bea."

"Is that why you left?" Their eyes met. Bea's dark ones concerned.

"I had to do something." She wouldn't tell the woman who raised her that she was practically kicked off of Legba. There was no telling what Bea would say or do to the royal family when they arrived.

"You were told to leave it alone."

"She's my sister, Bea."

"Your sister was responsible for half the trouble you got into as a child. Her and that demon prince." Bea shuddered. "I for one am grateful you'll not have to bond with Kedric."

That made two of them. Liliana shuddered. "It wasn't as bad as that."

"And the arguments?"

"Sisters argue, Bea." The knockdown drag-out fights they had could hardly be classified as normal behavior.

"I'll never understand this hero-worship you have for Kita. She was a mean and spiteful child and I hated the way she was allowed to treat you."

"That's not true." But close. Kita and Kedric together certainly made her childhood hard. Hell, here she was well into her adulthood and they were still doing it.

"It's the truth." Bea's voice invited no argument. "You refuse to see it. Remember I'm the one who cleaned your various scrapes and bruises. I wiped your tears when they were mean to you."

"She's still my sister." It was lame, but the only argument she had. To avoid mating with Kedric, she would've traveled to Azreal herself.

"I wish you would let it go, Lily. There's nothing but trouble going down that path. Please, trust me on this."

She heard the warning in Bea's voice and flinched. What could the woman know that she didn't? "You know something."

A quick jerk of her head showcased Bea's aggravation. "Liliana, your stubbornness will get you into trouble one day."

"That day has come." Her mother's voice from behind her lowered the temperature in the room. "The king's messenger arrived. The royal family will be here in two hours. Let's be presentable, Liliana, and for the Gods' sake, try not to embarrass this family further."

Liliana swallowed the angry retort. "Yes, mother."

Arian left the room on silent feet and Bea breathed out a frustrated sigh. "That woman."

"I can't believe you still work for her." Liliana raked a shaky hand down her face. She wanted to question Bea more but she dropped it for now. She would talk to her later about it.

"Go do as she says, Lily. No need in the two of you fighting so soon after the first one." Bea turned her back and started straightening the kitchen.

Nausea rolled, the teacakes threatening to come back up. She had to face the prince. She could only pray they would not be left alone.

Chapter 8

LEO SHRUGGED HIS SHOULDERS to ease the tension gathered. He paced the room, edgy, the need to escape Legba at the top of his mind. His communicator beeped on his hip, he looked at the display.

He sighed. "Yeah?"

"How's everything going?"

"Just as we expected. They rolled out the red carpet." He didn't bother adding that they would have gladly wrapped him in said carpet and tossed it off the highest point of Legba.

"I suppose you couldn't possibly do what I asked you and take her to the royal family first." Xavier didn't sound particularly surprised or angry.

Rather than admit to his brother his concern for Liliana he opted for changing the subject. "Did you look into her sister's disappearance?"

Xavier let out a deep suffering sigh. Leo squelched the urge to laugh. Gods it was so easy to rile his eldest brother.

"Liliana was right. Kita was in the club. She disappeared from here."

"What did you find?"

"Nothing, at least not for around the time of her disappearance. We're checking earlier records next. For now, though, there are no portal log entries, no surveillance footage. There's a portal record of Kita coming through to Adro during the new moon five years ago. We caught sight of her once more when she came to Haven for a club night." Frustration and worry colored his tone. "We'll check the Oras, but so far nothing. She literally disappears, Leo."

That didn't sit well with him, but he could do nothing until he got back to Adro. "Thank you for checking." Now to figure out how he would tell Liliana. "Do you think their father knows anything?"

"Even if he did, we can't question him on a family matter. You know how the Eshu are about what they deem family matters. If he knows something, he has made his peace with the Eminzu or they would've helped Liliana when she went to them. The fact that he didn't come to the Amanda when she went missing is telling."

"What does Fallon say?"

"He thinks Kita's disappearance is the beginning of something, but it's hidden from him. It could be something going on in Legba, some family enemy, or something political."

Her father was a very wealthy merchant. It made sense, but still… it wouldn't hurt to be thorough. "I'll rush the di êjê along on this end. I'll be back on Adro helping in a couple of weeks or so, depending on if Liliana wants to take the bonding period here."

Xavier grunted, "Call us when the date is set."

"X." He hesitated, rubbing his hand across his hair. "Can I have your permission to speak with Rugaba?"

Xavier sighed. "I already intended to ask for an audience. Consider it a gift for your mating."

Leo's heart thumped in anticipation. "What do you think his answer will be?"

"Rugaba is unpredictable on most days and nasty as hell on the rest, there's no telling what he'll do. He may leave it up to the Eminzu, and you know the way they will go."

Leo suppressed a growl. Yeah, he knew the way the Eminzu would vote. Once mated, he would have to give up his position in the Amanda. Take something lower, and out of the line of fire. The Eminzu were crazy about mating and continuing the family line. The sole purpose of their machinations was to make sure a family line stayed pure and if not pure, as strong as they could make it. The ancestors wanted only the strongest to survive.

Xavier broke into his thoughts. "Call baba."

Dread pooled in his gut. "Does he know I'm in Legba?"

"Who knows what baba knows? I warned you all your dangerous hijinks would catch up with you."

"What the fuck does that mean?"

"You're about to be mated to a willful and stubborn woman. Good luck, it's no less than you deserve."

"Thanks for having my back, bro." He hung up on his brother's laughter. He stared at the phone as though waiting on it to bite him. He sighed and dialed his father.

He answered on the first ring. "Are you okay with everything, Leo?"

So he did know. Leo relaxed and shook his head at how fast gossip traveled within the world of the Demis. "I'm fine, baba."

Ranolph cleared his throat. "I understand how important your job is to you. I'll approach the Eminzu on your behalf and ask them to allow you to stay with the Amanda."

Touched, Leo swallowed the lump in his throat. "I'll handle it, baba. I've requested an audience with Rugaba."

Silence met his statement.

"It didn't work for me," his father said after a moment. "I hope it turns out differently for you."

"Have you told Sharine what happened?" He tried to keep the bitterness from his voice.

Ranolph scoffed. "I have not seen your mother in over six years. When all of you are mated, I will ask to be released from my own."

Leo's heart lurched. The consequences of his father's actions… all at once fear overwhelmed him. "Baba, you'll be banished." It came out a hoarse whisper.

"My sons spend all their time in Adro. I can't see the harm in living my final years where the primal source dwells and getting to see you and your brothers, besides I'll have no use for my magic with my sons to protect me. Once all three of you are mated, I won't have to worry about how my actions will affect your match. Goddess knows I don't want either of you to end up with a female like your mother."

Fury spiked. "She is no mother to me."

Ranolph sighed. "Leo, you'll be haunted by your mother's actions for eternity. I'm sorry about that."

"I'd rather not talk about it, baba."

"One day when I'm brave enough, I'll tell you the truth of your birth. Until then, please be careful. I look forward to meeting your mate."

"You will remain in Edin then?"

"I'm at peace with the decisions I've made in my life here, so yes, I'll live out my days here until I'm banished."

A knock on the door interrupted what he would have said. "I gotta go." He closed the communicator and walked to the door.

Liliana stood on the other side dressed in a formal gown of peach silk. Cinched at the waist, it draped her body perfectly. Doubts about their mating dissipated as she stood in front of him, her shy stance giving her a sexy vulnerability. Unable to resist, Leo pulled her into his room and closed the door. He leaned her against it and kissed her, possessive need driving him. She was just what he needed after the conversation with his father. He covered her body, pressing her into the door, yearning to be as close as possible. He cursed the small braids in her hair and debated tugging down the knot sitting atop her head. It shouldn't take her that long to redo it with magic.

As though she read his mind, Liliana pushed against his chest. "Don't you dare. It took me thirty minutes under my mother's watchful eyes to get the proper bun."

"I like your hair down." He nibbled on her ear, inhaling deeply.

Gods, the scent of her.

His hips jerked, grinding into her. All the blood in his body flooded south. Vivid images of taking her against the door flashed through his mind. He swallowed a moan.

"While we're on Legba I have to be presentable and respectable. No noblewoman walks around with her hair wild." She mimicked her mother's haughty voice.

Leo felt bad for her. Her body vibrated with anger. Of course, it did nothing to quell his arousal. If anything the fire in her eyes sent flames licking down his spine.

"What happened?"

A grimace tightened her face. "My mother and I don't get along. At all." She sighed. "We've had another fight. Don't worry about it."

She stared at him with a mixture of anger and heat. Her breath came out in short gasps and her body trembled.

He smiled. He could do nothing about the first, but as to the heat... "I could help you relieve that anger." His voice deepened. He gathered her gown in his hand, bunching the material, in an effort to reach her skin.

She traced the bronze lines on his arm lightly and his whole body reacted. Running her hands through his hair, she arched her body into his, grinding on his erection. "I'm having a hard time around you in your true form. Those Cagyn pheromones are making it hard to think past wanting you inside me."

Shit.

His cock bobbed in reaction. He could get with that.

"How long before the royal family gets here? Deal's off now that we've spoken with your father." He leaned down, sucking on her neck.

"Not enough time for what you're thinking." She tilted her neck to accommodate his kisses.

He growled and bit her neck. "Gods, you are gorgeous."

She lifted his head, and kissed him. Leo grabbed her leg through the slit in the dress, wrapping it around his waist. He could feel her mound beneath the silk and he rolled his hips. Her gasp of pleasure spurred him. He needed to feel her skin against his, needed it almost as much as his next breath.

He started to rip off her dress when there was a knock on the door. Leo snarled in warning, the sound pure animal. Liliana slapped her hand over his mouth to stifle the sound. He licked at her fingers intending to ignore the door.

With the second knock, her body tensed. Leo sighed in frustration. Panic in her eyes tugged at him and washed away his erotic plans.

"All right. Settle, baby." He rubbed her back and moved her from the door.

"Lily?"

"Yes, Bea?" She relaxed and reached to open the door.

Leo slammed his hand against the wood and shook his head. He sent a pointed look to his groin. Her eyes widened, the color deepening as a flush bloomed in her cheeks.

"The royal family will be here in five." The maid called through the door.

The color drained from her face. "Ok, we'll be down."

"Now, Liliana," Bea said.

"You have to dress up," she whispered, moving his hand from the door.

Leo growled. The impending meeting with the royal family was already becoming a pain in his ass. With a simple spell, he changed back into his dress uniform, forgoing the human skin he usually donned. It would be necessary to remind all parties involved of his parentage.

Liliana nodded in approval and opened the door. A Cagyn maid stood anxiously in the hallway.

"Cagyn?" Leo raised his eyebrows and gave her a pointed look.

She flushed in guilt from her earlier words about his race. "Leo, this is Bea. Bea, my mate, Leo."

He nodded to the maid and guided Liliana down the hallway. The back of his neck itched, and tension tightened his shoulders. Liliana stiff at his side, and the maid's soft tread at his back, the whole procession took on the tone of a funeral march. He hadn't seen the royal family since his mother dragged him before the king when he was a child. Permanently burned into his mind, the incident had kept him from visiting Legba long into his adulthood. He swore he wouldn't step foot on the realm for as long as he lived. He sighed. And here he was, back for this stubborn slip of a woman fate tied to him. If nothing else, the night was about to get very interesting.

As they rounded the corner into the receiving room, Liliana stiffened. The royal family stood as they entered, their expressions varying. The king's solicitor stood behind them, his face wary. The queen gasped and looked at her husband with daggers in her eyes. The king nodded to Leo politely.

He took a long look at the male who was his biological father. The resemblance between them was striking. They carried the same strong jaw, almond-shaped eyes, and proud nose. Leo's eyes were a darker shade of gray than the kings. Resentment bubbled and for a moment rage rose. Liliana's body brushed him, her hand gripping his tightly, and just like that the rage dissipated. Bitterness, however, was not easily set aside.

"Your highness may I present…"

"We are well acquainted." The queen cut off Liliana.

Kedric held his hand out to Leo and they shook hands.

The smirk on the prince's face was puzzling, as was the look he sent to Liliana. "You have done well for yourself, Leonalph."

"Allow your father to handle this…distasteful situation, Kedric."

"Mother, there is naught we can do. The Eminzu have marked them."

"He's right Kaylin, we're only here to dissolve the agreement between our families and put this business behind us." The king continued to stare at Leo, his eyes narrowed.

Fuck you. Leo's lips twitched with the urge to say the words aloud. Gods, he wanted nothing to do with this. Screw protocol, he would take Liliana, complete the bonding and damn the consequences. And if the prince kept eyeing his mate as though he had carnal knowledge of her, he would rip that fucking smirk from his face.

"Your highness, if you will sit, my mate has the required documents." Arian flitted around the room nervously, brushing imaginary dust off of their prized possessions. "We're completely embarrassed…"

"You should be," Kaylin narrowed her eyes. "This is no way for a noble family to behave."

"Mother."

"No, Kedric. I'll not sit quietly while you are disrespected by this usurper and his silly twit."

Leo stiffened. Tales of Kaylin reached well into other realms. She was feared as much for her sharp tongue as well as her quick temper. Liliana's mother looked stricken. It was said she shunned nobles from Eshu society for the slightest infractions. Their current situations would probably put Liliana's parents well outside of any acceptable social circles.

"Queen Kaylin, we never intended for this to happen." Arian rushed to explain.

"It's what happens when you allow your children to run around like trampy Dzivas. Had she kept her legs closed we would not be in the situation." Kaylin pursed her lips in distaste.

Arian paled.

Leo shifted, a subtle reminder of his presence in the room. Damned if he would let the queen disrespect Liliana in front of him. What was the penalty for knocking around royalty? He considered it, seething. His violent thought must have reflected in his eyes because the queen opened her mouth to say something, but closed it with an audible snap. Liliana stiffened, her nails digging into his hands. He didn't need to look at his mate to know she was angry. Her body no longer trembled in fear, power vibrated between them, little sharp stings traveling up his arm.

"Enough, Kaylin." The reprimand in King Leander's voice whipped through the room.

Evan rushed in with the documents, passing them to the king's solicitor standing quietly in the corner. The man read them over quietly.

Moments later he cleared his throat. "Your highness."

"Are they in order?"

The solicitor's eyes darted around the room. "Your highness, these documents are still valid."

"What?" Kaylin lifted an eyebrow and turned to the solicitor.

Leo winced at the venomous glare. He felt sorry for the lawyer.

"These documents were signed and witnessed prior to Prince Kedric's birth. There are no names listed."

"What is he saying, Leander?" Kaylin tapped her husband with one long tipped nail.

The solicitor swallowed. "The same loophole…er…loose wording that allowed for the switch between the Marcolev sisters apply. The contract only states that the families have to join."

Dark amusement filled him and for once, Leo could appreciate the cruel joke fate had played. "He is saying, your highness, that whatever you promised as a dowry still stands. The contract is still valid."

Kaylin ignored him and faced her husband. "Leander, you cannot allow this to happen."

"He is my son as well, Kaylin." Though Leander's tone was weary, a hint of pride slipped through his gaze.

Leo's body tightened like a bowstring. Hearing the king's statement was a bitter pill to swallow. He'd kept his Eshu form to remind the king and queen of his heritage, but hearing Leander's pride in him left a bad taste in his mouth. Liliana's hand brushed his back, the motion soothing.

"You will allow him to take what belongs to my son?" The chill in her voice lifted the hair on the back of his neck. He had firsthand knowledge of the lengths the queen would go to rid herself of problems.

"Mother, please." Amusement tilted Kedric's lips, his eyes finding Liliana's.

She shuddered. Leo tightened his grip on her hand to still her trembles. He assessed the prince through narrowed eyes. Kedric was a replica of the king. The same brown skin, squared chin, though his chiseled features slid into gaunt. The prince's hair was a riot of reds, from the palest shade of blush to the deepest of burgundy like his mother. His eyes were identical to Leo's and the irony of it staggered him. He hated that he looked like these strangers instead of the brothers he'd grown up with and loved.

"You set the terms, Kaylin. If you recall, I warned you against so generous a dowry." Leander said patiently.

"It was to go to my son," she objected.

"So what have I won?" Leo crossed his arms over his chest, all trace of amusement gone.

"You have been nothing but a curse to me." Kaylin narrowed her eyes, her hands clenched tightly into fists. Her caramel face was flushed, anger causing sparks in her eyes.

"I have been nothing to you, your highness. You made that distinctly clear when we last met." There was no respect in the title. Memories washed over him igniting his rage. He would never forget her words to a child who'd done nothing to earn her venom.

"Your mother stole what belonged to me. I'll not allow you to do the same to my son."

Silence choked the room. His vision changed, sharpening and expanding, signaling his loss of control. Only a thin thread of sanity kept him from the violence clawing at his chest. The touch of Liliana's cool fingers pulled him back…marginally. Only the strict training from his brothers kept his beast leashed. He would need to thank them later. Though, the meeting was not done yet. It remained to be seen if he could keep it together.

He took a deep breath. "Well, shall we see what exactly I have stolen from my brother?" His brother. It left a foul taste in his mouth. Leo released Liliana's hand and held it out.

The solicitor looked at the king, who nodded. He passed the forms to Leo. Liliana leaned over his shoulder and gasped.

"Dear Goddess." She whispered.

"You cannot let this happen, Leander." Kaylin snatched the forms from Leo's hand.

Leander stood. "It has happened and there is nothing to be done. It also means that the Marcolev family's portion of the agreement still stands." He gave his wife a pointed look.

She nodded grudgingly.

The king shook Evan's hand. "Do send word when you would like the *di êjê* to take place."

"We are not attending." Kaylin brushed her gown and stood.

"You may stay in your room if you like, but it will be held at the palace as befitting my son. Kedric and I will be in attendance. Let's go."

Kaylin gave Leo one last nasty look and followed her husband from the house. Leo doubted it was finished between them.

Kedric stayed behind. "Despite what you think about my mother, or I yours, I don't dislike you Leonalph. I've never harbored any ill will towards you."

"Nor I, you." At least not until he saw the way the prince looked at Liliana.

Leo ignored his outstretched hand.

"Well, I don't envy you your mate." Malicious amusement danced in Kedric's eyes. "She was something of a handful when we were growing up."

Leo's eyes narrowed. He shrugged in faked nonchalance and he fought his jealous urge to lash out. "I don't think that much has changed."

"Since we are going to be neighbors we should make the effort to get to know one another."

Not in this life. "My work for the Amanda will make it impossible for me to stay in Legba, it won't be a problem."

Kedric nodded, his jaw tightening at Leo's reminder of who he was. "Lucky for you then." He left quickly.

Leo brushed a hand over his face and reigned in his tattered temper. Only a few weeks and he could leave. The ceremony couldn't be over fast enough to suit him.

***

"Well, thank you, Liliana." Arian clenched her hands at her sides.

"Try to contain your pride in me, mother." Still reeling in shock, the words were automatic, the sarcasm a natural response to her mother's taunts.

Arian sucked in a shocked breath. "Sarcasm is common, but then, you've proven yourself to be just that."

Leo's growl closed her mother's mouth, surely stopping a flood of other insults.

Liliana pushed down on that well-aimed dart, shoving it into a dark place in her heart reserved just for her mother. "Since we obviously don't have anything nice to say to each other, I'll leave. Good night, baba, Leo."

She prayed her legs would carry her to her room. Her mother's angry words had struck their mark. After two hundred years she should be used to it, but nevertheless, it hurt. She'd always hated displeasing her mother.

Fickle fate.

The Eminzu had given both she and her mother what they'd asked for. Tears of relief stung her eyes. Her mother would get the palace wedding she so coveted and Liliana avoided mating with Kedric. Hysterical laughter bubbled at her lips. Too bad they would all be shunned because of it. She stopped and braced her arm against the wall of the hallway to give her legs time to stop wobbling.

The dreadful meeting played through her head and her knees weakened. She could barely focus on what had been said with the looks the prince threw her way. It was a look she knew well, it promised retribution. Bile rose and she lowered her head.

It was over.

Kedric wouldn't dare lay hands on her now that she was mated to Death's Messenger. Her back bowed as memories of his lashes snuck past her defenses. She could almost feel the sting. It didn't matter any longer. She took the memories and shoved them back into the black box of her mind. She would not be bonded to him, and now some other poor noble would bear the brunt of his sick pleasures. She thought of her sister and wondered if Kita had known what she was getting into with Kedric. She'd never seen him lay a hand on her sister, but that wasn't saying much. They never allowed her near them, and if they did it was to play some cruel joke on her.

Liliana sighed. It wasn't as though her sister was mean. She'd simply been used to getting everything her way. In light of their mother's pampering, it was no wonder. The clear favorite in their mother's eyes, Kita could do no wrong. Liliana stood straight and released the tight bun from the top of her head. She finger-combed through the tresses, leaving the small braids.

It was done.

Really done. She was mated, and her mother had no hold over her any longer. She'd searched for Kita to avoid mating Kedric, and now that was unnecessary. But… her sister was still missing. Her parents still suffering, could she in good conscience stop the search for Kita? She prayed Xavier would do what he promised and help.

Chapter 9

VERITY WATCHED THE ESHU noble as he nervously paced the club parking lot where they arranged their meeting. His dark multi-hued hair gleamed under the street lights. His tall rangy body stooped and bent into his coat to hide his face. She rolled her eyes at the cliché. Really, a dark parking lot? The noble certainly had a flair for the dramatic, but what did she care? His love of drama would make him easier to control. She ran her hands down the front of her mini skirt.

A spurt of anticipation added an extra sway to her hips as she walked over to him. She regretted the human skin she wore. It would keep her from using most of her powers, but one did the best with what one had. She had a feeling the noble had requested the meeting in a place humans frequented exactly for that purpose. Exposing the Demis to humans carried a heavy price.

She couldn't afford the Amanda's attention.

So she'd traded her iridescent scales for smooth skin the color of the darkest chocolate. Her normally long hair swung around her chin, black with highlights of her natural pale lavender hair. The noble's eyes widened as she approached him. Men were so easy.

"You are Verity?" He licked his lips and looked around.

She inclined her head in acknowledgment.

He rubbed his hands against the front of his pants. "I've never seen you in your human skin."

"You know we're not supposed to meet outside of the guild."

His eyes narrowed into slits. He crossed his arms over his chest. "We have a problem."

"What problem could *we* possibly have?"

He handed her a sheet of parchment with a single name on it. Cursing, Verity crushed it in her hand using her magic to burn it to a cinder.

That bitch.

Verity pushed down her aggravation. Leo had been a useful contact and damned good in bed. Her body tingled in remembrance. Though he'd not been a good source of information, being his lover did give her access to better informants. Now she would lose him.

And Verity did not lose.

"She needs to be taken care of." His pout did nothing for his handsome face.

"Why exactly? Getting rid of her would certainly cause more problems."

"She's still looking for her sister. What do you imagine will happen when she gets her mate to help?"

Damn.

He was right. The last thing they needed was the Amanda looking into Kita's disappearance. Although not directly affected, the scrutiny could cost them.

"She's mated, to royalty no less, it will cost you." She studied his face, using the nuances to determine how far she could push him.

"I'm told you are the best." He moved closer to her, anticipation shining in his eyes.

"Of course." No need to brag. A fact was a fact.

His lips tightened a fraction before the arrogant mask descended. "How much?"

She smiled. That would be easy to remedy. "Money is for common folk. There is something else I require from you."

He sneered. "I'm not stupid enough to trade favors with a Dziva. Trading favors for you is how I ended up involved in our guild in the first place."

She smirked at the reminder of how she'd recruited him into their group. "Not even for the removal of one very wealthy nobleman's daughter?" She put a hand on her hip and pushed her full lips into a sultry pout. "I mean, you caused this problem, I could simply allow our friends in the guild to deal with you."

Terror sprang into his gaze and she watched him weigh his options. "What is the favor?

"I understand that you are…intimate… with a few members of the Ajo council. All I ask is an introduction"

"That's impossible. You're wasting my time." He turned to leave.

Damn it. She'd counted on him being desperate to get rid of his problem. There were other ways to get what she needed. Shedding her human skin, Verity jumped and landed behind him. His start of surprise pleased her, almost as much as the feel of his neck under her knife.

"Perhaps you are not familiar with dealing with a Dziva?" She pressed the knife into his skin. She looked around the parking lot to be sure she hadn't been seen.

"I have gold in my pockets, take it and leave." The noble showed no fear.

"Must you continue to insult me?" Verity shook her hair.

The noble's eyes widened, his pulse skittered. Whispering a quick binding spell, she circled him, her scales glinting in the dim streetlights. His fear was a fine wine on the back of her tongue.

She smacked her lips. "Now, here I've come all this way to exchange business with you and you insult me. You now owe me for the inconvenience."

He swallowed, his eyes blinking, darting around the parking lot. "I don't owe you shit. We've come to no agreement."

She smacked her lips. "Not for the information I provided, no. However, you do owe me for information I've not yet disclosed. What do you think will happen when your secret comes out? I mean, we're talking about getting rid of a soon-to-be princess. Do you imagine your position in society would hold if this got out?"

His body, frozen in her spell, twitched. A noble with secrets was always useful. Verity slid her blade down his lips.

"You're as culpable as I in this matter. We're both fucked if you go to the Amanda." His eyes gave away his uncertainty.

He could have a point.

Putting pressure on the knife she watched a sliver of blood well on his bottom lip. "I'm only asking for your contact in the Ajo council. Surely your lifestyle is worth that much."

He struggled against her bonds. His panic burned through her senses. "If I give up my contact, I give up my leverage in the guild."

She smiled. Gods she loved secrets. The noble couldn't afford for anyone to know about the games he played. About the blood he spilled every week for the sake of pleasure. Nor about his attempt to kill a fellow nobleman's daughter. She licked his bottom lip, tasting his. "I'll keep your secret, and get rid of your female, all you have to do is introduce me to your contact."

Calculation replaced his fear. "Just an introduction?"

"That's it." For now. She backed away and released him from her spell.

He grabbed his jacket lapels and shook his shoulders. "And you'll kill her?'

"Right after you introduce me."

He nodded and walked away.

"You have forty-eight hours." She called after him. His shoulders stiffened but he didn't turn back. She smiled. One more to add to her bunch.

Verity's network of spies and informants was vast, once a contact was made, she never gave them back. She would use him for as long as he was useful and dispose of him when she was done. Freeing the master was the ultimate goal, the casualties did not matter. What was one merchant's daughter in the grand scheme of things?

She turned in the other direction, her change back to a human skin fluid. Pleased with tonight's outcome she dismissed the noble. The introduction to the Ajo was a big step. One that despite other tries had failed. It was how the noble had ingratiated his way into their group and convinced them to help him with his first 'problem'. His usefulness had run its course though. He'd promised that the Ajo council would come to heel, and he had yet to fulfill that promise. The guild bade her find her own way into the Ajo's world. They needed them for their plan to work. All she needed was an introduction.

She was a Dziva, it would take her nothing to bring the Ajos to their knees.

***

UNABLE TO SLEEP, Liliana sat outside on her balcony hours later, mulling over her problems. A cool night breeze played with her hair and cooled her overheated skin. With her mate two doors down, arousal sensitized her body to the point of madness. She supposed had she no memories of his touch, it wouldn't be so bad. But, every time she closed her eyes, the sight of his dark marbled skin flashed before her. The very moment the *di êjê* finished, she intended to wrap herself in his black hair and wallow in the soft strands.

It was disconcerting how much she wanted him. She couldn't fathom how some were able to cheat on their mates. How did one ignore the attraction between each other? The thought of anyone other than Leo soothing the heat turned her stomach. She knew once the mating frenzy left, that feeling would go away. But she still couldn't imagine. Her mind drifted back to the confrontation with the royal family.

An unpleasant bit of business.

Two families destroyed by unfaithfulness.

Her body warmed, her only warning that Leo had stepped onto the balcony. His scent wafted to her next and she closed her eyes and drew it in.

"You couldn't sleep either?" She kept her eyes on the stars. Maybe if she didn't look at him, she could get her body under control.

"Legba makes me restless." He sat in the lounger next to her.

"There is something quite stifling about it." She'd certainly felt strangled since she'd stepped through the portal. It had nothing to do with Legba, more her family.

A short mirthless chuckle was his only answer.

"I know my issue with Legba, but what's yours?"

A beat of silence passed. "My mother brought me here when I turned seventeen. Rather, I should say she dragged me kicking and screaming through the portal."

"That's terrible."

"She and my father were arguing again. Always arguing, those two. Anyway, she said she was leaving and my father told her she couldn't leave with his kids. She said 'fine, but Leo's not yours.'" He laid his head on the back of his lounger, eyes closed, his mouth pinched. "She snatched my arm and marched me to Haven's portal room."

She laid her hand gently on his. The pain in his eyes when he opened them clutched her heart.

"See, up until that point I'd had no idea Ranolph wasn't my father. My mother was almost always gone, and so I spent the majority of my time with my father or with the Amanda."

She hurt for the kid he'd been. Finding out something like that had to be painful.

He shook his head, and the pain in his eyes disappeared under anger. "She dragged me before the royal court and demanded King Leander give her a place to stay to escape her abusive mate."

"Oh no."

"My father never laid a hand on her and King Leander called her on it. He and my father were best friends, so of course, he wouldn't believe her. He told her if she had a grievance to go to the Eminzu. My mother refused and told him he had to provide for his son. Queen Kaylin exploded. She told my mother she'd rather kill me herself than allow my mother to use me against the king. The Queen still had not been able to conceive at that point. Over two hundred years into their mating and she hadn't provided the king with an heir. I'm surprised I wasn't killed on the spot." He smiled. There was no humor in the upturn of his lips. "That's not to say she didn't try. I had 'accidents' for years after that visit. Three hundred years later and I still avoided Legba for fear she would make good on her promise."

Liliana's closed her eyes to trap the tears.

"Long story short, my father came to pick us up. He told me that to him, I was his son and that was all that mattered. My mother and I don't speak, and I quite frankly prefer it."

"I'm sorry, Leo." The useless platitude her only offering, she stood and paced the balcony.

"What's on your mind, Liliana?"

Her search for Kita, her constant fights with her mother, him. Everything. She shook her head. "How did you get the name 'Death's messenger'?" she asked instead.

"I'm half Eshu. The messenger part sort of stuck."

"And death? Do you kill Demis?"

Their eyes met, his narrowed, but he shook his head. "I hunt those sentenced to death and deliver them to Azreal. In essence, I brought the message of death."

She nodded, relieved. Would it have made him a different person? Maybe not, but she was grateful just the same that he didn't kill for a living.

"Don't get it twisted though, Liliana. No one can enter Azreal alive. You understand that."

Her heart lurched. She gave a sharp nod.

"They are executed at the portal to Azreal, by Azra's servants." He met her gaze, his look needing her to understand the difference.

Her body slumped in relief. What he did was important. She couldn't, wouldn't judge him for it. Besides, it was not as though she moved about in society. She certainly didn't plan to stay here after their ceremony. It didn't matter what others thought.

The silence stretched between them until it became a heavy weight. Her body tuned itself to him, her heartbeat thumping to match the rhythm of his. She straightened her nightgown, doing anything not to look at him. A languid heat moved through her limbs, making them heavy.

"Come here, Liliana." His face was patient, with no evidence of the heat sapping her strength.

"How can you sit there so unaffected?" She growled.

Leo laughed. "Unaffected? Liliana, were it not for the fact that your parents were right down the hall, I would have you pinned to the nearest surface, making love to you until neither of us could walk."

Oh Gods. She gripped the banisters to keep from melting into a puddle on the ground. Lightning arced through her, firing her blood, her womb clenched in need.

***

LEO WATCHED THE HEAT playing across Liliana's face and adjusted in his chair, pushing his erection to the side. In her innocent nightgown, with her hair flowing to her back, she was irresistible. Her teeth worried her bottom lip. His attention was riveted, her lush mouth moved in a sensual pout and fire pooled in his gut. He'd tensed when she asked about his job, unsure of what she would think. He was used to getting two reactions from the women he ran into, fear and disgust, or lust.

Never anything in between.

A part of him had not wanted to see either on the face of his mate. Her relief at hearing he didn't kill soothed him.

His smile, a mere baring of teeth, showed a hint of his growing fangs. "Come, baby, I'm only asking you to sit in my lap. I'll behave."

Gods she was beautiful. Her dark lashes lowered and hid her eyes. When they lifted, the need reflected caught his breath. Moonlight filtered through her gown painting her curves in erotic shadows. She straddled his lap, the material of her gown bunching around her waist. Her scent wrapped around him and he buried his face in her neck.

"Do you have any idea what your scent does to me?" He kissed her neck, pulling her fragrant skin into his mouth.

She moaned. "I thought you were behaving."

He drew small circles in slow motion along her thighs taking delight in the shudders that shook her shoulders. He traced the lace at the bottom of her gown debating how far he could go. "I *am* behaving. You have no idea how hard it is for me to keep myself from sliding your panties aside," he bit her lip. "and sliding into the sweetest—"

"Leo," she whispered, cutting him off.

He chuckled, trailing kisses across her collarbone. Her skin warmed under his lips.

She moaned. Fire raced through his blood straight to his hard-on. Her hips wiggled, his control strained.

"How quiet can you be, Lily?" Leo fondled her breast, weighed it. His thumb brushed the taut peak pushing through the fabric of her gown.

A moan was her answer. She swallowed. Her neck working as she fought for air.

He pushed up her gown higher, trailing his fingers across the smooth skin of her stomach. The scrap of lace she called panties did nothing to hide the moisture gathering between her thighs. He slipped a finger underneath.

She moaned again.

"One more moan, Liliana and you're as good as fucked." He barely recognized the guttural tone of his voice. His finger lightly played in the soft curls covering her mound before he pushed into the warmth.

"Promise?" Her hoarse whisper traveled down his spine.

His dick throbbed, pushed against his pants. "I promise." He pushed two fingers into her warmth. "You'll find that I keep my promises, *iná.*"

He hissed as her inner muscles gripped his fingers. He captured her lips in a hot kiss, swallowing her next moan. He tangled his other hand in the braids of her hair and pulled. Her back arched, displaying her breast in offering to him. An offering he gladly took. He licked her through the gown, teasing the silk-covered pebble. Her mouth opened on a sigh of pleasure and he groaned. Magic flowed between them, her skin blushing, a dim light starting to build. Her light rivaled the glow from the bright moon.

He pulled her head down and shoved his tongue in her mouth, his grip on her hair tightening as she drew on it, sucking on it. He pushed the strap on her gown down her shoulder with his chin, exposing more of her body to the cool air.

"*Mi iná.*" She was his light. He watched as that light played across her face as her magic flared. Her caramel skin glowed, the warmth encompassed him and tightened his chest.

He separated their bodies, stopping his kiss only long enough to lift her and slide his pants down.

"Leo, I need you."

Her whispered words were desperate, her eyes liquid pools of emerald flames.

"You'll have me, baby." He positioned her over his straining shaft.

He pushed in slow, tortuously slow, biting down to contain his shout of pleasure. Her sex was tight, wet, and clenching around his shaft. Liliana arched her back, driving him deeper, her heat surrounding him. He pulled her head down for a kiss.

His hips lifted as she rode him, his strokes deep and her walls dragging him further out of control. Her neck called to him, instinct drove him as his fangs dropped, crowding his mouth. He scraped his teeth along her neck, so tempted to taste the blood flowing there, to seal them so no one could take his light. He closed his eyes and threw his head back, away from the temptation.

Liliana rolled her hips. She tightened on him, flexing and gripping the head of his erection. Finding his control, Leo pushed his hips in time with hers relishing every stroke. Edging closer to release, their passions consumed them. His hands released her only to take purchase down her back finding a place on her tight ass. He used his strength to lift her up as she drove herself down over and over again. Her hands gripped his strong shoulders balancing over his lap to drive her tightness home. The heat of her thighs burned his skin as their magic combined. Leo's hands squeezed tight as her wetness slid him effortlessly inside with each stroke.

He was a goner. He tried everything he knew to slow his climax but to no avail. His orgasm was a fire that raged down his spine and tightened his balls in pleasure. Her eyes locked on his as she rocked her body, grinding on him. Her orgasm rolled through her as her hands dug deep into his back nearly breaking the skin. She came, pulling at his throbbing erection and his control. He followed her over the edge, his hips lifting as he drove into her body. He was flying. Her mouth opened in a silent scream. A haze of pleasure fogged his mind, and he collapsed back into the lounger, dragging her down on his chest. Liliana burrowed into his neck her mouth on his pulse.

"No, baby" He pulled her from his neck. He couldn't allow her to bite. Couldn't allow the blood exchange before the *di êjê*.

She whimpered and wiggled and he hardened again. The mating frenzy would ride them until they completed their bond, and he planned to enjoy every moment on her beautiful body.

He stood up still joined with her body. He dragged the cushion from the lounger and tossed it on the balcony floor and laid her down, her hair spread out. He positioned himself at her entrance and drove in. She was beyond wet, her orgasms still sending tremors through her sated body. Leo closed his eyes and growled. Her nails raked further down his back and she lifted her hips, meeting him thrust for thrust. Yeah, he could do this all night.

Chapter 10

LILIANA DIPPED HER HEAD to hide the yawn threatening to crack her jaw. She'd been sitting in her mother's living room for the past two hours learning etiquette and history from the royal archivist. The woman was in charge of passing down Eshu history to future generations. It was required since she would be marrying into the royal family.

"Lady Marcolev!" The slap of the silver pointer against the table snapped her to attention.

The historian stared at her, her narrow lips pursed. The petite woman was Eshu. Her family had served the royal house since before recorded time. Metalie Yoru was dressed in the traditional gown of beautiful and sedate silver, marking her station as a royal employee. Her purple and blue hair was faded with age, but shinier than a polished diamond. A large, single braid trailed her shoulder reaching her stomach.

'Lady Marcolev, you need to pay better attention. Not only are you marrying into the royal family, but into the Amanda as well. The protocol I am attempting to teach will keep you out of more situations like the very one you're in now."

Liliana suppressed a sigh and the urge to jump across the table at the smug lady. "Why didn't I have to go through this when I was betrothed to the prince?"

The archivist eyebrows lifted. "If you'd successfully mated with the prince, these lessons would've been conducted once you took up residence in the palace. That will not be the case with this mating. If we make it to the ceremony that is."

The barb hit its mark, pissed, Lily crossed her arms over her chest. "We've been at this for two hours Mistress Yoru, and quite frankly you've just regurgitated history we learned in finishing school."

Metalie narrowed her eyes. "Very well. What do you know of the history of the Demi, and the start of the Amanda?"

"The Amanda started after our war with the humans. They were started as a way to control and monitor traffic to and from Adro."

A smug smile tipped Metalie's lips. "Wrong, that is the type of misinformation little girls fresh out of finishing school regurgitates to others. If you're to be the mate of Death's messenger, then you'll do well to pay attention and keep your bad attitude to yourself."

Heat climbed Lily's neck, the bite of her temper rushing through her chest. "Fine, tell me what you think I need to know and be quick about it. I don't want to hear any more about who beget who, and whose cousin had a million babies."

The two women stared neither breaking eye contact. Finally, the archivist rolled her eyes and turned back to her presentation. She moved through a few screens and pulled up an artist's rendition of the Great War. Lily sucked in her breath at the heartbreaking scene. Blood ran in a river at the bottom of the painting. Humans and Demi in various positions of death littered the ground, while the gods turning their backs were scattered throughout the darkening sky. Something not quite black, but dark enough hovered on the edge of the scene, sinister and waiting, almost happy at the destruction playing out. The artist captured the devastation in a way that brought tears to her eyes.

"Doesn't it break your heart," Mistress Yuru whispered. Clearing her throat she carried on. "The Divine were the first humans the gods and goddesses created. They were made from the soil of the Earth and given the breath of life. They were beautiful to look at and it wasn't long before the gods that made them started to lust after them. As it always is with lust," she gave Liliana a pointed look, "the gods were unable to keep their hands to themselves. That's where the Demi come in. Born from gods and humans. Demi-gods."

Liliana sat up. This wasn't the same history they were taught. They were told they were made by the gods.

"History tells us the death of the first Divine started the unrest among them. They were made by the gods, but not of them, so they were mortal. It was then they noticed the slow aging of the Demis. Jealousy started the first fights and the war soon after."

"The war between us was started because the Divine realized they were mortal?" Liliana sat stunned amazed at the disparity between the histories she was taught as a child.

"The fear of death is a powerful motivator, as Prince Leonalph knows. They did everything in their power, and it was remarkable power, to prolong their life. Experimenting with magic darker than anything belonging on Earth. In doing so they unleashed the ultimate evil." Metalie sighed and shook her head. "Soon the Earth ran with the blood from both races, gods and goddesses fought on both sides, driving up the body count until Adro herself cried out for an end. The primal source pulled the gods from the war, leaving two races to fight for themselves. Except, the Divine didn't play fair."

"Ofeeree," Lily whispered. Stories of the evil villain were whispered among the children at sleepovers. Used by nannies to keep wayward charges in order.

Metalie cleared her throat. "Yes. He was formed from pure black magic, no soul resides in that being, nothing to tie him to any type of humanity. He turned the tide of the war towards the Divine, and soon the Demi went into hiding. Adro created realms for each race to give them shelter. But Ofeeree was not content to just rule the Earth dimension, he wanted everything, every dimension to belong to him. To stop him from encroaching, the most powerful families of each realm got together, each giving a portion of their power. A binding spell was created from the magic, and after more deaths, more chaos, Ofeeree was finally bound."

"Why did the Demi not come out of hiding then?" Lily sat forward propping her elbows on her knees.

"You've seen the realms we were given, you've spent time on Adro, would you give this up for that?"

"But the primal source. We need it more than humans."

Every year families traveled to Adro to access the primal source, to soak up the sun as it were. Though the realms were made for the Demi, their dimensions did not hold the true power of the sun or the cosmic energy Earth held on its surface. Only an echo of that power.

"It was decided that to keep the peace, we would remain where we were. We would keep our magic and our technological advances to ourselves. Only venturing out once a year to pull in power from the primal source. It was why the Havens were created. To give us a safe place to pass through to Adro and to give the Amanda a way to keep track and accounting of who was where."

Lily frowned. "Why did it matter? Why keep track of who's going to sunbath for a week?"

Metalie crossed her arms over her chest in a rare showing of temper. "Would you want an Apophi demon roaming Adro unsupervised, randomly taking souls? Or shall we send a pair of un-mated Benu to seduce half the population of any city they enter, leaving the poor women enthralled and near death?"

Lily shuddered, neither sounded like a good idea. But, since she'd snuck onto Adro, she knew there were ways around the Havens. "So since I'm going to be marrying into the Amanda, tell me about them."

"The Amanda were created by Rugaba. He initially was given responsibility for the Demi, it's said as punishment from the primal source. During the war, because of the primal source's edict, he had to step back from both us and the humans. He created the Eminzu to govern us, and the Amanda to police. Along with policing the Demi, the Amanda are responsible for protecting the humans from us, and our magic. Your new brother-in-law is the current leader of the Amanda and has been in his position for close to three centuries. He took over for his father Ranolph Tegan, who had served for close to a millennium. According to tradition, Prince Leonalph will be asked to step from his position as Death's Messenger and take a less dangerous job."

Lily's heart dropped, and remorse filled her.

"Regardless, he will be known as Death's messenger for the rest of his life and you will need to act according to that station."

She rolled her eyes. And they were back to how she was supposed to act. "What else will I need to know? Can we wrap this up?"

"Goddess, but you are a rude female. We cannot just 'wrap this up'. Your lessons will take place every day until the day you're bonded. So you may as well get used to it." Metalie started to pack away the gear she'd brought for her presentation, her movements jerky broadcasting her aggravation.

"So I'm not the only one you drive crazy?" Leo's deep voice

broke through the tension.

She didn't hear or see him come in. Her heart thudded at the sight of him leaning against the door frame. He wore a black V-neck shirt with a pair of khaki-colored linen pants, looking impossibly handsome. Her fingers itched to touch him. The fatigue and boredom she'd felt with the etiquette lessons dissipated and were replaced with anticipation. The smile on his face sent heat through her body.

Metalie bowed her head. "Your majesty."

A look of surprise darted across his face before he hid it. "That's a first."

Leo's dry tone brought a barely-there smile to the archivist's face.

She grabbed her bag. "If you'll excuse me." She turned to Liliana. "We will resume tomorrow." With that threat, she left them alone.

Lily stood, wiping her hands along her jean shorts. "Hi." Shyness left her voice a whisper as she approached him. Despite last night, she was unsure of his reception of her.

"Hi," he said softly. He pulled her the remaining distance into his arms.

He dropped a whisper of a kiss on her lips, sending her heart into a tailspin. She melted at his sweet greeting.

"How did you sleep last night?" A mischievous grin converted his face from the stern handsomeness she'd grown accustomed to, into gorgeous.

She smiled, and looked up from under her lashes, "I slept wonderfully for some reason."

He chuckled, the sound sending a thrill to her lady parts. He trailed kisses along her neck. "We should get out for a bit," he whispered.

***

LEO CUDDLED HIS MATE closer. Aggravation from her etiquette lesson seeped through their connection. Getting out would be a perfect way to relax her. He sniffed right where her hair met her neck, inhaling against the warm spot, her smell turning him on like nothing he'd ever experienced.

"Maybe we can visit the market place, I've missed our pastries so much since my time on Adro."

He loved the smile on her face and wondered if he'd ever be able to tell her no for anything when she smiled at him. The oversized t-shirt she wore slipped off her shoulder and he couldn't resist a nibble. She tilted her head to the side, tightened her grip on his waist and moaned.

He hardened, pressing his body into hers. "You know what that sound does to me, *ina*." He reveled in the feel of her and wondered where they could escape her mother's prying eyes. Someplace they could sequester themselves so he would have her to himself.

Grinding into her a little more, he groaned. He didn't want a quickie with her. He wanted something slow…drawn out. He wanted space to devour her. "Go get dressed, before we get in trouble."

Reluctantly he stepped back.

"Let me change into something proper and we can leave." She kissed his cheek and slipped past him.

He eyed her retreating figure in the short denim that hugged her ass, giving him all types of ideas. The shorts showed off her shapely legs and damn if he didn't want to chase her down the hallway. He pushed down the predator within him and turned his back. If they didn't get the *di êjê* finished soon, he was going to explode.

***

"You're meddling Rue."

Rugaba stopped his pacing and stared at the intruder. Azra, the god of death sauntered across the courtyard, his steps insolent and leisurely. Rue came to his solarium to think, he had no need for company.

"What are you doing in Alafia?" The god rarely left his realm.

"I came to see what you were up to. There are rumors floating around, I thought I'd come to the source." Azra folded his arms over his lean chest and eyed his brother. "Something you want to tell me?"

"What could I have to tell you that you don't already know?"

"I'm to understand you're doing favors for an old friend…again."

Rue grimaced. To say Azra and Oya didn't get along was an understatement. "What has that to do with anything?"

Azra sighed. "Rue you know what happens when we meddle with the creatures on Adro. Not to mention, what happens to you when that viper is involved. Leave it be."

"They are not creatures, brother. Besides, they're our creation. You would allow them to die knowing we could help?" He cringed as he recognized the words Oya used with him when she defended her tribe.

"They are ours no longer, let the primal source deal with whatever it is."

"So you imagine *when* Ofeeree destroys the Earth, he'll not be looking for another place to take?"

Azra scoffed. "Please, he and what army?"

"Oya's tribe is the only thing standing between Ofeeree's followers and the army of souls he's going to try and take back. So scoff at my favor all you want."

Azra frowned and uncrossed his arms. "They're locked away, bound tighter than Ofeeree himself. Or don't you trust the magic your Oya so preciously covets?"

Rugaba ignored his brother's barb. "It's part of the prophecy. Ofeeree will search for a way to rebuild his army, most of whom were sent into the deepest reaches of this realm. Guarded by the very same woman you openly mock. Do you not think he'll come after those souls?"

"What prophecy?"

"The Mina…"

"The Mina have a prophecy every be-damned day. Why is this prophecy any different?" Azra cut him off.

"This prophecy concerns the Kokoro souls."

"The same souls Oya keeps guard over?"

Rugaba nodded. "She released them.

Azra frowned. "When?"

"I track time no better than you do. It doesn't matter, what matters is they've been released and we both know they're the only ones who can free Ofeere."

"Which begs the question, why did she release them?"

"I didn't ask." Rue lowered his head.

"Is that right?" The scorn in Azra's voice was easy to discern. "So she just decided one day to release three of the most powerful souls in the universe, and you didn't ask any questions."

Rugaba shrugged. "The prophecy…"

"You know how I feel about prophecy, Rue. By the time you're done chasing your tail, and playing with riddles, Adro will still be fucked."

"Even still, we can't ignore it. The Ajo are trying to get into Oya's temple, presumably to get access to Ofeere's banished army. The only souls able to free him are out in the world and there is magic darkening Earth. When is the last time you've tried to see beyond the veil?"

"I haven't. Your messenger brings my worshippers to me. I need not look to Adro for them."

Rugaba stopped pacing and stared at his brother. Unless invoked for vengeance, his brother was lazy, and did the least amount of work he could get away with. "Really, Az? By the gods how do you manage to keep Azrael in line?"

Azra gave him a wolfish smile. "Oh but, brother, I make the most spectacular examples out of Demis who don't cooperate. Eternity with me can be hell, or hellish, their choice." His smile disappeared. "Speaking of hellish, there is another reason I came to see you. Your messenger has been mated."

"What!"

"Yep, and I'm here to tell you, I'm not breaking in another messenger. Talk to your council, they can't bench him."

"Az, he can't take trips to Azrael with a mate. The Eminzu will throw a fit if he dies in your realm…"

"I'll strengthen my wards over him, but nothing has happened to him in two centuries."

Rugaba growled."Azra,"

"No, Rue. Three messengers died before the ink was dry on their assignments, two more died simply trying to cross the veil into Azrael. I'm not going through that shit again. Talk to your whiny ancestors."

"Fine, I'll see what I can do." There was no use arguing with Azra. His brother saluted him and disappeared, ending any argument he would have anyway.

Rue growled and continued his pacing. Unlike his brother's nonchalance regarding Adro's fate, Rugaba couldn't stand back and allow a war he knew would end the world to take place. Most of the gods' power came from their worshipers. If they were gone…

They would be weakened. Who knew what would happen then.

Chapter 11

THE RINGING OF HIS communicator interrupted the naughty thoughts racing through Leo's head. He saw his brother's I.D. and connected the line immediately.

"We looked through the Oras for the last time Kita visited Haven." Xavier wasted no time on pleasantries.

His heartbeat picked up its rhythm. "What did you find?"

"It's more what we didn't find that has me worried for you. Magic corrupted the Oras."

"How is that possible?"

"Exactly my question," Xavier growled. "One for which I will enjoy getting the answer. We have her last movements coming into Haven during a fight night, she wanders around a bit, does some quite frankly questionable things and then the feed dies."

Leo's gut churned, a bad feeling drying his mouth. "It takes an inordinate amount of dark magic to slightly interrupt the feed, I can't imagine what it would take to erase it altogether. That's magic over Adro itself."

He mentally went through creatures who would have powers over the Earth, and only one came to mind. Except, the Gu were the last to mess with dark magic. They used their magic to form weapons, armor. The iron giants mined the Earth for its precious metals and minerals, they would never manipulate the magnetic fields in order to tamper with the Oras. Doing so could affect their metallurgy. But who if not them.

"Listen to me, Leo." Xavier's voice broke into his musings.

"I'm listening."

"Kita came in with Prince Kedric, and the last images were of her with the prince. If ever there was a person with the influence and perhaps the money to get the Oras erased…"

Leo cursed. Instincts that kept him alive in his post as Death's messenger flared to life. Fear for Liliana bloomed in his chest.

"On another note, Fallon spoke to Rue, he's giving you an audience after your ceremony."

A sharp exhale was the only answer he could give his brother. Gods, he needed his meeting with Rugaba to go well. "Thank you, X."

"I know how important your job is to you, Leo."

"I gotta go." Leo snapped closed his communicator cutting off his brother, and the emotion threatening to swamp him. Just the thought of losing his job was carving a deep hole in his soul. He had no memories of wanting to be anything other than in the Amanda. His whole life he'd watched the soldiers, his life's goal to join their ranks. There had to be a way to keep both his job and his mate, and he would find it.

Liliana walked carefully down the stairs. He turned his attention to her. Dressed in a long flowing gown tied around her exposed neck, she was beautiful. The soft peach color made her brown skin glow, and the sleek, loosely draped fabric clung to her curves. Her hair was piled high atop her head, leaving her neck and shoulders bare. His body tightened, heat pooled low in his belly at the sight of her. How the in hells of Azreal did he get so lucky? She smiled as she made her way over to his.

"Will you be able to walk around in those?" He took in her dainty feet in the gold sandals she wore.

She curtsied and laughed. "Of course. Ladies the world over are trained to walk around in uncomfortable shoes. All for the sake of looking pretty."

He shook his head and smiled, grabbing her elbow. "I'll never understand females." He escorted her out to the family's lift pad.

Liliana typed in a code and they stood to wait on a travel pod. "You're not meant to." She lifted on her toes and kissed his cheek as their ride pulled up.

They entered the travel airlift laughing. It wasn't long before they were zipping through the skies of Legba. Liliana spent the trip pointing out her favorite places as they backtracked towards the city. The multi-colored stone towers of the temple she and her family attended. The whitewashed building with arched windows where she'd spent hours reading. The whole realm was a show of colors as they got closer to the city center. Bright colored brick buildings seemingly floating in the air. Stained glass windows from floor to ceiling in some, flags of other realms waved from atop many of the roofs. They passed through the business districts where dark-colored windows separated the bank buildings from the other commercial buildings.

Soon they pulled up to the travel pod at the marketplace in the heart of the realm. Outdoor vendors stretched as far as the eye could see. A rainbow of colored awnings covered fruit vendors, bakers, vintners, and various crafters hawking their wares in every language including English. Liliana's eyes lit and Leo was glad he'd thought of the trip. Always on guard, he exited the lift first, his gaze racking over both male and female, looking for threats. His brother's warning was uppermost in his thoughts. He turned to help Lily out of the transport, happy but surprised she'd waited inside. It must have shown on his face, her eyebrow lifted.

"I've dealt with security before, I know better than to move before I'm given the ok," she caressed his cheek before grabbing his hand. "I also know how to fend for myself, try to remember that as well, my mate."

He chuckled. Her words reminding him that she'd spent years alone on Adro, looking for her sister, while eluding soldiers. She was smarter than it seemed he gave her credit for. He released her hand, resting his on the small of her back as he guided her through the crowded market. His reputation often proceeded him when he went out and here was no different. He received respectful nods from some of the males, open staring from a lot more of the ladies than he was comfortable with and salutes from members of the Amanda scattered throughout the market for security. The more hostile stares he met head-on, the offender's eyes lowering quickly. He put a protective arm around Lily, keeping an eye out for anyone out of place. They randomly stopped at various shops, her happy chatter drawing a smile from him. She had an easy way with the shopkeepers, respectful yet firm as she haggled over prices. Her beauty robbed him of breath. She turned to him and smiled, winking in a shared joke over her negotiating. It punched through his heart and he was struck dumb by the realization that he might actually, really like his mate.

Liliana caught him staring as she spun in a happy circle in the middle of the baker's stall. A blush colored her cheeks as she reached over for her pastries. Her heart settled into a fast rhythm as his gaze caressed her face. Needing a distraction from the riotous feelings, she broke off a piece of her favorite *namo* bread and lifted it to his lips.

"You have to try this. I've only ever found these here at Mr. Aleah's stall."

He opened his mouth, waiting on her. The hunger in his eyes had nothing to do with the sweet treat. If he kept staring at her in that manner, they would need to find privacy, propriety be damned. She fed him the fruit-laden pastry, laughing as juice dribbled down his chin. She swiped it with her finger and put it in her mouth, her eyes on his as she sucked on it. He growled and pulled her close.

He nipped her ear. "Behave, *ina*."

What was the fun in that, though? She laughed instead, pulling him down the busy path to the next stall. They spent the next couple of hours wandering the market, him following her, one eye on her, the other scanning the crowd. The way his face softened every time he turned his attention to her made her feel unbelievably lucky. He was guarded with most they came in contact with, though never impatient with any child with the courage to approach him. She watched him lower to their level, answering their questions, no matter how outlandish. For the adults, especially males, he lifted his lips in a snarl sending them scrambling from their path.

"I realize the attention I garner when I go out, but you seem to have me beat." He remarked dryly.

Heat crept up her neck. She sipped from her frozen fruit cup to stall. He raised an eyebrow.

"I left a week before my mating ceremony with the prince." She ducked her head in embarrassment.

His lips twitched as he suppressed a smile. "A week? Runaway bride, then?"

She turned from him and cleared her throat. "Something like that." Had she known running was an option, she wouldn't have waited until a week before the ceremony to do so. She certainly wouldn't have waited until Prince Kedric whipped her and threatened her life if she stayed.

He turned her shoulders back to face him. "There's more to it than that, then?"

She nodded. "Can we drop it for now?"

He stared at her for a long moment before nodding and kissing her lightly.

Three hours into their trip, her feet decided they'd had enough. The pain wasn't what made her ready to leave though. A half-hour or so ago, the back of her neck started tingling, a sign she'd come to respect and heed. Someone was watching her, and she didn't mean the disapproving looks she was receiving from some of the older Eshu nobles.

She'd known as soon as rumors of her new impending mating started circulation, they would be shunned. She was prepared for it, and for the most part, ignored the tsking sounds and averted eyes they'd dealt with all day. This was different, malevolent, definitely more than just staring. She tucked closer into Leo's side, grateful for his size.

"What is it?" He tightened his arm around her, concern creasing his brows.

She started to shrug it off.

"Don't, Lily. You've progressively gotten quiet these last few minutes, something is bothering you."

"I have this eerie feeling I can't shake."

She expected him to brush off her concerns, instead, his eyes darted around them. Surprise and relief warred within her. She'd spent her life having her family dismiss everything she did and said. That he didn't hesitate or ask if she was sure…she rubbed her chest as affection for him blossomed.

"Can you pinpoint the feeling?" All business, Leo turned them back towards the transport area, his steps measured, but not rushed.

"Someone is watching us."

"Watching, not staring?"

She nodded, relieved he understood the difference. She slid closer to Leo, appreciating his warmth and the arm around her waist. She felt secure in a way she hadn't felt since...ever. She snuggled into his side not caring about etiquette. They were going to stare anyway. They were near the transport when she spotted the candies Bea loved and used to sneak to her when she was small.

Hand to Leo's chest, she stopped them at the stall. "I want to get some candy for Bea."

Handing him the bags, she stepped closer, grabbing a small basket to put them in. She scooped in a few handfuls, smiling at the memories evoked by the sweet smell. Bea would love these. She placed her basket on the scale, eyes roaming the stall as the shopkeeper weighed them. Candy jars of various sizes flanked the front counter, the ones below shaped like owls. She already pictured the smile on Bea's face. She reached down and grabbed it a moment before chaos erupted.

Blown back by a blast of air, confusion turned quickly to pain as she landed on her back. She blinked against the brightness of the sky, clutching the candy jar as she fought to make sense of what happened. Her ears rang, and Leo's face swam in and out of focus as he leaned over her. Pain exploded through her body as he lifted her, the jostling stealing her breath. Her heartbeat thundered in her ear loudly as he ran through the scattering, panicked crowd. Lily looked down at the jar, realizing she'd forgotten to pay. She glanced back at the stall and found it annihilated. Her eyes widened, her heart stopped, then settled into a rapid rhythm, the sound second to her harsh breathing. Lily closed her eyes in pain. What the hell had happened?

***

"Damn it!" Vanity cursed, bringing her hood up around her head.

Hours spent on that spell and she'd missed. Leo was moving at a fast clip, his precious mate tight in his arms. No way could she risk launching the spell again and accidentally hitting him with it. Yeah, there would be a stink if she took out the girl since she was a noble, but Xavier would pause the Earth on its axis if something happened to his brother. There would be no hole or realm where she could hide.

It took the Amanda no time to gather in force around the stall, cordoning it off to search for clues. She moved quickly through the still panicking crowd, not wanting to be anywhere near that stall once they started their questioning. She'd been following Leo and her target through the market place for close to an hour before they'd stopped at that empty stall. The shopkeeper had been far enough behind the counter that she'd decided to risk it. Her commission was for Liliana only, she refused to take out some struggling shopkeeper and his shoppers. Not because of anything having to do with morals or her conscience. Verity just didn't kill anything that didn't come with some form of payment.

Period.

She made her way through the thinning crowd towards the portal she'd used to enter Legba, cursing her bad aim. Well, not so much her aim. Someone had bumped into her as she set up her spell. She sighed in annoyance. She hated dealing with regular folk. Now, with this failed attempt, Leo would be more vigilant. Who knew what type of protections he'd set around his mate. Getting a second chance at Liliana just went from slim to damn near impossible. She had no time to think about it now, she was late. Glancing around to ensure she remained unseen, she pressed her palm against the sagging stall towards the back of the market, activating the illegal portal. The cloying smells of vegetation threatened to choke her as it opened. Verity took small shallow breaths through her mouth and cursed the Mina and their decaying forest.

Stepping through the portal she hot-footed it, heading towards the single structure on their realm, a small cabin used as a meeting place. Between the creepy forest with eyes and the claustrophobic cabin where she met with her partners, Verity had a crushing need to escape. The meeting place had been non-negotiable. Meeting on Minona would keep the precognitive race from seeing their plans. This godforsaken cabin was their only blind spot on the planet. Fucking Mina and their all-knowing, all-seeing eyes.

"Dziva."

Her partners greeted her with suspicion, her lateness noted and filed away, sure to come back and bite her in the ass. She cursed Liliana anew.

She blinked, refocusing on the faces standing around the room regarding her curiously. "Yes?"

"How did the meeting with the Ajo go?"

She lowered her hood and pushed the heavy fall of hair over her shoulder. Would it be too much to ask for a freaking breeze in this place?

"Dziva." Impatience tinged the sharp bark of her name.

Her eyes narrowed on the speaker. Dark eyes met hers, the yellow strip down the middle widening, encompassing the dark orbs of the creature. The Apophi's slender waif-like body was protected by scales much like hers, but very much impenetrable. She palmed her dagger anyway.

She debated taking him to task, but knew he'd simply feed on any anger she directed his way. Not worth the effort. Besides, the Apophi would amplify the anger until the eight of them were all going at each other's throat, and nothing would get done.

Yeah, best to let it slide.

"They're on board, though somewhat reluctantly." Though she dreaded every meeting with the guild, the one with the Ajo was worse. They were completely psychotic, and no amount of wheedling had worked. In the end, she'd had to promise them something she wasn't altogether sure she could grant.

"What? They're benefiting from this arrangement as much as we are. If we have the amulet, the Aje will be unable to reform their tribe, thus expanding their miserable life." The Benu flapped his large phoenix wings in aggravation.

Someone scoffed.

"What do you expect? They're insane. Logical thinking is a luxury for those creatures." This from the Cagyn in the group.

Verity eyed the female. She'd certainly earned her place in their merry band. The group consisted of eight beings, each powerful in their own right. The only goal of this group was to find Ofeeree and free him. They each had different reasons for doing so. It was an unspoken rule that no one asked. She certainly wouldn't tell another her reasons.

No names were exchanged to keep them from telling on each other. At least that was the theory. Verity didn't do business with people she didn't have dirt on. She looked around at those assembled. "Despite their insanity, for the time being, we need them. Getting the amulet is the key to getting into Oya's temple. That should be our goal for now."

"I disagree." An Abiku challenged. The demon met the eye of every being at the table, catching their attention. "The Kokoro souls have been released. Finding them should be our priority."

A heated argument broke out as the others added their two cents. Verity rubbed her temples, grimacing at the headache already forming.

She held up her hand for silence. "Once we have the souls, then what? We hold them until someone tells us where Ofeeree's hiding place is?"

"Our plan to find his location failed. I agree with the Dziva, we can't move without it." The Apophi licked his lips, his eyes raking her body.

Verity suppressed a shudder. Nasty creature. Out of the eight members of their group, the Aphophi was the only one she feared. That was saying much in light of the fact that a soul-eating demon was in their ranks. Something about the creature made her skin crawl.

"Do we have another plan for getting the location?" The Benu asked.

"I have one in place," the Cagyn said. They all listened as she outlined the plan.

It was clever, and could definitely work. Verity grudgingly gave the woman respect. But there was a slight problem with their plan, in that she'd almost killed the woman they planned to use to get Ofeeree's location. She eyed the Eshu in the corner and shook her head slightly at him. She failed in the job he'd hired her for, but perhaps it was for the best. With Leo stepping up security on his soon to be bride, getting to her would've been impossible.

"The plan will take some time. But between that and the Ajo, we're well on the way to freeing Ofeeree." The Cagyn smiled, her dark marbled skin glowing in anticipation.

"Gaining entry into Oya's temple will allow us to free enough powerful souls for an army that can't be beaten." The Apophi rubbed his hands together in anticipation.

Chapter 12

LEO PACED HER PARENT'S living room, angrily barking orders into his communicator. Despite his obvious anger, he wasn't shouting. Somehow, she found that scarier. She sat perched on the edge of her mother's chintz armchair, tightly clutching the owl-shaped candy jar she'd picked up at the candy store. Her fingers were cold and clammy where they met in the middle of the jar. Her ears had stopped ringing, but she was freezing, lightheaded, all signs she recognized as shock. All of the near misses she'd had over the years on the run had made her an expert on the symptoms.

She breathed deeply, closed her eyes and went through the techniques she'd learned to calm her body down. When she opened them a few minutes later her heartbeat was a little slower, and there was feeling in her fingers again. Leo's hair was longer, darker, his body thicker as he paced. Growls rattled his chest as he continued barking orders. She watched him, her heart rate speeding once more when he turned those beautiful eyes to her. The silver had completely enveloped his pupils. He murmured something she was unable to hear and closed the communicator. He stalked to her, his large body dominating her parent's common area, his chest heaving.

She set the jar next to her on the chaise and lifted her chin. She could and would be strong in the face of his anger. The non-submissive gesture could set him off, but damn it she almost died. She wouldn't cower from her mate.

She swallowed hard.

Even if he was close to changing into his Cagyn form. He growled and stalked to her, lifting her by her arms. He took her mouth in an aggressive kiss, blotting out panic, near misses, hell, all thoughts had disappeared. She wrapped her legs around his waist and held on for dear life.

He turned and walked down the hallway, his lips never leaving hers. He pushed her back into a wall, the picture frames rattling. She came up for air, her lower back throbbing, reminding her of the injuries from the blast.

"Leo, we can't, not here."

He trailed his teeth along her neck and the thought of him biting her, bonding the two of them bounced through her mind. She stopped herself from once again pleading for him to bind them. He sighed, kissing her one final time on the base of her throat. His touch gentled and he pulled back, running his hands over her body, checking for injuries. The claws on his hand gave away how close he was to losing control of his beast. She let out a hiss of pain as he raked his hands across her back. Now that the fog of passion and panic had lifted, the pain of her body was becoming apparent.

He hissed, the rage coming back momentarily. "You are not to go anywhere alone until I can figure out who did this."

She started to protest. Words from a few of the human women she'd met ran across her mind. *Start as you mean to go on.* They couldn't start their relationship with him dictating her every move. But at the same time, she did almost get killed, could she really argue? She opened her mouth but closed it when she saw the look in his face. Anger, more like rage was apparent but she saw the worry there, the tenderness bleeding his eyes back to their normal color. She somehow felt the way she handled this could set the tone for their mating. Pain shot up her back and she closed her eyes. She'd distract him from his orders for now.

Her moan of pain snapped him back from the edge. Leo shook his head to shake away the anger as worry for her once again jumped to the forefront. He eased her down from the wall, his claws receding as he calmed down.

"What hurts, baby?" He gentled his touch and watched her eyes for a reaction.

They widened when he got to her back. He turned her and saw the bruises blooming from the middle of her shoulder blades to her lower back disappearing into her dress. His heart stuttered and his beast slammed to the forefront. His body burned and stretched, the Eshu form seamlessly replaced by his Cagyn one. His already dark skin darkened, the bronze whirls coming to life as power flooded his body. His fangs crowded his mouth, the incisors cutting into his lip. Lily turned around, her eyes meeting his. No trace of fear lurked in her eyes and that satisfied him on a level he never thought possible. No one faced him in this form. The Demi he was sent for knew his Cagyn form meant death. Despite the fact that his hand spanned nearly her entire waist, the black-tipped claws finishing the distance, Lily stood before him unfazed. Fear for her took hold of his heart.

She raised onto her toes and grabbed his face. "Calm down, Leo, I'm fine. Just a little pain."

He growled low in his throat. "I will find and kill whoever is responsible for this."

Her eyes widened. A gasp from the hallway had them both turning. Leo pushed his mate behind him, facing the interloper. It was the maid, she clutched a canvass bag to her chest as she observed them. He eased down minutely.

"What has happened?" She dropped the bag and rushed towards them.

Leo growled again, the menacing sound stopping the maid in her tracks. Liliana's hands moved on his back, the upward motion soothing.

"I'm fine, Leo." Her voice went through him like a cool breeze.

He exhaled with a hard shudder. The whorls on his arm brightened, the light pulsing with his increasing heartbeat. If he thought handling the mating in his Eshu and human skin were hard, his Cagyn form was worst. The beast was simple, his mate was near, and in danger. No one and nothing would be allowed near her. The urge to mark her, and bond them sent blood straight to the perpetual erection he had around Liliana. First, he needed to get rid of the Cagyn woman standing in the hallway rightfully looking at him as though he were a dangerous animal. The maid's fear appeased him if only a little. Liliana made a small sound of distress and he whipped around to her. Her eyebrows were lowered, her body shaking, her pain obvious. He lifted her, pushed past the maid and took her to her room. He laid her gently on the bed and whipped out his communicator. As soon as the dispatcher at Haven answered he ordered him to find the nearest healer and send them to Liliana's father's house.

"We have a family healer, Leo." She adjusted in her bed to sit against the headboard.

He shook his head, waiting for the dispatcher to confirm his order. Once he received confirmation he hung up.

"Leo, you're overreacting, I'm fine."

He towered over her in his form, making her look smaller and more helpless than ever. "You will rest until the healer looks over you."

"Are you going to watch over me in beast mode for the rest of the day?" Her small smile melted him.

Wiping a hand across his face, he bade his beast to calm. Deep breaths brought his magic back under control and he transformed into his Eshu form. "Better?"

Leaning forward, she grabbed his cheeks and pulled him in for a kiss. "You're sexy regardless of your form."

He deepened the kiss, magic dancing between them, lighting her hair and the whorls covering his arms. Someone cleared their throat from the doorway. Leo had sensed the soldier the moment he entered the house, but nevertheless, he turned and shielded Liliana with his body.

"Who is that?" Liliana pushed his shoulder down to see the Amanda soldier standing at the door of her room.

"I want someone watching you while I go investigate this."

She frowned. "You're leaving me behind to do it?"

He angled his head to the side. "You have investigatory skills I don't know about?"

"Leo." She slapped his arm. "You don't know my skill set."

He couldn't stop the smile from forming. "You're right."

She reared back in surprise.

"What? You want me to be an ass about it?"

She crossed her arms over her chest. "I didn't expect you to be okay with me going."

"I'm not okay with you going, and for now, I will have my way on this." He held up a hand to stem her argument. "Perhaps later you will get your way. But, today, with you injured, I insist you stay in bed."

Expressions flitted lightning-quick across her face as she thought through his words. At some point, defeat settled and her body loosened the tension she was carrying. He knew the time she'd spent on Adro would keep her from being the perfect submissive mate. If he were being honest with himself, he didn't want one. He liked the fire of Liliana. Though he was happy to have won this mini fight, he didn't like the slump of her shoulders. He nodded the guard out of the room and stared at her.

"What? You won, I'll stay."

He leaned over and kissed her lips softly. "There is no win or lose in this, *mi ina*. Today scared the shit out of me. I want you safe, is that a bad thing?"

She sighed. "Now you're trying to make me sound petty."

"Am not." He chuckled as she narrowed her eyes at him. "Can we compromise?"

"I'm listening."

"You stay in bed until I get back, and I will tell you what I find out."

"I want to know everything, Leo. I deserve to know who's trying to hurt me. No leaving out what you think I can't handle."

"Promise."

She sighed in relief. Anxiety was still there in her eyes, but the spark he'd come to love about her was there as well. The compromise cost him nothing but made a world of difference to Liliana. He wanted her safe, but he didn't want her to feel stifled by him. He kissed her a final time and left the bed.

"Be careful, Leo." She called to him as he left the room.

He smiled and gave her a small salute. Leaving instructions for her guard, he hurried to the waiting air lift.

***

The scene was just as bad the second time seeing it as when he'd experienced it. A hard lump gathered in his throat as he took in the scorched ground. A crater the size of…Liliana was at the epicenter. Candy and various treats scattered the ground, some burning still an hour after the explosion. Every soldier he passed straightened, their face serious. He located the duty commander by the gold bars on the sleeve of his uniform. Walking up to him, Leo waited as the officer finished examining the site.

"What do you know so far?"

"A spell for sure." The soldier stood, brushing his hands on his pants to clean them off.

No bomb could kill the demi and he was pretty sure whoever threw it knew that. He refrained from snapping at the commander's slow movements. "Kill or stun?"

The male grimaced. "This is some dark magic, sir. We're waiting on a Kira to be sure. The shopkeeper isn't dead, but that means nothing. From what we can tell, there is no debris to indicate a device was left here, so someone cast it live when your mate arrived. The brunt of it was centered here." He motioned his hand in the area blackened from the explosion.

Leo nodded, swallowing hard. Liliana had been inches from the spot the commander indicated, right as it hit. It was the reason she was alive. His phone beeped and he answered it with a growl.

"What has happened?" Xavier's gruff voice held a wealth of worry.

"I don't know for sure, X. Someone threw a bomb, a spell, something at Liliana. It exploded, badly injuring the shopkeeper and…" He broke off and took a shuddering breath.

"Liliana?"

"She's fine. Stunned, she was bent over when the blast hit, so whatever it was missed her." And he thanked all the gods he knew for it.

"I'll get with the commander there for detail, you take care of your mate."

Leo nodded, though he knew Xavier couldn't see the motion.

"I'm calling the king and moving up the *di êjê*. I don't want you on that realm any longer than you have to be." Xavier was angry if his tone of voice was to be believed. "Gods knows I didn't want you there in the first place. I don't like you anywhere near that bitch."

Leo knew the bitch to whom his brother referred. They both were silent a moment.

"Do you think she could've done this?" Xavier asked.

Leo cursed and looked around. "The queen hasn't tried to kill me in years. What could she possibly gain from it?" He saw the funny looks from the other soldiers at his words. He walked further from the group for privacy.

Xavier grunted in answer.

"It was aimed at Liliana, X. The royal family won't get a dime if she's killed."

"Especially not before the *di êjê*." Xavier sighed. "I'm sending Fallon there to help you. I want whoever did this sooner rather than later."

Leo agreed. "Thank you."

He spied the Kira circling the crime scene. The seven feet tall male was nut-brown like the trees that inhabited Edin, their realm. Braids resembling tree branches, with leaves at the end of them, trailed his back. The Kira was shirtless, as most of the males of their race usually were. Rings, like those on a tree, covered his chest and shoulder showing his age. He got to the blast site and stooped over the burnt ground. He ran his hand through the sand there, letting it fall through his fingers. He reached into his pouch at his side and extracted a gold chain, a stone on the end. He set the stone in motion, quietly watching as it swung in circles. He frowned heavily then stood. Leo opened his mouth to ask…

"Kill." The Kira said quietly. "Dark, dark magic."

Leo's ripe curse made the male cringe.

"I'll sweep away the magic, but I want to get a better sense of the spell before I do."

"Call me with updates." He ordered.

The Kira nodded, turning his back to Leo. Kira were never one for conversation. The introspective race kept a tight lid on their thoughts. All at once the urge to get to his mate struck him. Rushing back to the lift station, he cursed the slow transit the Eshu used.

Chapter 13

LILY CLOSED HER EYES wincing as she turned to her side. The healer Leo sent had checked her over and deemed her aches and pains small enough that healing was not required. She should've insisted Leo called her family's healer. The one from the Amanda was used to dealing with soldiers, of course, her bumps and bruises were minor to him. She sighed once she found a comfortable position. Reaching for the comms tablet on the bedside table, she perused through the news stories. She groaned at the breaking news story, bearing a picture of Leo running with her in his arms. His face was set in an intense expression, with her cradled close to his chest. She ran her finger across the image. She barely remembered the race back to her parents' home. She certainly didn't remember this stricken face whoever had taken the photo captured. His worry for her was there for the world to see. A small smile of pleasure ghosted across her face.

"Do you know how I know you left the house, Liliana?" Her mother didn't bother knocking.

Arian stood at the door of Lily's room, all aggravated scowl and pinched lips. A scarf covered her hair and hid her face in its shadows. It was a strange look for her mother, who took exceptional pride in her hair.

Raising an eyebrow, Lily said nothing. Feeding into her mother's nastiness got her nothing but hurt feelings. She'd learned not to take the bait. Though, it never stopped Arian.

"There are rumors flying around about you blowing up a market stand!" Her mother snatched the scarf from her hair and balled it in her hands.

Lily sat up straight, instantly regretting it. "That's not fair, and it certainly isn't true."

"Why can't you go somewhere without making a spectacle of yourself?" Arian took a step into Lily's room, her hands fisted at her sides.

"How is this my fault?" Why she bothered, she'd never know.

Arian ignored her question, pacing back and forth in front of her bed. "I can't wait until you leave this house, nay, this realm."

Hurt crystallized her blood, tears involuntarily springing to her eyes. "You can't mean that."

"We managed to go four years with no one mentioning an embarrassing thing you'd done. No whispers behind my back about poor Arian and the daughter she was stuck with. I'll never understand why Kita was taken and not you."

Lily's body trembled, the pain of her mother's words had found their mark. Her mouth opened but no words formed around the lump in her throat.

Arian's eyes widened as she realized what she'd said.

"Get out." Liliana's strangled words were barely a whisper.

Her mother backed from the room. "Lily, I'm sorry. I shouldn't have gone that far."

Liliana bit her tongue to keep from groaning in pain as she dragged her body from her bed. She walked slowly to her mother and slammed the door over her stricken face. She couldn't stay here. Her promise to Leo was the only thing keeping her from racing from her parent's house and to the portal station. She conjured a box and slowly made her way around the room packing only the things she couldn't conjure with magic. The necklace Bea had given her when she'd finished school, pictures of her and her father, and of her sister. Small trinkets of sentimental value all went in the box.

Leo walked in on her a few minutes later confusion written all over his face.

"Baby you're injured, you can do this later." He grabbed her elbow, guiding her away from her closet. "Has the healer come to see you?"

She nodded, pain tightening her lips as she sat on the edge of the bed.

"Then why are you still in pain?" He brushed a hand across her hair.

She waved off his question, breathing through the pain in her back.

"We're going to rush the *di êjê*, but it'll still take at least a week. Why are you packing so soon?" He looked around her room.

"I can't stay here." She whispered.

"What do you mean?"

"I can't stay here with that woman!" Her voice ended on a shrill scream.

Leo gathered her onto his lap as he sat next to her. He pulled the phone out, but she couldn't hear what he said over her sobs. She hated crying, especially over something her mother said. She should be used to the cutting remarks and blatant disregard for her feelings. In the years on her own, she'd grown to rely upon and trust in herself. She'd gained confidence her mother had spent previous years undermining and within a day of being back home she'd been reduced to this. Leo stood with her still in his arms and walked out of her parents' house. A lift was already waiting for them and she was thankful. She fell into an exhausted sleep as the transport left the pod.

***

THE NEXT MORNING LILIANA ROLLED OVER, in a giant, unfamiliar bed. Incredible smells permeated the air, bringing her out of the fog of sleep. She tentatively sat up, the aches in her body were gone. She twisted, testing her body further. Not even a twinge. She sighed in relief, thankful for the healer Leo had had meet her when they'd arrived last night.

The whole trip to the officer's quarters at the Legba Amanda station was done in a fog of pain and sadness. Leo had arranged everything, for which she was grateful. She peered around the elegant chambers, searching for signs of Leo. Spotting none, she left the comfortable bed conjuring a robe to cover the simple nightgown she'd slept in. Following the smell of breakfast, she spied him sitting at the small table in the surprisingly spacious kitchen.

He was focused on the comms pad in front of his eyes. As though he sensed her, his eyes lifted and met hers. He motioned with his hand and she joined him at the table. She pulled out a chair intending to sit, but he pulled her into his lap.

"How do you feel?" He whispered the words against her cheek as he kissed her.

"So much better." She ran her hand through his short hair, marveling at the difference between his forms. His hair was prickly as though freshly shorn. She loved the dark mahogany of his skin in his human form. She turned his head and kissed his lips softly.

"Your father called to check in on you. I told him you were okay."

She groaned. Her father was probably in the market when it happened. He was, no doubt, going out of his mind with worry despite Leo's reassurances. She made a mental note to call him.

"I'm glad this healer actually helped you. The guard I posted on you told me what the first healer said." He frowned and ran a hand over her hair.

She scrunched up her face. "It's fine, I'm sure the healer is used to dealing with hard-headed soldiers."

"Yeah, and it seems he had contradictory orders. No matter, he'll not make the same mistake again."

She rubbed a finger over the frown lines forming on his forehead. "Did you hurt him?"

"Just a little," he smiled mischievously.

She tried to hide her smile, not wanting to encourage him, but his overprotectiveness was very much a turn on. She looked down to find out what he'd been studying so resolutely and her stomach plummeted. Images of the candy stall where she'd been attacked were displayed on his comms tablet. She sucked in a breath at the decimation. Scattered wood shards and blackened Earth were all that was left of the stall.

"My God," she whispered.

"Yeah, it was pretty bad. There wasn't much to find out yesterday when I went down there. It was definitely a spell. I received confirmation from the Kira that it was specifically targeted towards you. I'm thinking he or she followed us waiting for an opportunity." He sighed, running a hand over her tangled hair. "Had any of the magic touched you, you would be dying."

She shuddered, her hands shaking as she flipped through the images. "Someone tried to kill me?"

His grip tightened on her waist and he leaned down, his breathing harsh as he pulled in her scent. "It won't happen again. I'll protect you."

"You'll try." She said absently, spotting the picture of the shopkeeper's gruesome injuries.

He turned her to face him. "You don't know my skill set."

She smiled at him using her words. Sobering she glanced back at the tablet. "How is the shopkeeper?"

"Alive. Just barely, but the healers have been working with him for hours and are positive he'll recover."

Liliana's stomach lurched at how close she'd been to dying. Leo's hands weaved a complicated spell over the tablet making it go dark.

"That's enough of that."

She blinked up, breaking the trance the images held over her. "Yes, definitely enough."

"Tell me what happened yesterday with your mother."

She sighed. "I don't know how to describe the relationship between my mother and me without sounding childish."

"Childish or not, tell me."

"My mother has always liked my sister better." She held up her hand to stall any argument. "I know people say that as hyperbole, but I mean it. She's always worshipped Kita and tolerated me. If you don't believe me, any number of our servants can back me up."

"I wasn't going to say anything." He leaned back in his chair and rested his hand on her back. "Finish telling me."

Liliana shrugged. "My whole life, I've never been able to do anything right for her. I was too loud, too common, and too clumsy. She used every opportunity to tell me how I was an embarrassment to her and our family. She takes everything I do as a personal affront. Bottom line, she was mean to me and her friends encouraged it. By the time I'd reached maturation, I stopped going to social events with my family. My life got a whole lot easier after that, let me tell you. If it weren't for Bea, I don't how I would've made it through childhood."

"And yesterday?" He prompted.

"She said it should be me missing instead of Kita. I mean, not a surprise, but it hurt all the same. I'm done letting my mother talk to me like that. My years on Adro have helped me find my self-confidence. No way am I letting her tear it down again."

"I'm sorry I wasn't there when she came in."

"It's better that you weren't. It was embarrassing as hell."

Leo sighed. "Don't worry about your mother. As soon as we're done with the *di êjê*, we're leaving and you won't have to deal with her if you don't want."

She smiled. "I can't wait."

"Are you hungry?"

"Starving." She whispered, looking into his eyes.

He cleared his throat, adjusting her on his lap. But, not before she felt his hardness pressing into her hip.

"No time for that. There are women here from the palace who want to go over plans for the *di êjê*. They've been waiting for an hour now, so their mood is…not nice. Since we're moving it up, they're a little peeved by the lack of time for planning."

She groaned and looked down at her appearance. She'd had no plans to get dressed for hours. She'd hoped to talk Leo back into bed for the rest of the morning. Mistress Yoru was probably behind the brigade of women waiting for her. She dreaded sitting through another etiquette lesson, but she didn't have a choice. According to her mother, gossip had her blowing up a market stall, no need to add further fuel to the fire. She would pass her remaining days on Legba with zero incident. Even if she had to suffer through the next few hours with the archivist and whatever other servants she brought along to torture her.

"Let me at least wash my face and change my clothes."

"Also, the stuff you bought while we were out was delivered." He pointed at the bags over in the corner of the sitting room.

She scrunched up her face. "I'd forgotten about that stuff. Most of it was gifts for my family. I'll go through it later." Much later.

He shrugged. "I'll take you to the conference room, I have plenty to do to keep me busy. Do you need me to stay for the planning?" The grimace on his face said he'd rather not.

She was touched he volunteered. "I can handle it. Are you okay with simple?"

He pulled her into his chest. "Were it up to me, we'd be bonded already somewhere locked in a room."

A thrill of heat went through her body. Gods, but the man had a way about him. She cupped his cheek and kissed him, moaning at his taste. He opened her robe, his hands spanning her waist.

He pulled back, nibbling on her lips. "Don't start nothing."

"Just a little something," she murmured, resuming her kiss.

Their tongues danced, the heat building between them. A knock on the door interrupted their play. Leo growled, the menacing sound its own turn on.

"Go." She stood, closing her robe. "I'll get ready."

Liliana quickly washed her face and brushed her teeth, smiling as she heard Leo grumbling about the interruption. He continued to surprise her and she actually looked forward to their mating. She found herself excited about their life together. She was anxious to get the ceremony part done so they could leave Legba.

The whole way to the conference room, Liliana held Leo's hands, marveling at the difference a few days made. He had been mad as hell at being mated, and now, he scowled at any male they passed in the hallway. A large frosted glass signaled their arrival at their destination. The large wooden table inside the room was another clue.

She frowned at the women gathered in the conference room. Taking a deep breath she dropped Leo's hand. Only a few more days to get through the traditions. It wouldn't be so hard. Expecting Leo to leave her at the door, her eyebrows winged up in surprise as he charged through the door.

"What are you doing here?" His voice was brusque as he halted at the oak table separating him from the women.

Liliana studied the one he'd addressed, her expensive clothing standing out amongst the palace workers gathered in the room. A Cagyn, the female's onyx skin was supple, the copper lines running through her skin pulsating with power. Her long jet black hair was partially pulled into a small bun on the top of her head, while the rest skimmed the back of her silk dress in a shining curtain.

"Leonalph." Her voice was deep, gravelly in a way that should've been unattractive, but made the mysterious woman sexy. Cagyn pheromones laced her voice, making Liliana mad with jealousy, yet drawn to her at the same time.

She stepped closer to Leo.

"I ask again, mother, what are you doing here?" He stabbed a finger onto the table.

Mother. She sucked in a breath of surprise.

"The *di êjê*, Leonalph. According to the harpy who hunted me down, the mother of the groom is required to speak with the bride before the ceremony. Impart wisdom." The smirk on the woman's face seemed to make Leo madder.

Mistress Yoru sniffed in offense, and Liliana couldn't help but like the woman a little bit for getting under the archivist's skin.

Years of etiquette training moved Lily from Leo's side, extending her hand before she could process the motion. "I'm Liliana Marcolev, mate to your son. It's a pleasure to meet you."

His mother sized her up before clasping Lily's hand in a strong, but gentle grip. "A pleasure, Liliana. I'm Sharine Tegan, mother to Leonalph, whether he likes it or not."

Leo growled.

Wanting to stall an impending scene, Liliana waved the palace servants from the room. Hell or high water, she would not be responsible for more gossip getting back to her mother.

She turned to him, placing a hand on his chest. "We're fine here, Leo. You had errands with which to occupy yourself, right?" Social Tone and accent in place, Liliana knew how to play the game. Despite what her mother or any other thought. She waved a hand in front of his face to break his eye contact with his Sharine.

Leo glanced down at her, blinking. "I can stay here. I don't want to leave you alone with her."

"Well, pesky customs dictate otherwise." She pasted on her most cordial smile, turning back to face his mother. "I'll be fine. I promise."

He stared at Sharine another full minute in silence before he nodded. "I'll be in the surveillance room, call me if you need anything."

"I will." She grabbed his face to bring his attention back to her. "Hey, I can handle it."

He lifted a finger and pointed at his mother. "If you so much as…"

"Enough, Leonalph." Sharine cut him off. "What do you imagine I can do to your mate in full view of the palace servants?"

Liliana groaned and turned. Sure enough, the women all stood at the glass wall making no attempt to hide their curiosity. Her mother would hear about it for sure. Luckily for her, she didn't have to go back home and be subject to the disappointed stares. Why did these things happen to her?

Leo gave his mother one last forbidding look. Kissing Lily's hand, he left the room, taking the majority of the tension with him.

"I would apologize on behalf of my son, but seeing as how you're mated to him, you'd best get used to his temper." Sharine waved her hand towards a chair.

Liliana sat, curiosity burning through her.

"My son and I haven't spoken in years. As you can see, he prefers it."

At a loss for words, Liliana clasped her hands on top of the conference table. Sharine had no problem filling the silence. She went on as though input from Liliana was not needed.

"Now, according to tradition, I'm supposed to tell you all about how to take care of my son." Sharine sat across from Liliana, fidgeting with the gold bangles climbing her arm.

"I'm not one for tradition. If you're uncomfortable with this, we can skip the formalities." Lily certainly didn't want to stir up anything that could potentially hurt Leo.

Sharine waved away her concern. "I don't have any insight to give you about my son. What I can tell you though is to be careful."

Lily sat back in her chair in surprise. "Leo would never hurt me."

His mother nodded. "You're absolutely right. He'd never lay a hand on you, and for the most part, should treat you wonderfully. Except…"

Liliana's back stiffened. "Except what?"

"Leonalph has wanted to be in the Amanda for as long as I can remember." A small nostalgic smile tilted her lips. "He followed those soldiers around asking a million and one questions. Gods, he was such a sweet and serious child." She cleared her throat and shook away the smile. "Now that he's mated, he'll lose his position."

"I'm aware of that." Defensiveness added a snap to her voice.

Sharine nodded. "Of course you are. What you're unaware of is the bitterness that accompanies the loss. Bitterness he'll take out on you."

She folded her arms on her chest. Leo would never hurt her, and the certainty in his mother's voice would not shake her faith in him.

"You're sitting there smug because you know Leo so well, right? If you knew half the ways his father..." The woman took a shaky breath. "The head of the Amanda used to be able to hunt. Did you know that?"

Liliana shook her head.

"Yes, Ranolph enjoyed the hunt. It gave his beast an outlet. He would take his men out and hunt down those who committed crimes. At least the ones who weren't sentenced to death. He loved that job, and because he was mated, he was required to give up that part of it."

"Leo is not his father. Our relationship will not be the same."

"Whatever you say." Sharine stood and adjusted the skirt of her dress, her bangles tinkling with the motion. She leaned forward, arms on the table. "Call me when you're pregnant, stuck at Haven, unable to leave."

Lily frowned. "Mates or not, the Amanda can't hold me hostage."

"No?" The nasty smile on her face gave Lily chills. "Is my son not charismatic enough to suggest you stay inside the walls of Haven for your own good? He cares so much for the safety of his mate, surely you won't object to a couple of guards keeping watch over you."

She thought over the conversation they'd had just yesterday. "You're wrong."

"Am I, sweetie?" Sharine stood straight, shaking her head. "Those Tegan men can be quite persuasive. My bitterness is living proof of how charming they can be."

Fed up with the conversation Liliana stood. "Is that the 'wisdom' you came to impart?"

Sharine laughed, genuine amusement lighting her face. "Oh no, my dear. I only thought to give you a little warning for appearance's sake. In actuality, I'm here to stir shit up. I'll try not to get any of the splatters on you."

Liliana frowned in distaste. Leo's mother just smiled and left the room. Gods, why did these things happen to her?

Chapter 14

LILY WIPED THE STEAM FROM the bathroom mirror hours later. Her wet hair trailed her back, the darkened colors still bright against the white towel wrapped around her chest. Rivulets of water chased each other down her shoulders dampening the towel. Leo crossed his ankle and leaned against the door jamb watching her. She rolled her shoulders and sighed. She brought her wet hair to the front using another towel to dry it. Exhaustion rode her shoulders, slumping them as she attempted to towel dry her hair.

He must have made a sound, because her head popped up, her eyes catching his in the mirror. He came up behind her and took the towel. Moving the hair off her neck, he laid a small kiss to her shoulder. Without saying a word, he rubbed the towel along her head, pulling her hair into it and rubbing vigorously. The need to care for Liliana was a compulsion. He wanted to make her feel better, and selfishly he could admit, caring for her would also calm the beast raging through him.

Once he heard the shower stop, something compelled him into the bathroom.

Finished with the towel, he tossed it aside. Spotting a hairbrush next to her hand resting on the counter, he grabbed it and held it up. She nodded at his unspoken question. Starting at the bottom of her hair, he methodically worked through the tangles, much like when he brushed through his hair in his Eshu form. She sighed in pleasure as he reached the crown of her head. He brushed in long, sure strokes, massaging her scalp. His brows furrowed in concentration as he worked through her hair. He said nothing as he brushed the tangles out, the intimacy in the action robbing him of words.

He'd sensed her aggravation from the moment he'd picked her up from the conference room. Her stiff gait as they walked back to their temporary quarters told him all he needed to know about how the planning went. He imagined dealing with anyone from the palace was stressful, especially after the day she'd had. Then to add his mother on top.… Just the thought of his mother alone with Liliana pissed him off. He could well imagine the nastiness she'd shared with his mate. Lily said nothing about it though, and that worried him.

Finished with the tangles, he braided her hair starting from her nape. He moved the braid to her front, once again baring her neck to him. She adjusted the towel knotted on her chest, the motion sensual in the silence enveloping them. He then kissed her neck, wet kisses, dragging his teeth along her neck. Days ago he'd cursed having a mate, now with her in front of him, her vulnerable beauty reaching out to him, he couldn't imagine life without her. He nipped her neck, using his teeth, telling himself he wouldn't break the skin. Her moan did nothing to help his self-control though. What it did do was channel the tender feelings from moments ago into hot, drugging passion.

One hand gripping her waist, he used the other to release the knot holding the towel over her breasts. It pooled at her feet, its thump the only sound other than her heavy breathing. Humming in approval, his hands skimmed her curves, tracing across her budding nipples. Her breath caught, encouraging his exploration. He licked a path up her neck to her ears. He trailed his fingers lower, ghosting over her stomach with the lightest touch. He reached her center and looked into the mirror at her. Their eyes met and she let out a rough exhalation, nodding her consent. Slowly inserting his fingers, satisfaction spiked through him when she shuddered. She closed her eyes, leaning back into his chest.

"Uh-uh." He bit her ear lobe. "Watch."

Her eyes popped open, the lids hooded as she watched him slowly stroke his fingers in and out of her. He studied her face, picking up the pace of his fingers. Her orgasm was right around the corner if her choppy breaths were anything to go by. Her body tensed, and a long moan left her parted lips. He used his thumb to stroke the numb of her clit and she exploded. Gods she was beautiful. He turned her face with his other hand, kissing her deeply. Her body went limp, weak with satiation. He lifted her up and carried her to their bed. Neither of them exchanged words. He lay her on the bed naked, tucking her under the covers. He brought the blanket up to her chin, hiding her beautiful curves from himself, in an attempt to keep temptation away.

"I'm going to take a shower first, then I'll join you in bed." He leaned over her, braced on his arms.

She nodded her assent, her eyes lowering as sleep overtook her. She stirred as he lifted from over her. He stood still until she'd settled back to sleep. Leo walked back into the bathroom, setting the water on a comfortable temperature. Shucking his clothes, he entered the warm stall, grateful for the water beating down on his tired body.

He leaned his head against the tile, his breathing harsh puffs of air. His body was tight with tension, both from the stress of the last few days, and the lust thrumming through his bloodstream. He could do nothing about the stress, but the lust was easily assuaged. Taking his length in his hand, he pictured Liliana's face as she orgasmed a few minutes ago. He vividly saw her full lips parted, her head thrown back in ecstasy. He moved his hand up and down, wanting those lips wrapped around his shaft. He imagined her cheeks sunk in as she pulled him deeper. Her scent surrounded him from her earlier shower adding to the memories of her breathless cries. It all crowded his mind sending him over the edge. He came with the thought of her blanketing his thoughts. He sank to the tile floor, his body spent.

He released his human skin, letting go of the magic keeping his body constrained. Finally relaxed, he leaned back against the wall, letting the hot water pelt him. He'd nearly lost Liliana. Agony at how close he came to losing her seized his breath. Pictures of the damaged stall threatened to take over his relaxed mood but he banished the thoughts.

He'd find the person behind the threat to her and he would end them. There was no other recourse. No other outcome was feasible to him or his beast. He'd spent hours going over every bit of surveillance they'd had available in the market and hadn't seen anything out of the ordinary.

He wished they were on Adro. He'd be able to look through the Oras and find out exactly who cast the spell. Since the magic was based on the Earth's magnetic field and their realms were merely ghosts of the Earth, the field didn't reach them. Thus no Oras. He didn't realize how heavily they'd come to rely on them. He growled in frustration. Old fashion hunting would take longer, but hard work never scared him.

Chapter 15

THE NEXT MORNING LILIANA AWOKE, stretching, savoring the delicious feeling traveling through her body. Leo woke her up late into the night, frantic to have her and her body was still humming from their lovemaking. She smiled. She didn't want to leave the bed. Her smile turned into a snarl as she remembered she didn't have a choice in the matter. Palace servants would be in the conference room, Mistress Yoru's severe face pinched in disapproval, waiting to shove more etiquette down her throat.

"Ugh," she said aloud. The woman was so snotty.

She briefly wondered if she herself had been that way before Adro had hardened her. Had she been the prissy noble, concerned only with rules and the who's who of society? Gods, she hoped not. Now that the mating ceremony had been moved up, they were double-timing the lessons. Information overload. Still groggy, she shook her head, squealing when a noise sounded in her room.

Kedric sat in a chair across from her bed. She gasped and scrambled into a sitting position up against the headboard.

"What are you doing here?" Oh gods, didn't Leo say he was leaving security at their door? Where were they? Her eyes darted to the door.

"Don't worry about the guards they're currently being entertained by my own."

Pissed Liliana pulled her blankets up her chin. How dare they? Allowing a male into their rooms when her mate was gone was a severe breach of propriety. If it got out that she'd entertained someone other than Leo in her bedroom, gossip would bury her and her family. Gods, didn't just yesterday, she promised herself she'd stay out of scandals?

Fear reared its ugly head as Kedric smiled at her, flexing his fingers. Disgusted with herself, she growled. He wouldn't dare touch her now. Leo would kill him. Manifesting sweatpants and a t-shirt like the ones she'd normally wore on Adro, she threw the covers to the side. Standing from the bed, she glared at the prince.

"I'm not having a conversation with you in my mate's bedroom." She walked into the sitting room on rubbery legs.

He walked in behind her, a stupid smirk on his face. "When have you ever cared for propriety?"

"What do you want, Kedric?"

"No title, Liliana? Surely you're not so bold as to disrespect me." He closed the distance between them.

Liliana sat on the sofa and pretended nonchalance. "If you'll remember, I'll be a princess in a few days' time. I'll use your title when you use mine." She raised an eyebrow and dared him to challenge it.

"Mating to a bastard does not make one a princess, but it's of no consequence to me either way."

"Why are you here, Kedric?"

He stared at her for long moments, his eyes roving her body. "You came back without Kita."

Fear choked her. "I searched for her for years." Damn it, why was she explaining herself?

"And you found nothing?"

She shook her head.

"Well, then, it's not to be. Leave it alone, Liliana and move on with your life."

Her eyes narrowed. Was he serious? "What?"

"That's what I came to tell you. There's no need to further look for your sister."

A sick feeling circled her gut. Why would he give up the search for her sister so easily? "Excuse me?"

"Don't be naïve, Liliana. We both know Kita is dead by now. Now that you're mated, we no longer have to go through the mockery of a courtship. I wish you nothing but the best, but I for one am glad to have the noose from my neck."

Liliana struggled to digest his words. "What are you saying? You don't know that Kita's dead." She refused to believe it.

His eyes narrowed, a calculating look entering them. He sat back in his chair. "Do you think your sister would run away and never come back? She would've eventually become queen. Does that sound like something your sister would do?"

He had a point. But the leap from believing Kita ran away and didn't want to be found, to believe her sister was dead was a huge one. One she wouldn't take without proof first.

"Face it. Your sister is dead, and you looking for her won't bring her back."

She reeled at his callousness. Her chest tightened, and she thought she would pass out from the pain "You thought my sister was dead, yet you sent me to Adro anyway?" She swallowed the scream burning the back of her throat. She'd lost four years with her family. Not to mention the shame her friends and family endured because she left. Her life had been turned upside down as she roamed Adro, running from both the Amanda and the queen.

"You couldn't very well stay in Legba." He shrugged his shoulder. "Once our mating failed, it would've come out that I had already bonded with your sister. And if I couldn't mate with you, then my mother would've lost the dowry to which your father had already so generously given us half. I would've been disowned. You know how my mother is."

"You selfish bastard." Her throat hurt, raw from the tears of anger she kept back by sheer stubbornness. He would not see her cry.

"Let's be realistic, Lily. I couldn't let the circumstances of my mating get out. You know my family was in need of money. My mother would have flayed me."

"All for money." She whispered.

"My father smartly turned that money into riches for the kingdom. Would you have really wanted to let the whole kingdom down, Lily?"

"Don't call me that."

He scoffed. "You're being dramatic. It's for the best, the gossip would've been excruciating. Do you want people talking about you like that?"

"They're probably already talking about me. If you haven't heard, I was nearly blown up in the middle of the market square. Between that, and me running away from our mating, what's one more thing for them to gossip about?"

He waved away her words. "*I* took the brunt of that gossip. One sister runs away to avoid mating, then fine. But two sisters? Everyone scrutinized my every move. Had it not been for me being the prince, I would've been shunned from society."

Liliana blew out an indignant breath. His nerve! "Then maybe I should tell them why I left. I can explain in explicit detail how you had your security drag me to the condo you keep in the business district where you whipped me for hours. Hours. And when I no longer had the energy to heal myself, you dumped me at an illegal portal and threatened my life. I think their prince's predilection to violence would be a suitable distraction, don't you?" She spat.

His nails dug into her skin as he grabbed her arm, snatching her from the couch. "No one would believe you."

She gasped as he tightened his grip on her arm and used the other hand to pull her hair. "I can't imagine I'm the only person you like to hurt. I'm sure you've left a trail of palace servants who've suffered your beatings. I'll tell everyone who will listen how their next king likes to beat on women."

He loosened her hair and grabbed her throat. "If you value your life, and your mother's position in this society, you will keep that bit of gossip to yourself." He flung her against the wall.

Air whooshed from her lungs on impact. She slid to the floor with a whimper. She coughed, fighting to get air to her starved lungs. "If you touch me again, I'll shout it from the market square."

He pulled her up by her hair. "By the gods, you've never known when to shut up. Your whipping was twice as long as it should've been because you wouldn't shut the fuck up. Maybe I'll stay for a while. What do you think Death's Messenger will do if he comes back to this room to find the guards chatting amiably in the hallway and the two of us in his bed?"

Her heart lurched. Leo would kill them both. Nausea rolled, bile clogged her throat.

Kedric smiled. "Yeah, that's what I thought. It's over Liliana. Consider this your first and final warning."

"Fuck you." She spit in his face.

His slap snapped her head back. She thought vaguely of screaming for the guards, but he squeezed her throat, cutting off her air. Black dots danced before her eyes. She clawed his arm, fighting to free her neck. Noise in the hallway was louder as the door crashed open. Liliana closed her eyes in relief when Kedric was pulled off of her. She slid to the floor gagging, heaving in gulps of air.

The light dimmed and Fallon's figure swam before her. She watched with a sense of detachment as he slammed Kedric against the wall. The plaster cracked behind the prince's head from the force.

"Touch my sister again and your life is forfeit. Do we understand each other?" At Kedric's nod, Fallon tossed him to the front door.

One of the guards lifted the prince, the others headed towards Fallon. One growl from him stopped them in their tracks. Walking backward, they carried Kedric from the room.

Fallon kneeled next to her. His hands were gentle as they roamed her body for injuries. Finding none, he sighed. "Trouble."

She coughed. "I didn't mean to…"

He lifted her gingerly. "Yeah, I was told these things just happen to you." He placed her on the sofa, and disappeared, coming back a moment later to sit across from her. He passed her a dishtowel wrapped around ice.

Liliana hissed as she brought it up to her cheek. "Yeah, well, I may have helped it along this time with my smart mouth." She grabbed the glass of water he offered gratefully. She winced as she swallowed. "What are you doing here?"

"Occasionally I get visions. After what happened yesterday, Xavier and I thought it prudent to be closer to you and Leo."

She set the cup on the table and lowered her head. "Leo will be furious."

"Furious? We'll be lucky if my brother doesn't burn this kingdom to the ground." Fallon stood and rubbed a hand over his face. "Shit, Trouble."

Lily rubbed her neck, closing her eyes tight. He was right, Leo would kill the prince.

He sighed. "Stay here, I'll replace the guards at your door."

He left the room, and Liliana let the tears she'd been holding stream down her face. Gods damn it she was tired of crying. She got up and washed her face in the bathroom sink. She was done crying. The next person to hurt her would regret it.

***

Leo left the surveillance room, no closer to finding out anything than when he went in this morning. It was frustrating as hell. He looked down at his watch realizing how many hours had passed. He cursed. Lily was probably beside herself with boredom. He made a beeline to the conference room to rescue her from the wedding planners. Finding the conference room empty, he frowned. He stopped a passing servant.

"Has there been anyone in this conference room today?"

The servant shook his head. "Earlier the archivist was here, but she left once informed Lady Marcolev would be unavailable today."

"Unavailable?" He asked sharply.

The servant shrugged. Dismissing the man, Leo rushed for their room. What could possibly have Liliana unavailable? The guards at her door were different, giving him the first clue that something had happened. Opening the door a little harder than he planned, he called her name, pausing in the doorway as he spotted Fallon sitting in an armchair. His brother's face was lined with worry. His heart sped its rhythm as he scanned the room for Liliana. She came out of the back wearing sweats. A blooming bruise colored her face along with fingermarks staining the skin of her neck. He rushed to her side.

Fury exploded through him as he got a full look at her. Fangs burst from his gums, his claws grew, and cut into his hands. His vision went straight infrared, the beast tearing from his body. He leaped back from her to avoid hurting her, but his voice was a dangerous growl.

"Who touched you?"

Eyes wide, Liliana backed up a step. "Leo?"

He turned to his brother. "Who put their hands on my mate?"

"Calm down, Leo, it was handled." Fallon kept his tone low, placating.

"I didn't ask if it was handled. I want to know who. Put. Their. Fucking. Hands. On my mate!"

Liliana looked up at him and stepped closer. "I'm okay, Leo."

But his beast was far from appeased. He scooped her into his arms, careful of his claws.

"Put her down, Leo and calm yourself." Fallon knew better than to step any closer to brother in his Cagyn form.

"I want the guards I left on her in the commander's office, now!" The deep growl of his voice showed how close he was to losing control.

Fallon looked like he wanted to argue but Leo's look silenced him. Leo fought for control as he walked Liliana back into their bedroom. He lay her on the bed, his hands clumsy as he searched her for other bruises. He backed himself into the corner of the room as he fought to control his baser instincts. His beast was urging him to mark their mate, to mark her so every male near her knew to whom she belonged. The threats to her were numerous and the beast had had enough.

"Baby," her voice stroked over him. "I'm fine, Leo."

He breathed hard, his chest heaving up and down as he fought to subdue the beast and change back to his human skin. He clasped his hands in front of him, fighting the need to snatch her into his arms. Liliana rolled from the bed.

"Don't." He closed his eyes and fought harder. "Give me a minute."

She kept coming until her cool touch brushed his arm. He opened his eyes and stared into hers. She didn't say anything, simply looked at him until his body settled. His claws receded along with his teeth and he breathed easier. He changed back to his human skin on a shuddering sigh. She opened his arms and stepped into his chest. Her body trembled and Leo rested his head on her hair and held her.

"Don't cry, *ina*, I didn't mean to scare you." He felt self-conscious. He'd not lost control of his beast since he was a boy, and twice in her presence, he'd done so.

Liliana hit his arm. "I'm not scared of you. I've just had a shitty couple of days, ok." She sniffled and snuggled back into his arms.

"I'm sorry for losing control. The mating instincts have me on a hair-trigger."

She shook her head at him. "It's okay."

"I need to go take care of this."

"Let it go, Leo. It's over."

He grunted in answer, he disagreed, but he'd let her think otherwise. "You should lie down."

She sighed. "You're always trying to get me into bed."

"Of course." He waggled his eyebrows. "I'll be right back."

"Fine." She pushed him out of their bedroom.

He smiled back at her and waited until she closed the door. Once he heard the click he turned back to his brother, the fake smile dropping from his face.

"Leo…" Fallon started.

"I don't want to hear it, Fallon. You'd do the same."

"Of course." Fallon stood, no use denying the truth of that. "Xavier is waiting for us in the commander's office."

Leo paused at the front door of the apartment. "You called X?"

"The prince was involved."

"What?" Rage simmered again below his skin.

His beast rumbled, his fangs aching his gums as jealousy ripped through him. The prince was in their room. Had she invited him? Was there something he'd missed? Insecurity flashed through him, his normal distrust and cynicism taking over his concern for Liliana. They had been betrothed, could they still have feelings for each other?

He closed his eyes and breathed through his nose.

No way.

He didn't imagine the heat between him and Liliana, and he certainly didn't mistake the look in her eyes when they kissed. Not to mention the terror on her face whenever the prince was mentioned. There couldn't be lingering feelings between the two.

"I'll fill you in on the way to the office," Fallon said grimly.

He let go of a string of curses. Shaking the last of the jealousy. "We're not leaving until I put guards I trust on her."

Pulling out his communicator he called the Atlanta Haven looking for men he'd personally trained. He didn't want ones from this realm looking after Liliana. Especially if the problem was Prince Kedric. He picked two men he knew wouldn't be swayed by the Legba monarchy. Quiet men, but vicious. A Benu and Cagyn, he'd been training them for a couple of months now. Xavier was worried about him when he left Haven, Leo thought having the men with him would alieve his brother's stress. Until he could find a permanent solution to security for his mate, he wanted them to shadow her every move. He was no longer taking chances with her life.

It only took the soldiers half an hour to reach the officer's quarters. Leo let them in, grateful for their haste. He quickly briefed them on what had happened in the past couple of days.

"I have to leave for a little bit, no one is to enter this room until I return. Understood?"

They nodded in silence. He went back to check on Liliana and found her asleep on top of the covers. Satisfied, he and Fallon left his temporary apartment, marching with quick feet to the commander's office. The two guards he'd originally assigned to protect her stood in the office at attention. Xavier sat on the commander's desk, his arms crossed over his chest, and his legs crossed at his ankles.

His rage exploded at seeing the males' faces, but he kept it under wraps. That is until he saw the smug look they gave him. Neither guilt nor remorse showed on their face.

Oh, that wouldn't do at all.

Changing into his Cagyn form, he used his magic to slam one of them into the wall. The other he grabbed around the throat, lifting him off the ground.

"Leo, mind the furniture please." Xavier uncrossed his legs. "We did borrow this office after all."

He nodded. It was a valid point. "Explain to me how my mate got hurt under your watch?"

The guard was gasping, clawing at Leo's arm.

"He can't talk while you're choking him. Maybe let enough air in for him to talk." Fallon suggested as he took up a spot on the other side of the desk.

Leo smiled and lifted his claws a fraction. The guard hissed and sucked in small huffs of air.

"Well?" Xavier barked.

"The prince said he grew up with Lady Marcolev. We thought—"

Leo speared the soldier on the wall with a hard look. "I didn't ask you. You're hanging on that wall because I can feel your remorse. So, close your mouth before I open your gut."

The male shut his mouth and grimaced.

"Now this piece of shit, you're not sorry at all are you?" Leo lifted the guard and slammed him down into the carpet. He picked him up and threw him into the wall, watching with disinterest as he slid down into a heap on the floor.

The soldier changed into his true form, and Leo bared his teeth. The Eshu struggled to stand. Leo walked over and grabbed the yards of green and aqua hair to help the soldier up.

"We're going to have us a bit of fun, brothers."

Xavier and Fallon both stood. Leo smiled. Yeah, the Eshu had a lot of explaining to do and Leo had no problem making the conversation as painful as possible.

***

Liliana lifted a groggy eye and felt the bed next to her. Empty. Damn him and damn her for going to sleep. She'd slept more in the past two days than she had the entire four years she was on Earth. She scrambled from the bed and rushed into the living room. A uniformed soldier stood next to the bedroom door and Liliana backed away.

"What are you doing here?"

The soldier blinked but said nothing.

She sighed and marched to the intercom on the wall. "What's the number for the commander's office?"

Getting no answer from the guard, she searched the emergency numbers on the intercom pad to no avail. Growling in frustration, Liliana eyed the soldier and debated her next move. Leo went to punish the security officers even though she'd told him to drop it. That wasn't what had her upset. The guard hanging in her room, not speaking, was the source of her anger. He stood over the door like a prison warden.

"Am I allowed to leave?"

Sharine's taunting words echoed through her mind. She hadn't wanted to believe the woman, but here she stood, stuck in the room 'for her own good'.

The Amanda soldier tapped an earpiece and spoke quietly. She tapped her feet and wrestled her temper down.

"I've only been told to keep others from entering," he said.

Benu, his accent gave him away. Though his human skin disguised his true form, his small eyes and pointed nose gave him bird-like features, so common to their race. Liliana growled and stomped to the door. She opened it to find another soldier there.

"Lady Marcolev, do you have need of something?"

"Are you supposed to keep me locked up in here?" Irritation sharpened her voice.

The soldier shot a confused look to the Benu behind her.

"I asked you a question."

"No, my lady. We're to guard you, not keep you locked up. If you have somewhere to go, we will get you there." Perfectly polite, his answer annoyed her all the more.

"Like what, an armed escort?" She worked to calm herself. After all, she'd nearly died…twice. She rubbed her neck, imagining the bruises still marring her skin. Okay, so perhaps the guards were needed. "Where is Leo?"

The soldier spoke quietly into his earpiece. "In the commander's office, if you'll calm yourself, we'll escort you there." The Benu's voice held no emotion, his face gave nothing away.

She sighed, she wasn't being held prisoner. She knew better to let Sharine get into her head. The woman said herself she'd come to stir up trouble. Liliana refused to feed into the other woman's mischief. They walked her down the hallways to what she assumed was the commander's office. The Benu held out his arm at the door, stopping her movement.

"We cannot enter until we get the okay." He knocked quietly on the door.

Fallon peeked out of the office. "Liliana, you shouldn't be here."

"I want to see Leo, now." She crossed her arms over her chest. Fallon continued to block the door and she wanted to know why.

"Hold on." He disappeared back into the room, closing the door tightly behind him.

She growled and kicked the door, the small move petty, but made her feel better. The soldier next to her snickered. She shot him a deadly look.

Leo slid out of the door a moment later in his Cagyn form, his black hair around his shoulders in disarray and his eyes meeting hers, no remorse.

"You left me." It slipped out. She winced at the hurt in her tone.

"*Ina.*" He dismissed the soldiers with a flicker of his head. He pulled her close. "I needed to take care of this."

"I asked you to drop it."

"No one hurts you and gets away with it. Would you rather I kill Kedric?"

She searched his eyes and shuddered at the chill in them. He was telling the truth, he would kill Kedric despite the punishment he'd suffer for it. She didn't want that for him. Not to mention all manner of skeletons were sure to pop out of Kedric's closet with his death.

"No."

"Your guards were responsible for you, and the Eshu allowed the prince to push his way into our room. This after the healer was given instructions to let you suffer your injuries. Clearly, the monarchy has a lot more power in this station than they should. It stops today. I plan on making a staggering example out of these two so it doesn't happen again."

The anger etched on his face was implacable. Talking him out of punishing the guards was not going to happen.

She sighed. "Fine, I'll leave you to deal with it." Not like she had a choice. But for the sake of her pride, she would pretend she did and leave while there was a minuscule amount of dignity left.

Leo motioned the guards over. "I'm not locking you up, sweetheart. The guards are there for your protection only. I swear."

He kissed her cheek and went back into the office, the door cutting off any other conversation. Her protection only, huh? Still, Sharine's words were there taunting her. She could only hope once they were back in Atlanta everything would return to normal and she would get some semblance of freedom.

Chapter 16

THE SURVEILLANCE ROOM WAS EMPTY, as usual around this time of night. It certainly suited Verity's purpose just fine. She'd heard Xavier had left the Atlanta Haven to take care of something on Legba. Security all around would be a tiny bit more lax with him gone. She planned on using the opportunity to clean up behind herself a little. There was a meeting with a certain noble she needed to hide. She smiled at the soldier who let her in, and blew him a kiss, shaking her hair a little to dazzle him. Men made it so easy sometimes.

Dismissing the gullible male, Verity spied her reason for sneaking into the surveillance room. Adding an extra sway to her hips, she sidled up to the captain in charge. His cubby sat at the back of the room, the walls gave her privacy for what she had in mind. He smiled as she perched herself on the edge of his desk.

"To what do I owe the honor?" He sat back in his chair, clasping his hands behind his head.

Sliding a finger down the front of his chest, she purred. "Can't a girl just visit?"

His eyes widened and his pupils dilated in lust as she weaved a spell over him. "You're always welcome."

She hooked the belt loop of his pants and slid his chair closer, careful to complete the spell she was murmuring under her breath. The captain's breathing evened, and his eyes glazed as she finished. She leaned into his space, stopping a hair's breadth from his mouth.

"I need to see the Oras."

For a moment, the captain's heart rate picked up as he fought through her magic. But it was useless. Verity had honed the magic native to her race. There wasn't a Dziva faster than her at enrapturing their prey, nor one as thorough. The captain would be under her spell until she dispersed it.

But just in case…

She pushed a little more of her magic into it.

The captain's jaw slackened a bit and she knew he was completely under. Satisfied, she ordered him to pull up the Oras from the date of her meeting with the Eshu noble. His hands lifted, if a bit slowly, weaving a spell only he and maybe three other people knew. She'd tried to use the spell outside of Haven's surveillance room and it not only changed every day, but the magic didn't work outside of Haven. Unfortunately for her, it meant that anytime she needed to corrupt them, she had to do so from here. It increased her chances of being caught, so she made sure to make each time count.

She sighed in relief as the images from her meeting floated in the air in front of them. Pulling out a crystal given to her by a shaman she used, she laid it on the captain's desk. She pulled out a piece of parchment and read the spell quietly. The images wavered and blinked out. She was never sure what the stone was for, but each time Sergio weaved a spell for her to erase the Oras, he had her bring it along. One of these days she'd get around to asking him. Satisfied that she'd completed her task she kissed the captain on the lips and left.

She would drop the stone off to Sergio, along with his payment and leave Adro. She didn't necessarily hate the Earth realm, but she hated the restrictions of being in her human form. Her cellphone beeped at her hip. Her frown turned into a grimace as she realized who was trying to contact her. Not wanting to take the call at Haven, she made quick steps to the exit.

"Yes, mother."

"Verity, your grandmother wants to see you." Her mother didn't bother with a greeting.

She sighed as she unlocked the Porsche she drove on Adro. "Will she be sane?"

"I doubt it, but it doesn't matter."

Verity rolled her eyes, happy her mother couldn't see. Of course, it didn't matter to her mother that her grandmother was insane. The woman had given up half her power to contain Ofeeree, that type of sacrifice demanded respect. Which meant, every time her grandmother yelled jump, they were to ask, 'How high?'

"I don't have time."

"You will make time." Was her mother's simple answer.

Not bothering to argue, Verity locked the doors of her Porsche and walked around the back of Haven. There was an illegal portal nestled in the forest behind Haven's back door. That the Amanda continually missed the portal baffled her. Though, in their defense, a lot of care was taken to keep it hidden. Weaving the spell for Uhlango, her home realm, Verity stepped through the portal and into complete darkness.

For some reason, time on this realm ran differently than other realms. Not bothering with a cab, she walked the mile to her grandmother's house, using the cool air to center herself. Meeting with her grandmother was always a chore. According to family legend, one elder from each realm gave a portion of their power to bind Ofeeree to stop him from taking over the world. Those elders and their families were heralded as heroes, each of them given riches incomparable. Unfortunately, her grandmother was paying for her contribution with her sanity. She was going insane, and each decade it got worst. It didn't help that the loss of her grandmother's power made her an outcast in Dziva society, despite the money and property.

She didn't know how the other families lived on other realms, but on Uhlanga, power ruled. And giving up your power voluntarily…Her family was ridiculed. Dzivas were a matriarchal society, a cut-throat one who saw noble deeds as useless unless they garnered favor. And money, unfortunately for her family didn't count. Verity had spent her formative years dressed in the finest money could buy but shunned because both her mother and grandmother were weak. It had taken her a while to hone her magic and a lot of shady deals to build her power, but she had. She'd clawed her family back up the rungs of Dziva society and made examples out of anyone who got in her way. Now the same ones who looked down on her family, wouldn't dare look her in the eye, for fear of what she'd do.

Not bothering to knock, she entered her Grandmother Helen's home and called out for her.

"In the living room, dear." Helen's voice sounded strong, so clearly it was a lucid day.

Verity rounded the corner, surprised to find her grandmother not only lucid but combing through old family albums. She leaned over and gave her grandmother a perfunctory kiss on the cheek.

"I don't have time to waste, darling, I don't know how long I'll be lucid." Helen's hands shook as she flipped through pages.

"What's going on, grandmother?"

"You're working to free Ofeeree, right?"

Verity gasped and sat down in alarm. "Grandmother, you can't go around…"

"Never mind the lying, child. You want the family's power back and Ofeeree is the only way that will happen. You will need to know the names of the families who gave up their power. Likely the Kokoro souls will be born to them."

She nodded. It was the same thought she and the rest of the guild were counting on.

"I have those names here in this book," Helen mumbled absently. "They swore us to secrecy, but you know a Dziva could never resist having that kind of information."

"I would've done the same," Verity said, leaning forward to look in the album her grandmother was searching.

Old pictures and family announcements were taped into the scrapbook.

"Of course you would've. You're nothing like your weak mother. I love her dearly, but she would never have the power or the audacity to return us back to our rightful place in society."

Pride swelled her chest and a newfound wonder for her grandmother filled Verity. She too loved her mother, but Helen was right. Her mother had no time for politics, and no desire to mingle in society. She'd been content to live with her father on the outskirts of both the city and Dziva society. Verity would never settle. She watched her grandmother flip through the pages. A few moments later, the page turning slowed down, and then finally came to a halt. Helen looked up at her granddaughter, her once sparkling violet eyes, clouded with confusion.

"Verity, darling, shouldn't you be in school?"

She cursed, standing to pace Helen's small but opulent home. Not bothering to answer, she simply marched into the kitchen and called the nurse they'd hired to care for Helen. Answering the first ring, Verity arranged for the woman to come back and sit with her grandmother for the rest of the evening. According to the nurse, Helen had given her the night off. She'd known it was only a matter of time before the woman submerged back into the murky confusion where she spent the majority of her days, so she hadn't gone far. Just down the street to visit a friend.

Walking back into the living room, Verity kissed her Helen goodbye, grabbed her family album and walked out. Perhaps her grandmother did have the name of the families where the Kokoro souls could possibly be born too, and perhaps she didn't. There was no harm in checking.

***

Between the plans for the *di êjê* and chaos of being attacked, Liliana had lost track of the days. It had taken two weeks to get the ceremony planned to the royal family's exacting expectations. The bonding ceremony had been an intangible concept until she'd awakened this morning. Now with the ceremony looming in just hours, her nerves were all over the place. She stood in the middle of her and Leo's room being prepared for the ceremony by Bea. She fluttered around Liliana, making last-minute adjustments, fretting over every minuscule flaw. Liliana eyed her reflection in the floor to ceiling mirror on the wall in their bedroom.

The gown she'd chosen was the palest yellow, with gold thread in geometric shapes throughout. Strapless, it displayed her shoulders shining from the hours spent in traditional preparation. She didn't want to attend another bathing ceremony for as long as she lived. She'd been scrubbed, lotioned and invigorated within an inch of her life. The invigorating process was especially joyful. Overeager maids with small, flat straw brooms briskly tapping her body until her brown skin glowed. Liliana curled her lip in remembrance. Some were more eager than others, no doubt at the instruction of her mother. Arian had had a week's worth of admonishments for her while she watched on in glee. From the ever-unfolding story of the market stall bombing to the drama between Leo and his mother, Arian covered it all as the palace servants tapped her body. The results could not be denied though. Her skin felt like silk.

Bea grumbled behind her as she used magic to finish her hair. Liliana rolled her eyes as her hair changed styles with the flick of Bea's wrist. Leo would have her tresses down her back soon after the mating. Bea's work would be for naught in a few hours.

She smiled secretly. He liked her hair down. He'd told her so every time he yanked out her pins during the moments they'd had these past few days. The planning and his investigation had kept them both busy, but the nights were theirs, and they'd not wasted a single one. Liliana clamped her mouth shut, trapping a moan. She looked forward to the rest of her life with him.

"It's important you not upset your mother today, Lily." Bea's words brought her back to the present.

She sighed. "My mere existence upsets my mother. There's nothing I can do about that." Liliana closed her eyes and put a hand to her stomach. Butterflies fluttered, making her anxious.

Beatrice clucked her tongue. "You shouldn't say things like that, my love."

Liliana shook her head in impatience. "You know it's true, Bea. My mother loved Kita more. I'm resigned to merely being a thorn in her side."

"That's not true, Lily." She met Liliana's eyes in the mirror. They both knew the truth. Bea looked away.

"You've always been more a mother to me than she." Tears gathered and Liliana blinked them back.

The fact that Beatrice helped her prepare and not her mother testified to it. Tradition dictated her mother be here, helping her dress, giving her last-minute advice and soothing the nervous bride. That her mother was not, was proof of their tumultuous relationship. The room should be filled with both friends and family, but no one wanted to be seen with a social pariah. She understood her friends being absent, not that she'd ever had a lot of friends. The few she had, had mothers as strict as her own. They wouldn't allow their daughters near her. Her mother's sisters were another story. Her mother, their baby sister was not here, so they wouldn't be. In fact, none of the women from her mother's family were there, especially the ones with daughters unmated. Whether or not they showed up to the ceremony at all was questionable.

She'd lost a lot when she'd left. All at once anger filled her. That Kedric would ask her to just drop her search for her sister after everything she'd lost pissed her off anew.

"I've always thought of you as my daughter, and I couldn't be more proud of you." Beatrice's voice pulled her from her thoughts.

She turned and pulled her into a tight hug. "I love you, Bea."

"Oh now, let's not start the waterworks." Bea backed up and ran a critical eye across Liliana's appearance. "Just beautiful." She wiped her eyes.

"Thank you for everything." Liliana stepped into her shoes.

"Be sure to visit me once in a while. I know your mate will be taking you to Adro straightaway." Bea fanned her face, looking up to trap her tears.

"I have a better idea. Come to Adro with me. You can stay with Leo and me. Not as a maid, but as my family. Think about it, Bea. Leo wouldn't deny me this."

Bea fussed with her own gown. "I've not much use for Adro. Can't stand the crowds if you must know."

"You can help me with my children, be there for them as you've been for me." Liliana wheedled.

"My place is here." Bea wiped her cheeks and turned Lily to face the mirror.

"What pray tell is taking so long." Arian breezed into the room, looking over Liliana and dismissing her all in one glance.

"It's your daughter's mating ceremony, would you rather me let her leave looking like a ragamuffin." Beatrice snapped.

Liliana's eyes widened at the woman's sharp tone. The women shared a look she didn't understand and came to some sort of unspoken agreement.

"She looks fine, let's go and get this over with."

Arian's words stung, but she was determined not to let her mother see. "Thank you, mother, you're so gracious."

For a moment, albeit a very short moment, something akin to remorse flitted across Arian's expression. Recovering, her mother gave her a thin smile. Liliana took comfort in the fact that she would go back to Adro after the *di êjê*. Being free of her mother was worth all the trouble she'd been through.

They left the Amanda station, her parents, Bea and she, piling into a private sky lift decked out in the royal colors. Red and orange livery covered the lift, the King's insignia displayed prominently. All they passed would know its inhabitants were favorites of the royal house. What they wouldn't know was the so-called favorites were actually persona non grata. Anyone attending the ceremony would only do so out of morbid curiosity. The thought sent a fresh wave of nausea through her. Despite what her mother thought, she hated being a spectacle.

Arian gathered her cloak closely, preening under the attention. The royal palace peeked from behind the clouds. The structure surrounded by fog looked the part of every human fairy tale. The white parapets topped with gold glittered under the sun. Nerves attacked her full-blown and the urge to run made her legs twitch.

You can do this, you like Leo. Just get through it.

She took deep breaths through her pep talk. It was how she had gotten through her years on Adro, and it would get her through today. In through her nose, out through her mouth, just a small ceremony and she would never have to deal with the scrutiny of Legba.

Right.

She could do this.

***

Despite the size of the chamber room, Leo was suffocating. He adjusted the collar on his dress uniform. Moments from the start of the ceremony, he was ready to flee.

Fallon clapped him on the back. "Stop fidgeting. You're well and truly stuck, bro."

Leo grimaced. "Great pep talk."

Xavier walked over to them. He adjusted Leo's sleeves and checked over the rest of his uniform. Leo swatted his hands.

"What are you, my valet? I'm nervous enough without you two fussing around me."

Xavier clucked his teeth. "I'm just trying to make sure you don't go out and embarrass us."

"It's way too late for that." Fallon laughed.

You know what…"

"Boys." his father cut in. Ranolph narrowed his eyes and pointed a finger at the three of them from across the room.

They straightened, the argument immediately ending. Their father used to be the leader of the Amanda, the authority in his voice came from years of wrangling stubborn warriors and boisterous boys.

Xavier cleared his throat. "You have a meeting with Rue when you return to Adro."

The room keeled and Leo sucked in a breath. Hope and fear sent his already jittery nerves into overdrive. He had to make the god understand. He needed the Amanda. He'd grown up following the soldiers around, learning everything he could. He couldn't remember a time when he was not with the Amanda. It was all he'd ever dreamed of being. Being assigned the hunter's job had been surreal, and he'd worked his ass off to keep it. He knew hunting would probably be out of the question, but he hoped to talk the god into anything but a desk job.

"Thank you, Xavier." Now more than ever he was anxious to be done with the ceremony.

"Everything will work out, Leo." His father crossed the room. Ranolph's gruff tone betrayed the emotion in his voice.

His brothers left to give them privacy.

"Baba." Leo grabbed his father's hands to still their motion. "My uniform is fine. I'll be fine, whatever the decision."

They stared in silence until his father finally nodded. "Your mother is here."

Damn, he'd forgotten to give him the head's up.

"Well, it should make for an interesting reception." Between his mother, Liliana's and the Queen, they would surely have to put away any sharp objects. Leo sighed. They should've skipped the damn ceremony. As it was, the planning had taken a lot longer than he'd wanted. Luckily, no other attempts to attack his mate had happened, and he breathed a little easier.

The king stepped into the room. He nodded politely to Ranolph and faced Leo. "The shaman is here, and Liliana has arrived. It's time to start the *di êjê*."

Leo curled his lip at the king.

His father sighed. "Leo, you cannot blame Leander."

"I don't want to talk about this now, *baba*."

"He and I are friends you know."

"Yes, your 'best friend' slept with your mate." Leo's dry tone conveyed his disdain.

Ranolph shook his head. "You don't understand. We were both bloody civilized about the whole thing if you must know."

He scoffed. Sure the king was happy to keep things civil. His father's fighting skill was known across all seven realms. His father was naïve if he thought the king didn't make nice for convenience's sake. No one wanted to be on the bad side of the Amanda.

"We all had our part in the debacle." Ranolph cleared his throat and clapped Leo on the back. "We'll talk later."

Leo clenched his fist. There was no use talking about it later. Would it change the way he felt about Leander? No. Too much time had passed. Besides, Leo knew if his father had not been head of the Amanda, the king would've looked the other way as his wife made good on her promise. His illegitimate heir would've no longer been a problem.

"I have the father I want, there is no need to discuss what's in the past, *baba*. Once I leave Legba, I've no plans to rush back."

Ranolph sighed. "My only advice to you, son, on this day, is to take care of your mate. Put her before all others because eternity with a bitter woman is a very long time."

"Way to put me in the mood for the *di êjê*."

Ranolph held up his hands in surrender. "Fine. I will say this, you are going to enjoy the ceremony and the next few hours after it." With a twinkle in his eye, his father left and Leo stood alone in the chamber room.

He closed his eyes, thankful for the few seconds of silence.

"It's time, Leo." Xavier smiled and held the door open.

They walked down the small hallway in silence. Xavier left him at the door of the throne room that had been transformed for the mating ceremony. The king and queen sat at their thrones on a raised dais in the front of the room. A sea of people filled the seats and stood along the walls of the chamber. The jewels and bright colors dazzled the eye, as nobles fought to outdo the other. A black tide of the uniformed Amanda lined the walls of the chamber and Leo smiled. They looked out of place amidst the stained glass windows they stood along. Winged folk frolicked in various scenes from the walls stretching to the high ceilings, all meeting in the middle of the chamber ceiling to worship the sun and moon.

His eyes roamed the scenes until the door on the other side of the chamber opened. The crowd quieted as Liliana stepped into the doorway. Leo dared not blink. His stomach rolled, a long liquid tumble as their eyes met. She glowed from head to toe, more beautiful than anything he'd ever seen. He observed the quick movements of her hands as she fidgeted, read the nerves on her face and his heartbeat sped. He thought wistfully of love.

Would it come for them?

He looked to the front row where his family was seated. His father and mother were separated by his brothers, and from the tense set of his father's shoulders, words had already been exchanged. He looked back at Liliana. Uncertainty and a small trace of fear reflected in her eyes. He made up his mind. There would be love, he would make sure of it. There was already affection between the two of them. Surely he could build it into more.

They would not be like his parents.

I swear it.

His ears rang, pressure built in his head, and from his mind to the gods, his oath was accepted. The music cued, and Leo began his march to the stone altar. Liliana walked from the opposite side, and they met in the middle. The shaman smiled at them both and started the ceremony. The ancient chant relaxed him, and tendrils of magic wound around them as the binding spell began. The shaman joined their hands. Magic circled them, a shining rope that wrapped around their arms, their heads and then their bodies. A solid line shimmered between them chest to chest and he smiled.

There would be love.

The binding magic sensed it and displayed it for all to see. A cheer went up from the soldiers lining the walls. A low hum started, the shaman chanted louder and the rope spinning around them sped up. Light emanated from them both, blocking his peripheral vision until it was just he and Liliana encapsulated in a circle of amber light. His body heated, his teeth grew in his mouth. They both stepped closer to each other until only a breath separated them. The shaman stepped back and Leo bent his head to Liliana. His teeth scraped her neck and he bit down until he tasted her blood. The *di êjê*, the blood binding, would bond them in the eyes of the gods and ancestors. The exchange of blood sealed them, soul to soul.

Gods, the rush. Her taste crowded his senses and rushed straight to his head. Everything else faded to the background. He luxuriated in the taste of her, his heart racing, fire burning through him. All of that blood immediately raced to his growing erection, hardening him to the point of madness. His teeth receded and he laid a gentle kiss to his mate's neck, licking her to seal the wound.

Liliana leaned forward and he bent to accommodate her. From the moment her mouth touched his neck, he went up in flames. Her small bite weakened his knees and he closed his eyes.

***

His taste.

Gods, lightning arced through her body. Magic seared her senses until there was nothing but Leo. Her soul soared, merged with his, and her skin tingled, her clothes too restricting. She now understood why the Cagyn ceremony was performed in the nude. She wanted to tear the clothes from her body and meld with him, skin to skin. Though it only took a few seconds to exchange the blood, it felt like hours until she pulled back from him. Drunk off his power, and filled with lust, her eyes met his. Molten mercury clashed with her gaze, and trapped her in place as he leaned down and kissed her.

Liliana cursed their bounds hands. She wanted more than anything to touch him, to hell with the gathered crowd.

The elder cleared his throat. The crowd chuckled and Leo backed away from Liliana. She shifted impatiently as the elder completed the ceremony. Magic lit the room, sparks raining from the ceiling as the ancestors accepted the match. Their bound hands were released and the elder ended the ceremony. Leo walked Liliana out through the crowd, nodding at well-wishers, ignoring the gossip mongers.

She barely heard the congratulations, her heart pounded, her focus solely on her hand in Leo's. His grip was warm, the skin of his hands soft despite the work he did. The moment they were out of eyesight he pulled her into the nearest room and pushed her against the wall. Liliana gasped. His hands moved on her body with his eyes full of the same heat coursing through her. He bunched her skirt, pushing it up to her waist. He ripped off her underwear and entered her, swallowing any protest she may have had. Not that she had any. The residual magic from the ceremony had her body tight as a bowstring, and throbbing to the rhythm of their combined heartbeats.

Liliana threw herself into the kiss, so turned on her legs barely held her up. Leo solved that problem by wrapping her legs around his waist. He drove into her and she clawed at his back. The taste of him lingered in her mouth, exotic and intoxicating.

Leo finally lifted his head and she gulped in air.

"You're going to kill me aren't you?" He growled.

She arched her back, driving him deeper, her husky laugh echoing against the walls. "What a way to go, though"

There was no gentleness, just pure concentration on his face, as he drove her up and over the edge. She came and tasted her own blood as she bit down on her lip to keep from screaming. He tensed, thrusting one last time before he bit into her shoulder to stop his own scream. He buckled and Liliana laughed as they tumbled to the floor.

"Gods, woman. We'll be dead in a decade if we keep this up." He pulled her on top of him.

She laughed and looked around the room they'd just snuck into. "There is a perfectly good bed not even three feet away from us, Leonalph." The empty bedroom looked like a small guest chamber.

He groaned and reached down to stroke a finger through the damp curls protecting her sex. "I couldn't have waited another inch to be inside you." He whispered against her lips.

She sighed in pleasure as he pushed her thighs further apart. He kissed her skin over her newest bite mark from him.

"It's a good thing the mating ceremony is completed. I won't have to worry about your fangs anymore." She touched her shoulder gingerly. "No more biting for you."

Leo kissed the spot gently. "I apologize, *ina*. I get carried away. Does it hurt?"

"If I say yes, will you kiss me and make it better?" She shifted her hips, teasing him.

He growled, growing hard again beneath her. "Do you think they'll miss us at the reception?"

"Are you thinking of skipping our reception and sneaking onto Adro?"

"Perhaps not as far as Adro. We can stop at our room at the Amanda station until we're sated." Leo lifted her and positioned her over his shaft. "Which I think will take some hours."

A knock on the door froze them. She jerked away from her and rushed to get up. She smothered her laughter as Leo pulled her back to him.

"Oh no you don't, Leonalph. Put that thing away." She scrambled from atop him, giggling trying to fix her gown. No way was she going round two on the hard floor with someone at the door listening in. While it was hot sneaking around having sex in the palace, having an audience was different.

Leo grabbed her ankle and pulled her back. "I'm officially your lord and master. Get back over here woman and obey me."

Liliana laughed outright and kicked her feet to loosen his grip.

"If you two are finished, there is a room full of people waiting at your reception." Xavier's dry tone sent her into another peal of giggles.

"Go away, Xavier." Leo wrestled her until he pinned her to the floor. "I'm trying to ravish my mate."

"Oh gods, get off. Get off now." Liliana pushed at his shoulders, fighting embarrassment and mirth.

"I'll be sure to tell her father what you said." Xavier shook the doorknob.

"Get off, Leo, I mean it." Her stomach hurt from laughing as she scrambled from under him. She raced to the door grabbing the knob and shoving it open.

Xavier raised a brow. Liliana adjusted her dress and used her magic to fix her hair. He looked at her, his eyes puzzled.

She touched her face. "What?"

"Thank you." Serious, with a little smile playing at his lips, Xavier continued to stare.

"For what?"

He inclined his head towards the door of the closet. Leo came out of the room smiling, his eyes seeking her, traveling her body. She'd had him not even five minutes ago, and still, her body reacted to him. Her nipples tightened, her womb contracted in need.

"Xavier, I do believe I hate you." Leo tucked the shirt of his uniform into his pants.

Xavier saluted them. "My pleasure, brother."

"Come here, *ina*. I'm not through with you yet."

His voice wrapped around her and Liliana took a step towards him. His nostrils flared, his eyes swirled with energy and she was drawn. Xavier stepped between them. Leo growled.

"An hour max, Leo, and then you can have your mate." Xavier rolled his eyes.

Leo reached around his brother and snatched Liliana into his arms. He tangled his hands in her hair, pulling down the bun she'd hastily erected. "One hour," he grumbled, sealing their lips together.

Liquid flooded her center, the nerves throbbing, aching for his touch. She parted her lips and moaned as his tongue entered her mouth.

"Enough, you two," Xavier growled from his position by the door.

She smiled and grabbed Leo's hand. "Just a little longer, my love."

Smiling, he kissed her one final time on the forehead. Nodding to his brother, Leo straightened his uniform and put on a blank face.

She sighed, just an hour, surely they could do that with little drama.

Chapter 17

THE ANSWER WAS NO, no they couldn't go an hour without trouble. If she remembered correctly it took only mere minutes for Sharine to start the trouble she'd promised. Queen Kaylin refusing to come down from the dais seemed to challenge the woman, and she made it her mission to taunt the short-tempered queen. The gossips milled around the dance floor dutifully taking note of every gesture and word exchanged between the two women. Her mother walked around scoffing at the simple decorations and what she deemed tacky food, and her father did his best to keep Arian's voice lowered as she consumed the wine. The only thing about the ceremony of which she approved.

It was an unmitigated disaster.

She snuggled deeper into the feather down blanket and closer to Leo's body heat. This morning she would not be awakened to her mother's lecturing tone, flashing the latest headline in front of her. There would be no rushing to get up and beat the next wave of soldiers being sent after her. If she wanted, she could stay in this bed, her marital bed, all day. She would try her damnedest to forget everything about her reception and call herself lucky for having escaped fairly unscathed.

Well, there was the matter of her throwing up all over her new father in law's shoes. She wasn't likely to forget that anytime soon. She groaned, burrowing her head into Leo's neck. His chuckle vibrated against her face.

"It's not as bad as you're imagining." He kissed her forehead, rubbing his hands up and down her back.

"I wonder if your dad thinks the same."

He laughed outright.

She punched him in the stomach. For all the good it did. He grabbed her hand and brought it up to his lips.

"It's not funny."

"It's hilarious. Besides, that wine was crap, despite the fancy label on it."

"Thank the gods we don't have to go back there anytime soon." She intertwined her fingers with his.

"Here, here." He kissed her again. "What do you want to do today?"

She thought a moment through her options. Yes, she could lay in bed for the day, but it wasn't in her nature. She'd spent years on Adro searching for her sister, somehow starting her new life without knowing what happened to Kita didn't sit well with her.

"I have a few things to check on in my office, but it should only take me a couple of hours. You'll have me all to yourself after that." Leo interrupted her thoughts.

She smiled. There was plenty she could do in a couple of hours. "That sounds nice. I'll look around, get to know my new home."

Leo eyed her suspiciously.

"I promise, I'll stay out of trouble."

He scoffed and rolled from the bed. "I'll believe that when I see it."

She smiled and waved away his disbelief. She rolled onto her back and looked at the ceiling, listening to him move around their bathroom and bedroom getting dressed. Now that she had inside access to Haven, the question would be where to start looking first. She could try and question a few of the soldiers. See if they remember her sister. It was a long shot with how many years had passed, but she had nowhere else to start.

"Just promise you won't leave the Haven without telling me." His voice interrupted her planning.

She propped up on her elbows. "Deal."

He smiled and leaned over her. "See you in a few hours?"

She nodded. He dropped small kisses on her face making her giggle. Gods, Leo caught her off guard by how sweet he was. She wrapped her arms around his neck.

"Have a great day." She whispered.

"Thank you, *ina.*" He gave her one final kiss and left the room.

She waited until she heard the click of the front door to get out of bed. Showering and dressing quickly, she was out roaming the hallway in under thirty minutes. The hallways were bustling, uniformed Amanda soldiers of every kind moving to and from their destinations. She followed a group of people in white coats coming up on Haven's massive kitchen. It was as good a place as any to start. Servants heard a lot more than their masters wanted. The smells reminded her that she'd not had breakfast.

"You there!" A tall woman, her black hair pulled into a high ponytail pointed a wooden spoon at her. "What are you doing in my kitchen?"

Liliana put on her most charming smile. "I'm sorry, the smells brought me here. I just realized I hadn't eaten breakfast."

With narrowed eyes, the chef looked her up and down. Sniffing in disdain she pointed to a small table in the corner of the kitchen. "Sit. I'll bring you something."

Nodding her thanks, Liliana happily took a seat in the wooden chair. She watched the staff move around the kitchen, shouting orders and a few ribald jokes. The whole scene was fascinating.

Before too long, the chef set a plate of bacon, eggs, and croissants on a plate in front of her. A second plate, laden with fruits from different realms followed. Liliana rubbed her hands in anticipation. The chef sat down in the chair across from her.

"What brings the mate of Death's Messenger into my kitchen to eat? You could have simply called and breakfast would've been brought to you."

Liliana paused with the croissant halfway to her mouth. "You know who I am?"

"I'm Marta, head chef here at Haven. I see lots of things and hear even more. This is why you came into my kitchen, no?"

"I…"

Marta smiled and leaned back in her chair.

Liliana picked up a small fig and popped it in her mouth, studying the other woman. How much did she know about her? "What have you heard?"

Marta leaned forward. "I heard you sexed up Death's Messenger and got caught in a trick of fate."

She groaned. Of course, that bit of gossip was floating around Haven.

"I also heard you're looking for your sister."

Liliana perked up. "Go on."

Marta shrugged. "No one here has seen or even heard of your sister."

Her shoulders slumped. Damn, another dead end. And she'd been so optimistic. She picked up her fork and dove into the eggs on her plate.

"You're different than I'd imagined."

Cocking her head to the side, Liliana finished chewing. "How so?"

"I hear you're a noble, a very rich one. I don't know, I guess I expected you to be more…"

"Eshu?"

Marta smiled. "Yes."

"Well, let my mother tell it, I'm as common as they come."

Marta laughed outright. "You're sitting in the kitchen eating with the help, so you're not exactly giving off 'noble'."

Liliana snorted and continued eating.

Marta watched her silently, tapping her fingers on the table between them. "I tell you what." She said after a moment. "I will ask around. If I hear anything I'll call you."

She clasped the other woman's hands gratefully. "Thank you, Marta, that would be amazing."

"I'll leave you to finish your breakfast. You should try the surveillance room if you can get access." Marta stood, leaving her with that last bit of advice.

It was a great idea. They probably saw everything in the surveillance room. Getting access could be a problem though. She wondered if dropping Leo's name would help.

Couldn't hurt.

She'd try it. Feeling more optimistic, she smiled. She was off to a good start. Not great, but good. She scarfed down the rest of her food, grabbing a bunch of grapes to take with her. She waved at Marta on the way out the door. She would make a point to befriend the chef. Having a friend who knew things would always come in handy. Now to find the surveillance room. Using the same tactics she used to find the kitchen, she followed the soldiers in uniforms.

Before long she was at a door of what looked like a break room. Taking a deep breath she went inside. She received a few confused looks, but no one stopped her. Shrugging, she walked up to a group of soldiers standing around a refrigerator. She'd just ask a few questions. No harm done.

***

Twenty minutes later she was no further along than when she first started. Not only did they not have information on Kita, but they also wouldn't give her information on where the surveillance room was located.

Jerks.

There was no use staying in the break room. She turned to leave. Leo was blocking the entrance, his shoulder leaned against the doorjamb.

"What are you up to, *Ina*?"

Lie, or not?

Leo raised an eyebrow.

Not.

She pasted on a sunny smile. "You know, just getting my bearings, looking around."

"Oh yeah?" He moved from the doorjamb and leaned closer to her. "Because I heard you were asking questions about your sister."

She rolled her eyes and blew a raspberry. These men were a bunch of gossiping women. "Fine, you caught me."

He gave her a small smile and crooked his finger at her. She moved closer to him, suspicious. He grabbed her hand and tucked it into his elbow.

"Come."

She followed him through the complicated hallways of Haven until they arrived at an unmarked door. Pulling up a spell, Leo entered a passcode and the door opened with a quiet snick. Eyes wide, she followed him into the air-conditioned room, degrees colder than the rest of Haven. It was quiet here, with only the drone of machines to fill the silence and the occasional command or request chirping from a communicator. She was nervous with anticipation. He'd brought her to the surveillance room. Liliana's heart raced. True to his word he was helping her search for her sister. He pulled her further into the room, the men coming at attention as Leo passed. Except for one male. He scrambled from his chair, fleeing for the door.

Leo clotheslined him, the soldier slamming into the floor, wheezing. Leo put a boot on his chest to keep him from standing. "I guess I don't have to ask which one of you rat bastards gave Verity the code to my room."

The guy writhed on the floor in pain. "I can explain."

"I don't care." Leo leaned down into his face, putting pressure on his chest. "My mate was in my room."

"I'm sorry." He wheezed out.

"If you give out information on another person under Haven's protection, I will deliver you to death myself."

He nodded. "I swear."

Leo moved his foot and resumed walking. Liliana looked back at the male still on the floor but doubled her steps to keep up with her mate. Leo looked back at her.

"Sorry you had to see that, but that jerk gave out my room information, which is prohibited."

She blinked, unsure of what he wanted her to say. He put a hand on the small of her back and directed her to a small desk in the corner. It was away from the rest of the room, a frosted glass divider keeping the desk private from the other soldiers. He guided her into the leather office chair, pulling it out until she sat down.

"We can look at the Oras here."

"What are Oras?" She scooted the chair closer to the desk.

His hands worked through a complicated spell until hundreds of images wavered in the air in front of them, like holograms. "These are the Oras."

The images were too small to really see anything, but shock widened her eyes.

"There are spells to pull up images of anyplace on the planet. We use information in the Earth's magnetic fields and magic from the primal source to surveil the whole and breadth of Adro. It's better than satellites and the spell is nearly impossible to tamper with." He worked through the images he'd pulled up. "Do you remember the date your sister last came to Adro?"

Pushing aside her shock and the million questions she had, she focused on his one question. "It was so long ago. Kita and Kedric made so many trips to Adro together, I stopped paying attention."

"Hmmm. Was Kedric with her this last visit?"

Liliana ran a hand through her short curls. She'd donned her human skin to keep her appearance concealed as was her habit after so many years on Adro. Though Marta had seen right through her disguise. Her brows furrowed in concentration. "I honestly don't remember. I don't see why she would've left without him."

"Wait." Leo straightened. "Xavier and Fallon had already narrowed it down and found the last time Kita crossed the portal. I forgot with everything that has happened. Hold on a moment."

He left her in the quiet of the cubicle.

Moments later he came back and went through another series of spells. The light of the Oras flickered, went out, then came back, this time with fewer windows, each with a different view of the main portal of Haven.

"X put these aside separately to go through. The Oras miss nothing, so you should be able to trace your sister's steps through Haven."

"Do people know about these Oras?"

"No, only a few Demi have access and knowledge of the Oras. As long as you know where to look and a general timeframe, keeping track of Demi activities is a snap."

She sucked in a sharp breath. "If that's true, then how did I evade your soldiers for so long?"

Leo chuckled. "Don't remind Xavier of that. You were quick, each time we located you and sent soldiers, you were gone. Sometimes we missed you by mere minutes."

He was right. Her heart thumped just thinking of the near misses.

"Adro is vast, finding one tiny Eshu noble, who changed appearances often, I might add, is difficult. Besides, you weren't really a priority for X until a few months ago. The queen became uncomfortably persistent then."

"I can imagine."

Leo worked through the images, narrowing the views down until only six screens showed. "Okay. Start with these views. X saved them, so obviously he spotted Kita on one of them."

"There." Liliana leaned forward, thirsty for an image of her sister. She spotted Kita walking through the portal room alone.

"Okay, you work through these." He showed her how to move through the Oras to pick up Kita in other places. "If I remember correctly, Xavier said some of them were corrupted, so you won't be able to see everything."

She frowned. "Corrupted. How is that possible?"

"Takes some dark magic. X is still working on that."

"So these Oras aren't infallible?"

"For every spell, there is a counterspell. It's all about balance. Nothing is infallible."

He went through other spells with her, showing her how to maneuver and angle the images and how to check different places. Once he saw she'd picked it up, he straightened.

"I'll go grab drinks and snacks. There are a ton of these to go through. Will you be okay here alone?"

Engrossed, she nodded absently and waved him away.

Chapter 18

"YO, LEO."

Leo turned around, careful not to jostle the tray of food and drinks. Fallon stood in the middle of the hall, his face grim.

"We were looking for you."

"Why, what's up?" He walked over to Fallon.

"I heard you were slapping people around in the surveillance room." Fallon grabbed a sandwich off his tray and took a bite.

Leo growled. "Not people, person. One jackass who had given out my room information, code included."

Fallon stopped eating and frowned. "I'll take care of it."

He shrugged. As far as he was concerned, he'd handled it. He doubted the male would be likely to give out any other person's info. But Fallon would do what he saw fit. He didn't allow for mistakes.

"Is that why you hunted me down?"

Fallon finished off his sandwich as they rounded the corner to Xavier's office. "No, Rugaba is here to see you."

Leo stopped and his stomach lurched. Looking around, he thrust the tray he was holding at the first person to walk by. Running a hand down his chest, he quickly changed into his uniform and took a deep breath. "Why didn't you say that first?"

Fallon shrugged, and opened the door, motioning for him to go in first. He walked into the office with his head high, hoping no trace of his nervousness showed. Rugaba in all his power was there. Six feet six in his human form, very dark skin with dreadlocks that reached his back, the god was very intimidating.

Leo bowed low. "Thank you, my lord, for seeing me."

Rugaba nodded. "I know the purpose of your request to see me. You know I created the Eminzu to deal with these types of issues, right? And I'm sure you're aware of their very exacting rules when it comes to mated pairs."

His heart sank. "I'm aware, and I apologize for the inconvenience, my lord. I simply wanted a chance to plead my case." He searched his mind for words to use that would convince the god.

"You've served in your post for some decades, yes?"

Leo kept his eyes lowered. "I have served you and wish to continue to do so. It's all I've ever wanted to do."

Rugaba sighed. "Your position is a highly dangerous one, Leonalph."

"I understand the risk and will be extra vigilant." He dared not hope, but couldn't quite corral his optimism.

"My brother speaks highly of you, and does not wish to lose you as a messenger."

Surprise raised his eyes to stare at the god. Azra spoke highly of him? Rugaba shrugged. Leo lowered his eyes unable to hold the god's gaze.

"You do your job efficiently, and it has not gone unnoticed." He opened his mouth to say something else when the door burst open.

"Oh my God, Leo, I found something! I really didn't think I would, I mean there are a lot…" Liliana trailed off when she noticed who was in the room.

She dropped into a deep curtsy. "Apologies, my lord."

***

Rugaba sighed. "Rise, child."

She hastily straightened and stood behind Leo. He really didn't have time for this. He needed to find out who the other Kokoro souls were and give their names to Xavier for protection. Rugaba dismissed her and leveled his stare at the warrior, trying to hold on to his indifference. He wasn't supposed to show a preference for any one warrior, but this family was dear to him. They had served him with no questions or complaints for centuries, each father passing the leadership of the Amanda to the oldest. He agreed to this meeting simply because the Amanda could not afford to lose Leo. He was the best hunter they had. He knew the warrior wanted him to override the Eminzu's edict and allow him to keep his position.

Death's messenger was an apt description for Leo. He delivered Demi to Azreal and their death consistently and efficiently. Finding Demi sentenced to death was no easy task, yet Leo did it better than any warrior in the centuries prior to him. He regularly traveled the portals to hell and came back, a feat in and of itself. His brother was adamant in Leo keeping his job. He would trust Azra to strengthen the wards on his side of the portal and keep the warrior safe. In this case, he would override the Eminzu and allow Leo to keep his position.

He started to tell Leo that when the female's aura reached out to him.

Rugaba walked to her and reached passed Leo laying a hand on her shoulder. The contact brought her past, her future and her every thought into his head. He hissed. The simple touch burned, but her fate was now an opened book to him. Its pages littered with the peril she would face and have recently faced. She was a Kokoro soul. While he knew the Mina were almost always right, he was still shocked that this small female housed one of the most important souls on Earth. For a moment he stared, unable to fathom the pain that awaited her if some of the visions he saw came to life. She would need a strong protector, that much was clear.

He turned to Leo. "This is your mate." Not a question, he saw the strong bond of their souls.

"Yes." Leo looked from Rugaba back to Liliana.

"Your request is denied." No way would he allow Leonalph to traipse the world for his job when his mate was more important than any Demi sentenced to death.

He lowered his head. "Yes, my lord."

Leo's pain shot through him along with the lancing heat from his mate. It was one of the side effects of him touching her. They would be tied to him for eternity, their every emotion and thought a burden to him. But he wanted to keep tabs on the Kokoro soul, and would readily bear the burden.

"You will be needed to protect your mate, Leo. For that reason only I deny your request." He couldn't allow him to hunt. It was way too dangerous. He would talk to Azra. His brother could keep him as a messenger, provided he did as he said and strengthened his wards over Leo. It would be the only way to mitigate some of the danger of Leo traveling through the portals.

Leo's pain forced him from his thoughts. He sighed, he needed to explain his reasoning. He turned to Xavier.

"I wanted to talk to you anyway. For a while now, there have been blank spots covering Adro, voids we call them. It keeps us on Alafia from being able to monitor Earth's events. Only one being leaves those voids."

"Offeeree," Fallon said.

Rugaba nodded. "As I'm sure your father told you, to lock him away, some of the Demi had to endow their power upon three people."

"You're talking about the Kokoro souls?" Xavier sat forward in his chair.

"What are the Kokoro souls?" The female's eyes were wide with fear.

"The souls of the three people who bound and hid away Ofeeree," Leo told her.

Rugaba had an idea which soul she housed but kept it to himself. Three people were used in the binding spell and their souls alone held that knowledge. One soul held knowledge of the location where Ofeeree was bound, and he had a suspicion that this was the soul she had. He'd found a woman who had the book of divinity. So he suspected she held the second soul, the one able to read and decipher the spell used to bind Ofeeree. It was the third soul he worried after the most. That person would be most important, as they would be the only person able to access the realm in which Ofeerree was hidden. Only with that person would the rest be able to have even the smallest chance at freeing the evil.

"You have one of the souls."

"Me?" She backed away from Leo.

"Each soul is imprinted with the knowledge of how Ofeeree was bound," Rugaba told her.

"And in turn, would have the knowledge of how to free him," Fallon said grimly.

"I don't know anything about Ofeeree." She hugged her arms around her waist.

Rugaba grimaced. "You don't know now. But there is a ceremony, a very painful spell used to activate and unlock the knowledge imprinted on your soul."

"My God." She whispered.

He nodded. "It's exactly why I want Leonalph to protect you. With the voids increasing, and the Kokoro souls roaming Adro freely, it's in our best interest to keep you as well as the other souls, when found, protected." He turned and faced Xavier. "I've found one other who houses a Kokoro soul and will need guards posted on her at all times."

"The bookshop owner?" Fallon asked.

Rugaba nodded, Fallon already had the female's name and information, so he didn't have to go over that with him.

"Done," Fallon promised.

He faced Leo. "Azra has asked that you retain your position as the messenger, and I agree, you would be hard to replace. I will do battle with the Eminzu for you but, only on the condition you no longer hunt."

Pride straightened Leo's shoulders, his relief trickling through Rugaba's subconscious.

"Train someone to take your place. Hopefully, they will be as good as you were. One other thing, when you travel, you're to have someone there when you cross back."

Leo sucked in a sharp breath and glanced at Xavier. He nodded reluctantly. Satisfied he wasn't leaving chaos, he nodded to the room and took his leave.

***

Leo stood staring at the spot Rugaba disappeared from. He was stunned. Though stunned seemed too mild a word. His wife was a Kokoro. If he thought she'd been in danger before…

He took a shuddering breath.

There were those who would kill her to get the secret her soul was harboring and there were those who would kill her to keep it from happening. He rubbed a hand across his face.

"What did he mean, have someone there when you crossed back?" Xavier's sharp tone broke through his thoughts.

Leo shrugged. "I cross to Azreal in the same place I find my mark. Sometimes it's not the safest place. But I've set up a few areas as my safety nets."

Xavier eyed him, knowing he wasn't telling the complete truth. Luckily Liliana slumped against the door, her face was pale. It distracted his brother from his line of questioning.

"What's wrong?" Leo gathered her into his arms, checking her over.

She shook her head. "Nothing. I mean, that was Rugaba, you know. God of the sun, of fate. I can't believe I just walked in on him. On you guys."

Fallon snickered.

"And why did you bust into my office without knocking," Xavier asked.

"Oh." She pushed away from Leo, blushing. "I came upon the corrupted Oras Leo told me about and I had an idea."

"What kind of idea?" Fallon sat in the chair across from Xavier's desk and crossed his ankle over his knee.

"Well, I know a shaman who may be able to help with the corrupted magic of the Oras. I want to go see him."

"Absolutely not." Xavier quickly denied her.

"Why not?" Liliana asked, a stubborn gleam in her eye.

"Did you not just hear what Rugaba said about who you are? No. End of story."

She looked at Leo and he shook his head. He knew what Xavier's tone of voice meant, and it was nothing good for his mate.

"I need to go see this shaman."

Leo frowned. "Who is the shaman?"

"Sergio, he helped me with my papers, and his fake pass got me into Haven. He's pretty powerful and could possibly help fix the corrupted Oras."

"Is that right?" Xavier's tone should've been a warning to Liliana, but she ignored it and kept up her plea.

Leo tuned out their argument. The huge weight of what she was hit him again. He was already protective of her, with this new information…He sighed. It would impossible not to smother her. Liliana was already touchy about the guards he'd had on her in Legba. How in the hell would he be able to keep her safe if she insisted on traipsing across Atlanta into who knows what kind of danger? He shook himself from his thought as everyone turned to look at him.

He shrugged, not having kept track of the conversation. He had no idea what they'd asked so he gave a safe answer. "Let me think about it."

She growled.

"Gods almighty, it's like I'm talking to walls. None of you jackasses listen to me. What use is being head of the Amanda?" Xavier grumbled.

She tapped her feet and stewed for a few moments. He raised his eyebrow. No way would she rush him on the decision. No matter the nasty looks she sent at him. He needed to find a way to keep her safe, one they could both live with. Until he did, she was going nowhere.

She shook her head. "There was another reason I came here. I can't access some of the Oras from around the time Kita was here."

"Outside of the corrupted ones?" Fallon asked.

"Right, they aren't corrupted. It gives me some kind of clearance warning."

Xavier frowned and pull up the Oras. "You used Leo's codes right?"

Leo moved closer to his brother's desk. "Yeah, I put them in myself."

"Show me," Xavier ordered Liliana.

She moved behind his desk and went through the screens as Leo showed her. Then she moved through them in the same way she had earlier looking for the clearance warning. After a few minutes of her moving around the screens, a small buzzer sounded.

"See." She waved her hand in front of the message.

Xavier's eyebrows bunched in confusion. He gently pushed her aside and moved through three locking spells. "What the…" He moved through four others, murmuring to himself before finally, an image flickered to life.

Fallon leaned over Xavier's desk. "What happened?"

His brother frowned over the image, pulling up and discarding spell screens. "Someone from the Eminzu locked the Oras around the time frame Kita disappeared. Remember how we couldn't find anything?"

His hands swept through the air as he pushed around images, and worked through spells. Holograms and images of Kita walking through the front door of Haven flickered and passed. Finally, he settled on one image and the four of them leaned in to watch.

Chapter 19

LILIANA WAS RIVETED BY THE image of her sister. Kita looked so carefree, so beautiful, all the while not knowing she would disappear and leave her family in turmoil. But then Kita never worried about anyone or anything but herself. Life was always a party for her. Liliana shook her head, banishing the nasty thought, guilt making her contrite.

She watched as Kita flirted with Fallon and strode into the club. The image faded out and shimmered back to life, this time with her sister in the middle of the dance floor. Liliana reeled in shock. There were people wearing dog collars, in varying color leather outfits, and that was if they bothered to wear clothes. Manacles hung from the ceiling of the dance floor, and devices she had no names for lined the walls.

"What is this?"

"There is a night at Haven to cater to all. Some beings feed off the energy of sadism." Xavier moved through the Oras keeping track of her sister as she writhed along with the bodies on the dance floor.

She watched, stunned as people were whipped, and some chained down for others to feed on them. Kita showed no shock at the events happening around her. If anything, the smile on her face indicated she was enjoying it.

Leo cleared his throat, clearly uncomfortable with her reaction. "It's not for dabblers. Anyone who shows up on Tuesdays is heavily into BDSM."

"Did you know?" Fallon spared her a small glance.

She shook her head. "Kita never let me hang out with her. I never knew." She turned to Leo, her face displaying her shock. Up until now, she'd never realized how sheltered she'd been. Yeah, she'd spent time by herself on Adro, but she'd never imagined a world like this existed.

Her gaze flickered back to the Oras. "Who are all the people with the matching tattoos?"

Leo frowned. "For lack of a better term, vampires."

She sucked in a breath. "Vampires?" Her voice was barely a whisper.

"Haven is just that, a haven for all supernatural creatures. So long as the rules are followed and the Ajo keep to the treaty, they're allowed to be here." Xavier explained.

She put her hands to her cheeks, their heat warming her ice-cold hands. Gods, what had Kita been into? Embarrassment took over her shock as she watched her sister grab a vampire by his collar and lead him up a private stairwell towards the back of the club. They were likely heading to one of the observation rooms. Liliana's heart thumped in her chest at breakneck speed. She was surprised they couldn't hear it. Kita had been betrothed to the prince her whole life. Did he know she cheated on him? The room was silent as they were all engrossed in the hologram. Kita and the Ajo reached the door to the room and the Oras dimmed before completely going out.

Xavier's loud curse made her flinch.

"Has to be some powerful magic to disrupt the Oras." Fallon's grim statement mimicked Leo's earlier words to her.

"We have someone working to reverse the spells on the others, but I didn't even know these existed. I should've suspected something was wrong when I couldn't find her." Xavier squinted his eyes as he tried once again to get past the point where the Oras went out.

She nodded absently, numb from the behavior she'd witnessed. Not only had her sister been into scary dominance games, but she'd also cheated on Kedric. Had she and the prince both participated in the BDSM scene? What she knew of Kedric, sure he would be into that kind of stuff, but her sister? What had the prince gotten her into?

"I need to go lay down." She whispered.

Leo pulled her into his arms. "I don't like your color, babe. I'm going to send a healer to meet you at our apartment."

She ran a hand through her hair, releasing the magic holding her in her human skin. "That won't be necessary."

He guided her from his brother's office. "I insist."

Arguing with him seemed too much work, so she dutifully trailed him to their room. Footage from the Oras played in her mind as she tried to reconcile the images with the memories of her sister.

"There is nothing wrong with BDSM, *ina*." It was like he read her mind sometimes.

"That's not…I'm not upset about that." She bit her lip. "She was my big sister, it's hard to realize I knew next to nothing about her."

He nodded. "That makes sense."

"Of course it does." She snapped.

He raised an eyebrow.

"Sorry. I thought you were being condescending." She pursed her lips in chagrin.

"Thank the gods." He muttered at the sight of the Kira healer standing at their door. "I will leave you in the capable hands of the healer, and I will go find out what else X is doing about the corrupted Oras."

He scrambled down the hallway, making his escape. Liliana sighed in impatience. His habit of running away for work was becoming annoying.

"Please, come in." She motioned to the Kira.

"Thank you Lady Tegan. My name is Rosalia." The female Kira was beautiful in a simple strapless shift dress. Her brown skin gleamed, the dark rings on her shoulders displayed in her dress. Her hair was pulled into a high ponytail, the branches in her hair trailing her back as with all the Kira. Their forested realm held the most peaceful magic, making Edin highly sought out by weary Demi. Their race was healers of both the mind and body and the Amanda employed only the best.

Once inside, Rosalia declined refreshments and had Liliana sit down at their kitchen table.

"Relax," she told her. "From what I've heard, your body has been through a lot of punishment recently."

"Don't I know it." Liliana closed her eyes and fought to relax as the Kira's hands roamed her body.

Rosalia started at her head, humming softly as she massaged Liliana's temples. She moved to the pressure points of her neck, her touch soft and hypnotizing. Liliana was in a deep trance by the time the Kira reached her stomach. The humming stopped being musical and turned introspective.

"What is it?" She asked, popping her eyes open.

Rosalia smiled and pushed Liliana's lids back closed. "Relax."

She cracked one eye open. "Just tell me."

The Kira chuckled. "It's not good for the babe for the mother to be all over the place. You need to relax."

Liliana sucked in a sharp breath. "Babe?"

The Kira nodded. "You didn't notice the change in your body?"

"So much has happened that I didn't…are you sure?"

Rosalia's smile was soothing. "I'm very sure, maybe two weeks old at the most. He is already a strong soul, you should be able to start your bonding exercises soon."

"Bonding exercises?" Liliana touched her stomach in shock.

"Yes, meditations with you and your mate that allow you to bond with your child's soul. It will help reassure the babe, and certainly, make labor easier. The more peaceful and secure the babe feels, the less he will fight you."

"Fight me?" She felt as if she'd lost her wits, repeating after Rosalia.

"Yes, babies never want to leave the warm safety of their mother's womb, so they fight the birth. As strong as your son is, I'll wager he'll give you hours of a fight. You should start bonding exercises as soon as you're able. It's new to you now, but you should start no later than three weeks into your pregnancy."

Liliana was going to be sick. Sharine's words circled her mind. Damn the woman. She was right. Lily was going to be locked in Haven raising a bunch of babies and no freedom. Between this and Rugaba saying she was a Kokoro soul, she'd be lucky if Leo allowed her on the roof to take in energy from the sun. She did the mental math and cursed. It had to have happened the first time they slept together on Legba. Once again, had she adhered to customs, she wouldn't be in the mess she was in. Why hadn't she felt the changes to her own body?

She rubbed a hand over her face. In her defense, she'd been attacked twice in the time since she'd stepped foot on Legba. Surely she could be excused from missing a few signs. Gods, it was too soon! They were barely getting to know each other and now a baby. The dull edges of panic crept into her body, tensing it up. A soft hand on her arm brought her back to Rosalia's presence.

"There's nothing to be done about it, Lady Tegan. Panic won't help you."

Lily laid her head on the kitchen table. How did she feel about it? She had no clue, and now the walls of their apartment were closing in on her. She needed to get out of Haven. That would prove Sharine wrong, right? She thanked the Kira for her help and escorted her to the front door of their apartment. Guards she didn't remember asking for, stopped her at the door.

"Am I a prisoner now?" Her scathing tone carried down the hallway.

They shuffled uncomfortably. "We're only looking out for you." One guard answered.

"I'm going to find something to eat. Do you have a problem with that?"

They looked at each other in askance. One of them spoke softly into what she assumed was the communicator in their ear. Frustration burned her chest. She had hoped there would be no guards when they got back to Haven. No way would she walk around with a freaking entourage. She didn't allow her father to give her bodyguards, she for damn sure wouldn't allow Leo the pleasure. She changed into her human skin and pushed passed them.

They rushed after her and she took spiteful satisfaction at the frazzled look on their faces. She turned her head to taunt them and ran into someone. She looked up and groaned as Fallon steadied her.

"Where you going, Trouble?"

"None of your business. You're just going to tell my jailor." She crossed her arms in front of her.

Fallon smiled. "Let's go get some fresh air." He nodded behind her, dismissing her guards.

She sighed, and acquiesced, a reluctant bob of her head. He led her out of Haven and into the warm day. Neither spoke as they walked. Energy from the sun seeped into her skin, exposed from her sundress. It energized her and slowly tension dissipated from her body. They'd gone three blocks when they came to a small outdoor shopping mall. She was pleasantly surprised. She'd assumed the Haven was off by itself in the middle of nowhere. To know just a few blocks down the road was an entire shopping center was jarring and a little reassuring. She saw many walks to the mall in her future.

Liliana was drawn to a small café. They opted to sit outside along the sidewalk. She didn't know his reason for agreeing to the table, but she liked to people watch. Watching humans go about their daily lives was fascinating to her. They ordered tea from the waitress and she perused the milling traffic, not bothering to break the silence between them. He barged in on her alone time, so she didn't owe him any conversation. But she was thankful the guards weren't following her.

Their teas were brought to the table before she gave up her silent treatment.

"Just say it, Fallon."

"I don't have anything to say, Lily. You need air, we'll get air. I'm straight with just sitting here quietly." He shook a packet of sugar into his teacup.

"Yeah, right."

"I know better than to aggravate a pregnant woman." He dropped that bombshell and sipped his tea.

"How do you know that? I just found out myself mere minutes ago."

He shrugged. "Why haven't you told Leo?"

Liliana scrubbed at her tired eyes. No wonder she'd been so tired lately. She wondered why the other healer hadn't said anything to her. "Did you not just hear me say that I've only just found out myself?"

"When are you going to tell him?"

She growled. "I don't know, Fallon. What happened to just sitting here quietly?"

He raised an eyebrow but said nothing.

"Damn it." She sighed. "I don't want to end up like your mother."

He choked on his tea, spilling it on his shirt. "What?"

She handed him a couple of napkins. "I don't want to be locked in a room with only children for company, slowly losing my mind. I hate being cooped up, ask my family. I don't want a mate who'll smother me."

"Liliana, I don't know what my mother told you, but I'm pretty sure it's lies. She tends to fabricate things to engender sympathy. Between her and my father, they're fantastic storytellers. Besides, it's apples and oranges. Leo is not like our father, and you're nothing like our mother."

"But I'll end up locked in that room, all the same."

He sighed. "Trouble, Leo doesn't know what to do with you. Rather than fight with him, work with him."

She eyed him and thought about it. It wouldn't hurt for her to have a guard following her. She could concede with everything that had been happening to her lately, it was probably a good idea. With the bombshell Rugaba had just dropped on her, she was sure talking Leo out of guards would be impossible anyway. She shrugged. Childish, but she wanted to hold onto her mad a little longer.

Fallon smirked but said nothing.

The silence stretched between them a few minutes more.

"I'll talk to Leo about allowing you to see the shaman. The ones X has working on the Oras are getting nowhere."

She waved him off. "No, I'll talk to him myself. I can't start my mating with others fighting my battles.

"Good for you."

She gave him a droll look.

He laughed. "Gods, but you are going to be fun to have around."

Chapter 20

THE DOOR CLICKED QUIETLY, and he paused his work. He'd been going through their archives researching the Kokoro souls for the past forty minutes or so. What he'd read scared him shitless. The first three Kokoro died completing their spell. According to everything he'd read, the reborn souls would, in essence, go through the same thing. The amount of power needed to complete the dark spell would drain the persons performing it. The way the archivist wrote it, one person would be needed to open a portal into the realm where he'd been hidden away. It was a realm completely separate from Adro and the seven realms of the Demi. Only blood unlocked the portal, and only one person with the unique set of genes would be able to even access the magic needed.

The next person would know the location of Ofeeree's corporeal body within that realm. The texts were foggy about Ofeeree's body, some said it had been cut into pieces and scattered, some made no mention of the state of his body. It was hard to decipher between legend and fact. No facts even existed for how the realm looked, how Ofeerree was bound, or what type of vessel or temple housed the body. The only thing said regarding what type of prison held Ofeerree was that the third soul was the only one able to unlock his prison. Using both the book of Divinity and a spell, only that soul would know, were the only notations about it. What he couldn't understand was how someone could use this sparse information in order to free the evil being. It was nearly impossible to piece together enough of the texts to make completed instructions.

The refrigerator opened and closed, the sound jarring him from his thoughts.

"I'm in here, *ina*."

He listened to her light footsteps as she walked from the kitchen to his office. She looked weary, but the fresh air seemed to have put color back into her face. He waved her over, patting his lap. After what he'd read, he wanted her in his arms. He thought back on their ceremony. Just yesterday he'd wondered if there would be love for them, and today he realized he was already in love with Liliana.

She'd gotten under his skin, her naïve but stubborn personality drawing him in. Fallon had called him while they were out, his words cryptic. According to his brother, he and his mate needed to talk about his safety measures for her. He was at a loss with how to balance his need to keep her safe and her obvious dislike of the guards he's assigned to her. According to the guards, she thought of them as jailors. He had a feeling once his mate made her mind up about something, it would be difficult to sway her.

"Enjoy your outing?" He pulled her down for a kiss.

She moaned, pulling away reluctantly. "Yes, I needed some air. It was getting a little stifling in here."

He sighed, so they were going to get right into it then. "What would you have me do, my love?"

"We have to compromise in some way, Leo." Her eyes pleaded with him.

He was not immune to her charms. Nevertheless, he groaned, imagining how long they would argue. "I don't want to argue."

"Compromise requires an argument?" Her dry tone made him smile.

"You heard Rugaba, Lily."

"I've grown used to roaming free on Adro."

"Right, dodging soldiers and on the run." He interjected.

"Point to you." She conceded. "However, I was free all the same."

"I can't allow you the complete freedom you had. It's too dangerous."

"I understand that, and I will promise not to go anywhere outside of Haven without guards, but surely they don't need to be here in the room or walking behind me inside of Haven's protections."

He mulled it over. She had a point, the laws of Haven should prevent anything from happening to her inside its walls. Banishment from the Havens kept most from breaking its rules. His brothers' punishments served as a strong deterrent for those who needed extra incentive to behave. In theory, she would be safe within these walls.

"I can agree with that."

Her smile took over her face and warmed him. She trailed a finger down the front of his shirt, her eyes taking on a mischievous glint.

"What about the shaman, can I go see him tomorrow?" She trailed kisses down his neck.

"That's not playing fair, *ina.*" He adjusted her body so her legs straddled his. He lifted his hips slightly, pushing his growing erection into her center. She sighed and wiggled as her skin heated.

"Who said anything about fair?"

"I can't do tomorrow." Xavier wanted him to find and train his replacements as soon as possible.

She pouted, trailing her hand down the front of his pants. "I'll take as many guards as you deem."

He closed his eyes and fought through the haze of lust she was creating. He trusted Roy and Paul, the guards he'd assigned to her. They'd protected her on Legba, and did a great job of getting her through the rest of their stay safely. Hopefully, she wouldn't object to them. Surely they could get her in and out of a meeting with a shaman with little to no drama.

She bit his earlobe and the sensation shot down through his body. Pheremones from his Cagyn form wafted from his skin, covering them both in his scent. Gods, if Liliana dealt with all their compromises this way, he was screwed.

"You will do exactly as told." He lifted her body, tearing her underwear off of her. "No trying to lose your guards. Swear it." He brushed a hand over her sex.

Her sharp inhalation pleased him. Her head fell back, her lips parting on her sigh of pleasure. Drowsy eyes lifted to meet his gaze as she surrendered to his Cagyn magic. She was getting caught up in her own game. He chuckled and pushed one finger into her wet heat.

"I didn't hear you, Lily. Swear it."

"I swear." She hissed.

He added a second finger, amplifying his magic. Cagyns were often accused of using their magic to seduce innocents and mated women for their own needs, and perhaps some did. Their magic captivated its victim, relaxed inhibitions until nothing but assuaging their body's ache mattered. He was quickly finding out that nothing compared to sharing his magic with the woman he currently held in his lap. Watching his mate succumb to his enchantment was a heady feeling. Her mouth parted as sighs of pleasure escaped.

"You will be careful, right? If anything happens to you I will wrap you in cotton battening and lock you in our room."

"I'll be careful." Her voice was barely a whisper.

He lifted her, opened his pants and freed his shaft. He growled as he slid deep inside of her. "Is this how you plan to conduct negotiations from now on?"

Her smile was dreamy as she flexed her body. "Yes, definitely."

He would gladly negotiate with his mate if they all ended this way. He'd talk to her guards in the morning before they left. His instructions had better be explicitly followed. He didn't even want to think about what he would do if Liliana were hurt again.

***

Body buzzing, Liliana woke up the next day full of anticipation. Leo was going to let her see Sergio today. The shaman was one of the best she'd encountered in her years on Adro. Though, he had given her a hard time when she had him forge a ticket for her to get into Haven. It was understandable. Someone in his position couldn't afford for the Amanda to know who he was. She winced, he would hate her showing up at his door with soldiers as her bodyguards, but that was not to be helped.

She sat up as the water in the bathroom adjoining their room started. Smiling, she slid out of bed and went to join him. A fifteen-minute shower turned into nearly an hour and both of them scrambled to get dressed before her guards were scheduled to show up. Being in a rush didn't stop her from staring at her mate as he got dressed. She sighed as he covered his sexy body in the all-black uniform. He caught her looking.

"What?" His full lips turned up in a small smile.

She shook her head and covered her still nude body in a pair of ripped jeans and a cropped tee. "Just admiring."

He pulled her into his arms. "Is that what you're wearing?"

"Will that be a problem?" She wrapped her arms around his neck.

He kissed her neck. "No, you just look so young. It's scary."

She laughed at his scrunched face. She tilted her head to the side and whispered a quick spell. Air touched her back as her long hair was transformed into a shoulder-length curly afro.

"Better?" She'd added touches of makeup to her eyes and lips and from the heat in his eyes, he approved.

He growled. "You look hot. I'm doubly thankful for the guards you'll have." He sobered. "You will be careful, right?"

"I swear." She insisted.

He sighed and pulled from her. He walked over to a wardrobe in the corner of their room. She was puzzled as he brought back a small box. He handed it to her and she looked at him in askance.

"Open it." His mischievous smile intrigued her.

She opened the box and gasped at the beautiful gold watch nestled in velvet. Delicate filigree made up the band and diamonds surrounded the watch face. She carefully removed it from the box.

"It's beautiful." She handed it to him to put on her.

He fastened it on her wrist, his thumb tracing the pulse point there. "It was made by a Gu craftsman, so while it may look delicate, it's near indestructible. And, full disclosure, I have an ulterior motive."

She smiled. Of course he did. She waited on his explanation.

"It has a panic button here on the side." He pointed to a small gold button on the side of the watch face. "It will send a signal to me with your whereabouts."

She raised an eyebrow.

"It doesn't track you or anything. I only get GPS when that button is pressed. So if you're ever in a situation where you're on the move press it every few miles."

"That's not too bad."

"I like backup plans. Not that I don't trust your guards." He hastily added.

She nodded. "I can live with that." Anything to gain a little freedom.

"Great." He kissed her once more. "Let me walk you out."

Her guards met them at the door, their faces serious. They were different than the two from yesterday. These guards were the two who had guarded her in Legba. Leo guided her through the catacombs up to the ground level with her guards trailing them. They entered a large garage filled with various cars. He led them over to a black SUV, the windows tinted darkly. Fallon lounged against the truck, his arms crossed over his chest.

"What's up?" Leo handed the keys over to one of her guards.

Fallon straightened and turned behind him. He lifted a small, square, black box from the hood behind him. He tapped a button on top of the box and a hologram flickered to life above it. She gasped.

"This will only work for two hours give or take. It's only loaded with the moments after your sister arrived at Haven, up to the point where the Ora becomes corrupted. Though the spell is temporary, your shaman is not to put his hand on this, are we clear?" Fallon handed her the box. He took a few minutes to show her how it to make it work, and the spells required to pull up the Oras.

She nodded stiffly, committing the spells to memory.

"Be careful, Trouble." Fallon nodded to his brother and left the garage.

Leo sighed. "Be careful, my love." He ghosted a kiss across her forehead.

She bobbed her head in agreement, excitement making her nervous.

She climbed into the front seat and buckled in. Turning to the driver she smiled. "I apologize for my behavior yesterday."

He nodded and started the car. "Having guards can be disconcerting, Lady Tegan."

"Ugh, just call me Liliana, please. What are your names?" She turned to the guard in the back.

He reluctantly held out his hand. "Paul."

He was the Benu she'd snapped on when they were still in Legba. The snobbish look on his face was fitting. The Benu were an elitist bunch. She wondered what his family had done to have a son sent to the Amanda, but figured it was rude to ask. The Benu kept to themselves and only helped their family and other Benu. The mandatory service to the Amanda was a sore point to the race if she was remembering her lessons with Mistress Yoru correctly. She would definitely not open that can of worms.

"I am Roy. What is the address to where we are traveling?"

She turned her attention back to the driver. His human skin was seamless, no trace of his original form showed in his features. If she had to guess, she'd mark him as Cagyn. They were shapeshifters by nature, and thus better at it than any other race. She shook out of her musings and pulled up Sergio's address on her phone. Roy plugged it into the GPS and off they drove through the streets of Atlanta.

Chapter 21

"WHAT EXACTLY IS OUR purpose for visiting this shaman, if you don't mind me asking?" Roy broke the silence minutes later.

"I want to see if he can undo a spell." She didn't know how much she was allowed to tell them.

"The one blocking the Oras?"

Roy's question released her from her debate, and she nodded in answer.

"And what is your plan?" Though Paul's voice was curious, his face showed his skepticism of the meeting.

"We go in, you guys look intimidating, he fixes the Oras, and *'Roberto es tu tio'*." She shrugged.

"What does that mean?" Paul frowned, his dark eyebrows lowering over pale eyes.

"Bob's your uncle." Liliana rolled her eyes.

"No, Roberto is your uncle." His literal translation made her laugh.

"Yes, you know, Roberto is Robert in Spanish. Robert…bob…get it." She shook her head as he continued to stare.

"It's a human expression Paul, you've never heard it?"

"I don't deal with humans." His lip curled in disgust.

"How dreadfully snobby, we came from humans you know." She'd only found out recently herself, but he didn't need to know that. She had to grudgingly give Mistress Yoru a little bit of credit. She'd only been mate to Leo for mere days and already she was using the lessons the stern lady had taught.

"We are of the gods, humans are simply walking, talking balls of clay." He crossed his arms over his chest.

"Wow, tell us how you really feel, Paul." Roy's dry tone surprised a laugh out of her.

Paul shrugged. "I don't have any interactions with humans, Lady Teagan."

"Call me Liliana, and you need to get out more. You're not on Mulu. Unlike the other Benu, you're going to have to learn to get along with others." Liliana turned back to the window and watched Atlanta pass by as they headed to Sergio's home on the outskirts of the city.

Soon enough they were pulling into the quiet neighborhood the shaman had chosen as his hiding spot. It wasn't a bad choice. The houses were far enough apart that the neighbors wouldn't bother him, but they were close enough to deter unhappy 'clients' from displaying their powers. They parked on the street, walking up the cobble driveway to the large brick house. Paul and Roy sandwiched her in between them on their walk.

Roy held his hand up for her to halt as he first ascended the stairs. He stopped a hair's breadth away from the top step, one foot raised and paused midair. He lowered his foot back on the second step and pulled a circular device from his back pocket. Setting it on the step next to him, his hands moved in circular motions until a fine blue light encapsulated his hands. He took two fingers and stabbed it into the air in front of him. A small ping sounded and he lowered his hands. Picking up the device, he motioned for the two of them to join him.

"What was that?" She moved around him to the front door.

"A trap." Roy pocketed the device he'd used.

She frowned. "What kind of trap? I've been here before, and didn't encounter a trap."

"You were invited, no?" Roy raised an eyebrow.

Yes, she had been. She swallowed hard. She'd originally planned to come to see Sergio alone. She shuddered to think what might have happened. She touched her stomach lightly. She had to remember her decisions no longer solely affected her. She had another soul to think about.

"Can we get on with this, please?" Paul's impatience spurred her from her thoughts.

Lily knocked on the door and waited.

And waited some more.

She knocked again, this time in irritation. She knew he was inside, the shaman's energy practically radiated from the door.

Liliana banged on the door, looking around. "Open the door, Sergio, I'm not leaving."

The curtain in a window to their right fluttered. She rolled her eyes. Moments later the door opened a crack.

"Why would you bring the Amanda to my door? I knew I shouldn't have helped you get into Haven."

"I need to see you."

Still, he blocked the door, his head nodding towards the guards. "They have to stay outside."

Paul snorted. "Not hardly."

"They're my guards, they go where I go." She pushed on the wooden door, forcing him to take a small step in retreat.

"You didn't have guards last time." He pointed out.

"Yeah, well…" She held up her arm, showing him the mating marks on her wrist. She left out who she was mated to, knowing that would spook him.

Sergio stared at her for a moment before sighing and backing up to allow them entrance. Liliana paused in the doorway and waited until she received a nod from her guards. Roy inclined his head and she followed the two into Sergio's living room. She sat on a plush sofa looking out into his backyard. Roy and Paul stood behind her, each facing a different direction.

"What do you want?" Sergio stood at the granite island that separated his kitchen from the small sitting room.

"Have you ever heard of the Oras?" Not wanting to waste time dancing around the subject she got right to it.

His eyes narrowed into slits, his gaze darting between her and her guards. "What of them?"

She pulled out the square device Fallon had given her and sat it on the coffee table. "You're the most powerful shaman I've come across on this side of the portal."

She pressed the button on top and watched him as the Ora of her sister played out. Once it reached the end and the footage stuttered, his eyes met hers, his mouth pinched.

"You need to leave." He crossed his arms over his chest.

The knowledge of what happened to the Oras was on his face. She moved up to the edge of the sofa.

"Someone is corrupting Oras and I think you know who it is." She clenched her hands together. "I need your help."

"That's your problem, not mine. I can't help you." His gaze once again darted to her guards, fear in his eyes.

She growled, searching for words to use to convince him. Looking around, she noticed for the first time since she'd walked in, how empty his house was. Last time she was here, which was mere weeks ago, the house had been cluttered with trinkets and his experiments. Her eyes narrowed in suspicion.

"Where's all your stuff?"

Paul and Ross stiffened, their posture straightening at the tone of her voice.

"If you must know, I'm moving."

"To where?" Paul asked sharply.

Sergio fidgeted with the buttons at the throat of his shirt. "I've been invited to visit Legba."

"You've been exiled, you won't be allowed into the portal room." Paul's finger flexed at his sides.

"There are other ways."

Roy growled, and turned around, abandoning his gaze on the backyard. Paul changed into his form. The wings expanded and his sharp claws made a ringing sound as he pulled a sword. Where he hid a weapon that massive, she didn't know, but her heart's rhythm kicked into full drive.

Roy changed into his form, the dark marbled skin of the six-foot-seven Cagyn glowing in anticipation. "You wouldn't think of breaking our laws, would you? You understand as Amanda, we can't let that happen."

Crap, it was getting serious now. "Wait." She stood hastily.

Sergio's form flickered but steadied on his human skin. "You brought them into my house, I ought to curse you." He hissed.

"I will cut the first finger off I see move." Paul pointed his sword towards the shaman.

Liliana sucked in a nervous breath. Dear gods, now she saw why Leo chose the two. Their faces were set in granite, their expressions ferocious. Sergio couldn't possibly miss the deadly intent.

"Hands up, fingers apart," Paul ordered. "Even the smallest movement will get you beat down."

"It was simply a figure of speech, I would…I would never curse her." Sergio stammered out, his hands shaking as he raised them.

"What do you know about the corrupted Oras?" She'd better hurry and get what information she could from him before Paul and Roy made good on their threats.

Sergio shook his head. "The Amanda will only torture me, those responsible will kill me outright. You need to leave."

"We aren't leaving until we can get someone here to strip your powers." Roy threatened.

"You can't do that, I've done nothing wrong."

"You just admitted that you were going to Legba. You've been exiled, shaman. Sentenced to spend the rest of your existence here on Adro, in this human skin. The fact that you are obviously plotting and using your magic is grounds for its removal." Roy pulled out a cell phone.

"Wait." The shaman pushed his hands higher. "I can tell you what I know. Just please, don't take my magic."

Roy closed the phone. "Talk."

"Someone came to me years ago. When I was first exiled and asked me to distort the Oras." The shaman spoke quickly.

"Who gave you access?"

"I don't have access. I just provide the spell. The person paying has to find a way to get into Haven and disrupt them." He eyed the computer Liliana had with a hungry look. "You can't do anything with the Oras outside of Haven."

Liliana closed the Ora and snatched up the box from the table.

"Who comes to you for this service?" Paul asked.

"I don't ask for names." Sergio insisted.

"Not good enough, make the call Roy." Paul crossed his arms over his chest.

"Wait, ask her, I never ask for the names of my customers."

Liliana sighed but nodded. It's true, he hadn't asked her identity when she'd come to him for her fake papers, nor the pass to get into Haven. He just made sure she'd had payment.

"I don't know anything else." Sergio pleaded.

Liliana narrowed her eyes. "You're lying."

"I swear." His left eye twitched.

"Call, Roy." Liliana gathered the box and shoved it back into her bag. The visit was wasted. Clearly, Sergio wouldn't give them anything.

"Wait, wait, please. I kept a copy of it."

Everyone froze. The sound of Paul's wings snapping back into place broke the silence.

"Where?" Liliana's heart thumped. She put a hand to her chest to calm its rhythm.

"It's in the cabinet behind me." The shaman's body shook.

"Do not move," Paul ordered as he stomped to the cabinet.

The room was quiet as he searched the drawers. He opened the last drawer and found a wooden chest.

"They are in that chest." Sergio pointed.

Paul opened the chest, it was full of crystal stones. Liliana swallowed past the lump of fear. She would have answers.

Roy frowned. "How long have you been distorting the Oras? There are nearly one hundred stones in there."

Sergio lifted his chin. "I was banished to Adro. I have to make a living. It's not right for the Amanda to interfere with that."

Paul put the box on the table. "Find the one she wants."

The shaman's hands shook as he searched through the crystals. He pulled one out and handed it to Liliana. It had a date etched on it, three days after the day her sister had left Legba.

The blood rushed from her face. She was the closest she'd been in the prior years to finding her sister. Kedric assumed she was dead. Thinking back on the footage they saw yesterday and the fact that she was unable to find her sister anywhere else on the Oras, she was starting to give his thoughts merit. She didn't want to believe it but the evidence was looking grim. She nodded, and with numb fingers, went through the spells Fallon had taught her. The Ora shimmered to life. Kita smiled and led her vampire down the stairs. They laughed and Kita backed him into the wall and kissed him. The Ajo pulled her hair back and bit Kita. She smiled and the Ajo closed the wound, his face full of anticipation. Liliana could see the look in his eyes. Kita led him down the stairs into a small room. The Ora shimmered and went out.

Liliana looked at him. "That's it. That's what you were hiding?"

"I'm not hiding anything specific. I've kept these only as insurance. I don't look through all of them."

She felt let down. But, more than likely Sergio was lying. She'd comb through every last one of these crystals until she found out what happened to her sister. She grabbed the second box and shook the stones out into her bag.

"Let's go guys." She wanted to be safe at Haven before she looked through them. They changed back into their human skin.

Paul grabbed the shaman. "You're coming with us to Haven where your powers will be removed."

Sergio hissed in anger. "You lied to me." He snatched his arm from Paul and started to shed his human skin. His form flickered, and his body expanded, growing taller and thicker until the seven-foot plus Gu filled the space of the living room, his head skimming the high ceilings. Both Paul and Roy's change to their Demi form was seamless, the warriors pulling their weapons before charging at the giant. Sergio fought them in earnest, slinging magic throughout the enclosed space. Liliana barely moved before one of his spells obliterated the couch she'd been sitting on moments ago. She scrambled out of the way as Roy released his sword and blocked a spell aimed for him. Paul in his Benu form was magnificent. The colorful wings were spread wide, the red feathers dipped in black on the ends. He kept his eyes on the Gu expertly dodging his escape attempts. Sergio made the mistake of making eye contact with Paul. It took a millisecond for the Benu power to enthrall the giant in its gaze. Sergio froze, stunned. Roy pulled out a set of heavy lead-lined gloves and had them on the shaman's hands before he could shake off Paul's magic. The gloves would keep Sergio from being able to use his power. Roy handcuffed his arms behind him for extra measure and she watched, heart in her throat as Sergio's body shrank back down to size, his human skin once again covering his body.

"He shouldn't have been able to do that," Roy remarked grimly as he grabbed the shaman's arms to lead him out.

"Right." Paul agreed. "I'm sure, the commander will have questions for him as to how he was able to access his original form in exile."

Liliana leaned over, hands on her knees as she took her first deep breath in minutes. She'd told them Sergio was powerful, but she herself had taken for granted him being in exile and not having his full power. It had given her a false sense of confidence. Not that she'd be telling Leo that. Rolling her shoulders, she stood straight, grateful it was over, and anxious to be home.

Paul peeked out the front door to be sure they weren't being watched, then helped Roy guide Sergio to their SUV. They were all silent as they drove through the neighborhood on their way back to the highway.

Roy tensed next to her, his gaze darting to the rearview mirror. He cursed. "Hold on tight."

Alarm sped her pulse and she grabbed the door handle tightly. 'What's happening?"

"We're being followed." He sped up the truck.

Paul turned in his seat and sighed. "We're at a disadvantage too."

"In what way?" She fought to keep the panic from her voice.

Paul loaded a gun he'd grabbed from under the seat. "All of these roads lead back to the highway. Evasive moves will be useless."

"I'll try to outrun them, but it will get hairy." The SUV leaped forward at his words.

She double-checked her seat belt and braced herself. The black car trailed them closely as Roy turned through the neighborhood, speeding through stop signs. Two turns and the car fell behind until she could no longer see it in the mirror. They were moving at a fast clip towards the highway and for a moment she breathed a little easier. At least until the impact to the back of the car. She screamed as they were hit again, this time causing the truck to tilt.

They turned over, the air leaving her in a whoosh as the SUV landed in a ditch. Paul's loud expletives were the only sound in the car as an eerie quiet descended. Liliana, afraid for her baby, remembered the panic button. She hung upside down in her seat smashing the button repeatedly as someone in a black mask rushed up to the jeep. Roy fumbled with his seatbelt next to her, his movements slow and stiff. He dropped out of his seat, whimpering in pain as he landed on the driver's side door. The impact shook the car.

She froze in horror as the male in the mask pulled out some type of gun. As he got closer, she saw a dart sticking out the end of it right as he shot at first Roy, then Paul. Magic swelled in the air, a curse or spell thrummed and thickened the space in the car. Flipping back through her time on Adro, she recognized it as dark magic and fervently prayed as she tried to remember counterspells. Roy's life force was diminishing right before her eyes as fear threatened to take over her thoughts. First thing first, she needed to stop the masked man. She registered the death grip she'd kept on her satchel and ripped it open. She grabbed the small pistol she'd kept on her during her time alone on Adro. The bullets would do nothing, but it would distract him and buy Roy some time. The male's shoulder whipped back with the impact of the bullet, and she fired another one into his other shoulder. Dropping the gun, she started the counter spell that popped into her head and pushed every bit of her power into it. He staggered under the weight of the power, going to his knees. He clutched his chest, narrowing his eyes on her.

Her eyes widened as he stood, moving towards the SUV with purpose. He punched the glass of the back door and snatched Sergio from the seat. They held eye contact as he backed away with the shaman thrown over his shoulder in a fireman's hold. His sinister smile raised the hair on her arms. Her energy was waning, but she lifted her hands prepared to throw another spell at him. With a small mocking salute, he threw Sergio into his car and drove off. She gingerly moved her body, working to unbuckle her seatbelt and help Roy.

***

A high piercing alarm filled Xavier's office as Leo and Fallon went through personnel records looking for his replacements. He cursed and whipped out his phone.

"What is it?" Fallon asked.

"Liliana's panic alert." He hung up and dialed her number again, worried with every ring on her end. "Shit." He tried both Roy and Paul, his anxiety climbing with every missed call.

"Not picking up?" Xavier sat forward in his chair.

"No." He pulled up the GPS, her last three pings were from the same place. "We need to ride."

He rushed from the office, Fallon hot on his heels on the phone dispatching a patrol unit to follow them. He tossed his phone to Fallon as they climbed into his GTO. He gripped the steering wheel, speeding through the streets as Fallon called out directions. His heart was thumping, panic and fear for his mate making him numb.

"There, Leo." Fallon slapped the dashboard, breaking him of his trance.

His stomach plunged as he came upon what looked like an accident scene. The SUV the trio had driven off in that morning was turned on its side, a deep furrow in the ground from where the truck had slid. What the hell had happened? He rushed up the vehicle, breathing out in relief as he found Liliana still in her seat, leaning sideways, but awake.

"I got you, baby." He whispered, carefully inspecting her body.

"My seatbelt's stuck." Her voice was weak. "Roy needs help first. He tried to kill him."

His hands shook as he cut her from the seatbelt. He cradled her body against his chest. She struggled.

"Roy needs help, Leo. He put a spell on him, I don't know if I stopped him in time." She turned her body towards her guard.

"Fallon, has him, *ina*, relax, we'll take care of him." He walked her back to his car and placed her in the front seat. She smiled and touched his cheek. Her head lolled to the side as she passed out. "Fallon, let's move!"

Leo slid across the hood of his car and got into the driver's seat. His hands shook as he started the car. Fallon rushed with Roy in his arms, the warrior limp, his breathing erratic.

"Burn, Leo. I don't know how long he has."

He didn't have to be told twice. He prayed the whole way back to Haven, never taking his eyes off the road. He knew at his speeds taking his eyes off the road for a second would be dangerous. Fallon was in the back seat shouting orders into the phone, requesting a healer for the two of them. He didn't bother parking in the garage, instead, pulling his car right up to the front door. Careful not to jostle his mate, he rushed through the catacombs to their apartment.

A Kira stood at his door awaiting him. He punched in the code and guided her into their room.

"Lay her on the bed, please." The Kira's calm voice steadied him.

He gingerly placed Liliana on the bed. He paced the room, growls rumbling his chest as the Kira inspected her.

"Perhaps it will be better if you paced in the common area instead." The Kira smiled kindly.

He started to argue but stopped. She was right. His tension probably filled the room and distracted her. He knew he shouldn't have let her go. Knew there was a danger to her. Xavier would more than likely chew his ass out for it. It was reckless, and for the first time, Leo understood the worry X had for him when he hunted.

After what seemed like forever, the Kira joined him in the living room. Her footsteps were silent as she walked towards him.

"She and the babe are fine. Her sleep is from energy loss and not injury. Your mate should be careful with the expenditure of magic for the first few months."

He sat down on the sofa dazed. "Babe?"

The Kira's stern look softened. She pat his shoulder in a pitying gesture. "Your son is strong and taking more than his share of his mother's energy. She'll need to relax and stay out of high-stress situations. And as I told her earlier, you all will want to start your bonding exercises soon."

A son.

His chest expanded while his vision tunneled. He took quick shallow breaths in panic. Liliana was pregnant. So soon. He was blown away, a lump clogging his throat. All at once fierce pride brought tears to his eyes. Though he'd only known his mate a few weeks, he found himself very excited at the prospect of a child with her. A son. He blinked to try and take in the news.

The Kira smiled. "I'll see myself out."

He heard the quiet snick of the door as she left. Xavier snapped his fingers in front of Leo's face a moment later.

"Yo. What's up, how's Liliana?"

He shook his head and looked around, unsure of when his brother had even entered the room. "She's pregnant." He blurted.

A bemused smile lit Xavier's face. "Congrats. May she birth a hell-raiser."

Chapter 22

VERITY PACED THE FLOOR OF THE CABIN, concern, and aggravation broadcasting in the hard sound of her heels. One of their members called an emergency meeting and she was racking her brain to figure out why. She'd rather be at her house going through her grandmother's album. She'd yet to find a list of names like her grandmother had promised, but she would keep looking. It had been a rare lucid moment for her grandmother and therefore she was taking it seriously.

She turned her head at the shuffling sound at the door. The Apophi demon came in dragging their shaman behind him. Verity's heart took a hard tumble and panic threatened to overtake her. She'd used the Gu shaman for a lot of underhanded deals and she wondered if it was coming back to bite her in the ass.

"I keep a watch over the assets we use. I got a call a little while ago that the Amanda were visiting our friend here."

"Does he keep evidence in his home?" Someone asked.

"I've sent someone to go through his house. If there is evidence left, there won't be any for the Amanda to sift through. Unless they can bring back ashes."

A part of her was relieved to hear that. But what if the Amanda had gotten evidence already? She swore and clenched her fists.

"Did he have time to give them anything? How long were they there before you arrived?" Impatience made her words sharper than she'd intended.

The Apophi's jaw clenched at her tone, but he shrugged.

Her heart hammered as all the dirt she'd had Sergio conceal for her ran through her head. He could bury her. She looked up suddenly and noticed that not everyone is there.

"Where are the others?"

"Unable to get away." The Cagyn answered.

She ran a hand through her hair. "I have contacts within Haven. I'll go find out how much they know."

"We'll meet back here in an hour's time. Will that be long enough?" Someone asked.

"Plenty."

They all stood to leave, except the Apophi who stood guard over the shaman. She was moving to leave when the Mina in their group pulled her to the side.

"The Cagyn's plan will not come to fruition."

Verity reared back in shock. The Mina were precognitive, so she had to take her at her word. "What do you mean?"

"Firstly, she'll not allow harm to come to the girl, and we all know what the spell encompasses."

Verity nodded. They all knew. The spell was the darkest of magic, and akin to torture. Getting knowledge from a person's soul required extensive pain. The Cagyn had had no trouble with their plan for the one sister, she didn't think using the second would be a problem. She said as much to the Mina.

"She has grown attached to the younger sister. Trust me, she wouldn't allow us to do what needed to be done. More troubling than that though, is that the tide of the war has turned. With the mating of Death's Messenger to the girl, our odds have decreased. My whole realm is nearly split down the middle about who wins."

"If that is the case, then why are you still here?" Verity raised her eyebrow at the information.

"I keep my word, Dziva."

She nodded. That she understood. "Is there a way to increase our odds?"

"I have a plan to rid us of her."

"The Cagyn or the girl?"

"The Cagyn. We can get rid of her, and possibly divert attention from ourselves. You'll need to go to Legba when you're done at Haven."

Verity growled. When had she become the messenger for this group?

"Our time is coming to an end unless this works."

"You'll owe me."

"Of course." The Mina lowered her head demurely.

Verity snorted. Yeah right, she was demure. She shook her head and left the cabin headed for the portal that would take her to Haven.

***

The energy in Haven crackled as she stepped through the back door. Soldiers rushed through the hallways and she caught bits of information about Leo's mate having been hurt. Verity shuddered. Gods help the world if Leo was unleashed. She made haste towards the security office, frowning when she noticed her normal contact missing.

Damn it.

She put on a charming smile and sidled up to the guard manning the surveillance feeds. "What's all the fuss about?"

He frowned and shut down his displays. "How did you get in here?"

His gruff tone surprised her, as did his stony face. She cocked her head to the side and shook her hair a little. His eyes never left hers, her enthrallment going completely over his head.

"You need to leave." He motioned, and someone came over and grabbed her arm.

Snatching her arm from the soldier's hand, she walked from the surveillance room. She prowled through the hallways until she came up to one of their breakrooms. Spying someone she knew, she sighed in relief. She waved and his eyes darted around the hallway.

"What's going on around here?" She lowered the timbre of her voice and placed a hand on his shoulder.

He shook her off. "I don't have time to help you today. Two of our soldiers went down today."

She feigned concern. "Of course, that's terrible. I can wait in your room until…"

"That won't be necessary." He lowered his voice. "The commander has been on a rampage about giving out information. I can't help you anymore."

He brushed past her, not once looking back as he blended into the crowd of soldiers milling around. She cursed in earnest. Getting intel was out. She'd just have to make sure they were too distracted to do anything about any possible information the shaman gave them.

She made her way upstairs to the club level, sneaking past the employees prepping for the hundreds of guests expected to pour into Haven. It gave her an idea.

"Hey, what night is tonight?" She grabbed a passing servant.

"Fight Night." He inclined his head towards the ring being constructed in the middle of the floor.

Perfect.

She dismissed him, making her way to the VIP level, where they would host a variety of beasts feeding on the aggressive energy sure to be pouring from the crowd as they watched the fights Haven would put on for them. Walking through each VIP room, she whispered a spell of amplification. Every ounce of magic pouring out of these rooms would be multiplied. They would be breaking up fights all night, and not just in the ring.

She smiled.

That should keep them busy enough to forget about their shaman. She sneaked back down the stairs and out the door, her next stop Legba. She had some rumors to spread.

***

Where was she? Liliana opened her eyes, careful not to move. There was a weight across her stomach, and for a moment she thought she was still pinned. A whimper escaped and she jerked her body. Slowly the room came into focus and she forced her body to relax.

Leo lifted his head, his eyes dark with concern. "How are you feeling?" His deep voice calmed her further.

She opened her mouth to say fine but then thought of Paul and Roy. "How is Roy, did we help him in time? And Paul, is he okay?"

He kissed her forehead. "They're both fine. Roy is grateful to you for saving his life."

"I really didn't. I froze in fear for the first few minutes. I could've helped him sooner."

His answer was a small grunt. "Go back to sleep. You need to rest." He nuzzled her neck and his hand stroked down her stomach.

The tenderness in the gesture soothed her. His love and excitement trickled down their connection. She turned her face into his and kissed him.

"You know, don't you?" She rested her forehead on his.

He lowered his head and resumed his nuzzling against her neck. "The Kira told me. How do you feel about it?"

She looked down at his large hand stroking her still flat stomach. It would be flat for a few more months. Eshu pregnancy lasted a year. She'd have twelve months to get used to it.

"I'm a little scared. What does this mean for us? It's kind of soon, don't you think?" She closed her eyes.

"I love you."

Said simply, his words burrowed deep into her soul. Her heart skipped and tears gathered in the corner of her eyes. "I love you too."

He smiled and warmth flooded her body. Gods, but he was a good looking man. She grabbed his face and kissed him deeply. She sighed in pleasure as they separated.

"Now. Go back to sleep."

She laughed at his persistence. She lay back down, his head on her chest.

Wait.

She pushed him off and sat up. "I almost forgot, the crystals!" She rushed from the bed, bracing her arm on the wall as a wave of dizziness hit her.

Leo grabbed her around the waist. "You should be in bed. What are you talking about, what crystals?"

She ran a hand over her hair. "From the shaman. They're in my bag."

"It can wait, love."

She shook him off her and tried to use magic to change her clothes. Damn it! She was weak from the counter spell she'd used to save Paul and Roy. She turned to Leo. "I need clothes."

He frowned at her, making no effort to move from the bed. They stared at each other for a moment until her body started relaxing, warming under his scrutiny. She sighed, breathing deep as nerve endings along her thighs started tingling. Blood flow through her body heated, loosening her tense muscle, throbbing at her center. Her nipples beaded, poking through her nightgown and thoughts of joining her mate in bed pushed everything else into foggy oblivion. She'd taken a step towards him before she realized what was happening.

She shook her head, clenching her thighs together to still the burn. "No fair."

"Who said anything about fair? I believe you set precedent for our negotiation tactics."

Damn him. Yes, she attempted to seduce him into letting her see the shaman. She hadn't expected him to use his Cagyn powers on her.

"Please, Leo." She whispered and clasped her hands together in a pleading gesture.

His magic dissipated, leaving her still horny, but grateful. He snarled and made her a pair of lounging pants with a matching tunic. She smiled her thanks, rushing to put them on. "You brought my bag in right?"

"Liliana." He stepped in front of her as she headed for the door. "Stop, baby. Why is this so important?"

She took a deep breath, far more winded than she should've been. "Sergio was the one corrupting the Oras. He made copies of everything he did."

"Copies? What kind of copies?"

She waved off his question. "We didn't get into an accident. Someone purposely ran us over and took the shaman. They'll probably be back for the Oras."

He snorted. "Ain't nobody crazy enough to storm into this place. Xavier wouldn't even leave a stain for identification purposes."

"I'm sure with the amount of Oras Sergio was hiding, they may attempt it."

Leo frowned. "If they wanted the crystals they would have taken them and killed the shaman."

She shook her head. "I don't think they knew."

He reared back in surprise. "We need to see what's on those crystals."

"Exactly." She rushed into the living room and breathed out a sigh of relief at the sight of her bag on the coffee table. "Do you want to have your brothers meet us in the surveillance room?"

"No, Xavier's office. Fallon said he's having issues with information leaking from the security office." Leo shook his head in disgust. Along with the soldier who'd sold out his room information, Fallon said he'd found two others leaking information.

His brother was determined to root out each and every leak in his security. There were soldiers taking bribes and passing on confidential data. He felt sorry for the next ones they found. Fallon had not been light in his punishment so far. The deeper down the rabbit hole the leaks went, the harsher his brother was likely to be.

He walked over to the intercom on the wall by the front door. He should warn Xavier that they were coming.

"Hey, X. Liliana and I are headed to you with something big."

Static filled the air a moment before Xavier growled into the speaker. "Can it wait?"

"No, definitely not."

"It's crazy right now, Leo. Someone spiked the power coming out of the observation rooms and it's brutal on the floor. I don't recommend your mate being out in this, man."

Leo sighed. He turned to Lily, sighing as her chin raised. "No can do, X. Liliana's visit was successful." He didn't go into detail, in case someone was listening in.

"Shit." Was his brother's reply.

"Roger that."

"Shield her. Tight. I don't want my nephew subjected to this."

A nonplussed smile tilted his lips. He turned to his mate. One hand covered her mouth, her luminous eyes softened.

"Roger." He breathed out past the lump in his throat.

Leo strengthened the shield around his beast and gathered Liliana close to him. He prodded their mental connection, satisfied with the shield she'd built around herself. Prepared for the worst, they left the room. Leo winced at the level of power in the hallway. If it was this bad, so far from the club floor, he could only imagine how bad it would get.

"Tighten your shields, *ina.*"

She shuddered. "You don't have to tell me twice, I can feel it."

He put his hand on her belly and felt for his son. Gods, his son. He was scared as hell about what the energy could do to his child. A small tentative touch ghosted across his subconscious and he was floored. Their son was strong. Only weeks old, and his soul reached for him. He sent a reassuring wave of energy to the tiny being. He tucked Liliana closer, picking up their speed down the hallway.

They reached the end of the underground catacombs and the very minute they hit the ground floor of Haven, power swelled. His beast immediately put up a fight, bashing against his mental shields. Leo swayed with the effort to stay in his human skin. The commotion from the club floor was filling the space of the hallway and Liliana's eyes widened. Her fear trickled down their connection, stroking the beast more. He rushed her towards Xavier's office. His brother's office was shielded against the energy from the club nights. X said it was the only way he'd get any work done.

They were blocked from entering by a huge fight in front of the door. The two males are going at each other and Xavier and Fallon were working to break them up. Leo growled when one of the Ajos landed a punch, not on his opponent but onto the side of Fallon's head.

"Shit." He pushed Liliana through the gathering crowd into a side door. "Stay put."

She nodded and he closed the door in her face. Turning, he wasted no time wading into trouble. He released his beast and helped Fallon pull the two creatures apart. The Ajo Fallon was holding bit into his arm. Cursing, Fallon's beast emerged and with his massive arm, he slammed the guy into the wall.

Blood already covered the floor, and now the wall was splattered as Fallon slammed him again. His claws settled around the Ajo's throat, the black tips poised to sink into its neck. Everything in the hall came to a stop. Leo pushed the one he held aside and reached for his brother's arm.

"Let him live, Fallon." They couldn't kill him, it was one of the rules of Haven. Rules even the Amanda were bound by, including high ranking officers such as themselves.

Fallon shook his head and threw the Ajo to the waiting soldiers. "Make sure he's banned."

"Both of them!" Xavier shouted. "And find out who the fuck spiked the power and make sure you bring them directly to me."

Leo pulled himself back together and followed his brothers into Xavier's office. Liliana stood as they entered, her eyes roving his body to make sure he was ok. He pulled her into his side and kissed her. She spotted the blood on Fallon's arm and went to him.

She swept them all with a chastising look. "I need something to clean this up."

Leo smiled at her tone and walked into the ensuite bathroom to get a towel and antiseptic. She cleaned off the blood and tended to Fallon's wound.

"You don't have to do all that, Trouble. It will heal soon enough."

She still put on a bandage. "What happened?"

Xavier dropped his body into his chair behind his desk and shook his head. He ignored her question. "Now. Leo said your trip to the shaman was successful?"

Chapter 23

LEO GRABBED LILIANA'S ARM, pulling her into his lap. He rubbed her back as she repeated to his brothers what she'd told him. Xavier frowned and reached his hand out for her bag. Fallon passed it over, raising an eyebrow at its weight. He pulled the chest from her bag and frowned as he opened it. She leaned over his desk and pulled off a crystal from the top of the pile.

"What are they?" Xavier shuffled the crystals around.

"Copies of the Oras."

"How is that possible?" Fallon asked Xavier.

"More important, how is he viewing these outside of Haven?" Xavier asked grimly.

"He's not. I think they were more so for insurance. This is the first one he showed me. The one with Kita on it." She passed it over.

Leo kept a close eye on her. At the first sign of stress, he was hauling her to bed, kicking and screaming if need be. Xavier dumped the crystal into his reader and fired up the Ora. They were all quiet as he flipped through the images. He frowned when it stopped.

"This is nothing,"

Liliana sighed. "I know. But there are tons of crystals. There has to be something there."

Xavier grunted in answer and pulled out another stone. The quiet was interspersed with laden curses as he went through the crystals one at a time. There were various crimes committed and subsequently hidden by the erasing of the Oras they were viewing. Several, punishable by death. Leo shook his head.

"We'll have to go through all of these with a fine-tooth comb." Fallon murmured.

Xavier slowed down the playback as Kita's image filled the screen. She was in one of the viewing rooms with an Ajo. The door opened and Prince Kedric walked in, joining the two as they made out on the sofa. Liliana's breath caught, a small gasp escaping her. Kedric smiled at Kita, running his hand through her hair a second before he open hand slapped her across the face.

"Dear God," Liliana whispered.

Leo rubbed her back in a soothing motion, his eyes not straying from the footage. He didn't know how much Liliana knew about her sister, but from the tense set of her shoulders, she was in for a rude awakening.

***

Rolling his shoulders, Rugaba suppressed his sigh of aggravation. It was rare for the Eminzu to call to him. Even rarer to request his presence. He sat back in his chair and crossed his arms over his chest. According to the Elder at the other end of the long oak table at which he sat, they had an issue regarding Ofeere. He eyed the other ancestors, their jerky movements broadcasting both their nervousness and worry.

"Let me make sure I understand. There is a noble demanding an audience with this council regarding Ofeere?" Rue speared the elder with an impatient look.

"She also claims there is a danger to her youngest daughter regarding this."

Ru frowned. A noble family mixed in with Ofeere? He was curious. He waved a hand for the elder to proceed.

The elder inclined his head to the soldier guarding the door to their council room. The soldier turned and opened the heavy gold doors. A woman stomped in, her hair in a single braid trailing her back. She wore a simple black shift dress giving the appearance of a working-class member. The sheen of her hair and the obvious expensive jewelry around her neck and ears said differently.

She opened her mouth to speak, but he held his hand up and silenced her. He tilted his head as Leonalph's mate's distress flowed through his body. What was her name again?

Liliana.

Right. He pulled out a communicator he used to talk with the head of the Amanda. It would be his second call to him in the span of a few hours. What was that female getting into?

Xavier answered on the first ring. "We're taking care of it."

Rugaba grunted and ended the call. He trusted Xavier implicitly. He shoved Liliana from his mind and turned his attention back to the noblewoman standing in the middle of the council room. He nodded to start the proceedings.

"I want out of my mating and punishment. And I want that maid dead for what she did to my daughter."

He turned to the elder and raised an eyebrow.

"A little back story, my lord." The Elder cleared his throat. "Lady Marcolev came to us some centuries ago because her husband and their maid were having an affair. The youngest daughter is the result of said affair."

"And the punishment of which she speaks?"

She lowered her head in what Rugaba realized was a false shame.

"She ordered the maid, a Cagyn to take on her form and spend time with the mate in question. As punishment for her part in the affair, she was ordered to remain in her mating."

"And I was forced to raise their child." The woman inputted.

"Tread lightly in your words, Lady Marcolev. Don't think we aren't aware of the way you handled your 'punishment." The Elder snapped.

"You claim the child is in danger, explain." He didn't want to hear anything about a centuries-old affair.

"I overheard the maid talking to someone at our back door. She mentioned taking Liliana and forcing information from her." She fidgeted with her dress in nervousness. "I heard reference to a hiding spot, and freeing 'him'."

"With whom was she speaking?" Rugaba sat forward in his chair. If they were talking about the same Liliana, then he was definitely interested.

"I didn't see, but I knew the council would want to know right away."

He narrowed his eyes at her blatant lie. "I'm sure using the information as leverage to end your punishment had no bearing on your decision."

Cheeks mottled, she lowered her head again. "More than anything, my lord, I want justice for my other daughter. During their argument, they talked about how my daughter was killed and they helped get rid of the body."

"You are certain, this is what you heard?" The Elder's sharp tone caused the woman to flinch.

"I wouldn't have come before the Eminzu otherwise. I have proof."

Shock reverberated through the room. Rugaba had to admit to surprise himself. She pulled out a comms pad and turned it over to the guard, who in turn passed it to the elder. With a few swipes video was displayed against the far wall of the chamber. It was a surveillance video, from a kitchen. It showed the maid at the door, but not the person on the other side. The conversation was easily discerned, and the more he watched, the angrier he got. That something like this had been going on under his nose infuriated him. He knew the voids covering the Earth were multiplying. He just hadn't realized how much he was missing.

Talk of a council to free the most evil being to ever exist was bandied about as though the consequences of their actions wouldn't end the world. The ease at which they spoke about such matters was unconscionable. He'd hunt every member of their council down and he would end them. Starting with the one on video.

"Summon the maid."

***

Her fingertips tingled as numbness traveled through Liliana's body. She alternated between hot and cold as shock doused her system. She watched, bile rising to her throat as Kedric gripped his sister around the throat with a glove riddled with spikes. Blood beaded on Kita's neck, trailing her skin. Her sister smiled through it, licking Kedric's lips as he leaned in to kiss her. She turned her head into Leo's chest, breathing in his scent to calm herself.

She'd never really known Kita, but never would she have imagined her sister was into something that dark. She chanced a peek, relieved to find Xavier fast-forwarding past the sex. He slowed the video when the smile left Kita's face. Panic widened her sister's eyes. Leo's grip on her arm tightened as they watched Kita gagging, scratching at her own throat. The Ajo leaned over Kita, licking at her wounds in an attempt to close them. He backed up hastily when it didn't work. Kedric lay her sister down on the floor, his mouth moving in a jumble of what she imagined were panicked instructions to the Ajo. The two males argued, her sister flailing between them. Tears crested Liliana's eyes as she watched what she knew were her sister's last minutes. She now knew why the prince had been so sure her sister was dead. Kita's magic wavered, her form changing between her base Eshu form and her human skin. The Ajo held his hands up and backed out of the room, leaving Kedric and Kita alone. Kedric moved towards the door. Kita reached out her hand weakly, her lips moving in a plea Liliana was glad she wasn't able to hear. Kedric shook his head and grabbed the doorknob.

The image went black.

Liliana rushed to the bathroom and barely made it to the toilet before she threw up. Her stomach heaved, tears and saliva mixing as everything she'd eaten that morning dispelled from her body. She heard Xavier cursing in the other room, the low murmur of Fallon and Leo talking. The images of her sister's death played through her head again and she gagged, clutching the edge of the toilet. She held up her hand as Leo crowded the bathroom door. She shook her head at him, her body bowing as she threw up again. She flushed the toilet from the floor, waiting on nausea to leave.

It took only mere seconds after it passed for fury to overtake her body. Magic lit her skin, warmth flooding her. She stood shakily, walking to the sink. She washed out her mouth, running cold water over her face. The tears didn't stop. Only sheer stubbornness trapped the sobs tightening her chest. She dried her trembling hands and re-entered Xavier's office.

"I want Kedric punished. No. I want him dead."

Fallon sighed, Leo's mouth tightened and he looked away.

"There is protocol—"

"Screw protocol!" She cut Xavier off. "He killed my sister!"

"Leaving her to die is not the same as killing her, Liliana. I'm sorry."

She could hardly breathe through her pain. Only the matching fury in Xavier's eyes kept her from trashing his office. "You aren't going to do anything about it?"

"He didn't say that, *Ina*. We just have to go about it differently." Leo stood and gathered her in his arms.

"You can kill him now, Leo. I won't stop you." She whispered, clutching her mate tight.

"We have to go to the Eminzu, Lily." Fallon looked to Xavier for confirmation. His brother nodded.

She pushed Leo away. "They didn't help me before."

"Calm down, we'll figure it out." Leo reached for her again.

She slapped his hands away. If they wouldn't help, she'd take care of it herself. She turned and walked out of the office. The spiked energy hit her at the door, doubling her fury. Her form changed, her Eshu hair flowing behind her, alit with her magic. She opened her shields, feeding on the aggressive magic. She swayed as it saturated her. It strengthened her body, goosebumps covering her skin as power flowed through her.

She would kill Kedric herself when she found him. She headed for the portal room, growling at anyone who crossed her path. She dared someone to attempt to stop her. She was headed to Legba and the prince would pay for what he did to her sister. She would make sure of it.

Chapter 24

PACING HIS BROTHER'S OFFICE WASN'T WORKING. Leo took another lap anyway. He wanted to run after his mate, but Fallon had physically barred him from leaving. He rubbed his shoulder, still feeling his brother's grip.

"We have someone trailing her, Leo. She'll be fine." Xavier sighed. "We have to clear this up."

"I called ahead to the portal station in Legba. She won't get far. She can't go to the royal house. The queen will kill her before she admits her son did anything wrong." Fallon pointed out.

Xavier nodded. "We need to contact the Eminzu first. Nothing like this has ever happened before and I want to cover our asses."

Leo tuned his brother out as he pulled out his communicator and tried to contact Liliana again. He kept going back to the video, the images playing through his mind. How could Kita have bled to death? It was hard to kill a Demi. Only the darkest magic had the ability to do so. It was why his job was so effective. No one wanted to die, the Demi especially.

"Something is missing, Fallon."

His brother nodded. "No way had she died from the games they were playing."

Leo winced. What Kedric and Kita were doing could hardly be called games. Fallon's phone rang on his hip. He spoke quietly into it and hung up.

"Lily just came through the portal. She's safe."

He breathed a sigh of relief. Xavier waved his hand to get his attention. He scribbled some notes and ended his call with the Eminzu.

"Leo, I need you to request a formal meeting with the royal family. If it comes from me they'll get cagey and try to stall." Xavier stood from his chair. "Fallon go with him. I'll meet you both there. Rugaba has asked me to meet him in the council room."

He didn't need prodding. Worry for Liliana had him halfway out the door before his brother finished giving instructions. He pulled out his communicator and worked on getting a meeting set up as Xavier requested.

***

Rugaba's fingers drummed on the table in impatience. The two females bickered, their shrill voices riding his last nerves. He held his hands up, finally tired of it. The women went silent, not entirely of their own accord. They both clutched their throats, their mouths opening and closing in panic.

"Now that I have your attention." He intoned dryly. He released them from his spell, watching with disinterest as they took heaving breaths.

"I want to know about the danger surrounding your daughter." Rue addressed the mother, he didn't bother trying to remember her name.

She threw her hands up in frustration. "I want justice for *my* daughter. The Eminzu had us cover up her death for years citing bullshit about the bigger picture. Liliana is not my daughter, she was my burden."

The maid screeched and reached for the woman, going for her throat. Rue lifted the maid with his power, pinning her to a wall.

"There will be no violence here."

"She never deserved, Lily. She treated my daughter like shit!" The woman screamed. "I don't understand why she was made to suffer for our sins."

Rugaba sighed in relief as Xavier popped into the room, grateful for the interruption. The emotions in the room were heightened and made him uncomfortable. He let the maid down from the wall, slowly floating her to the floor.

"You've been accused of conspiring to kill one, Kita Iliana Marcolev, for that alone you are sentenced to death. I want details of your part in her daughter's death, and I want to know the circumstances of the danger surrounding the second daughter."

"I'm dead if I talk about that." The maid raised her chin in defiance.

Rugaba scoffed. "Just moments ago you were so aggrieved for that same daughter, but when given a choice between her life and yours, you, of course, choose yourself."

The maid looked torn. Worry and remorse shrouded her face. "They will kill me."

"You will die before the night draws to a close, so your worry is misplaced. Of course, death does not mean an end to your suffering. My brother is very creative about getting information, I'm told."

She spit in the mother's direction. "I will say nothing of Ofeere or anything to do with that, but I won't go down alone for getting rid of that whore Arian sainted as her daughter."

The council reared back in shock at her vulgarity. He suppressed a groan, clearly, this would take a while.

***

Leo rushed through the portal station, pushing past the crowd. Liliana had only been out of his sight for thirty or so minutes, and the need to reassure himself of her safety made him impatient. His heart settled into a slower rhythm when he saw her standing at the lift station. He nodded at the soldier in the shadows keeping an eye on her. She stood in the falling dusk, her feet tapping, arms crossed over her chest. Her aggravation and anger still burned across their connection, clearly, she'd not cooled off in the time she'd left.

She turned as though she felt his gaze and snorted in disgust. "I knew there was a reason a lift hadn't arrived yet."

Fallon shrugged. "It pays to know people."

She pinned her hands on her hips. "I'm going to the royal house whether you tag along or not. You're not stopping me."

She blew out a frustrated breath as a lift floated silently to a stop in front of them. Leo opened the door, waving for her to enter.

"I wouldn't dream of stopping you."

Her eyes widened in shock. Straightening her shoulders, she entered the airlift. She muttered a reluctant thank you and moved over for him and his brother to enter. No one bothered to break the silence as they rode to the castle. Nervousness had his leg bouncing though. His mate was angry, and rightly so. He only hoped she'd exercise caution in approaching the royal family. They had right on their side, but one thing he'd learned hunting, he could never fully prepare for how a cornered person would react. The queen was renowned for both her temper and the way she punished those with which she found fault. He couldn't imagine she'd allow them to sling around accusations at her son without reacting.

They were met at the royal station house by four palace soldiers in full dress uniform. Leo exited first, reaching back to help Liliana out of the lift. He guided her up to the castle with his hand on the small of her back. He mentally prepared for the confrontation ahead. Fallon stopped them at the door, quietly speaking with the guards. There was a bit of a ruckus, as the soldier refused them entrance.

The hairs on the back of his neck raised and he shoved Liliana back into the airlift. He called out to Fallon as the platform beneath them heated. He shifted into his Cagyn form, as flames erupted around him. Pissed, he manifested his sword and charged through the fire. He'd traveled through hotter temperatures than that every time he took a prisoner to Azreal. The soldiers stared at him openmouthed as he cut down the first one to attack him. He heard the whistle of air a moment before he ducked an arrow spinning past his ear. Pulling a gun from the back of his pants, he fired into the guards' tower, grunting as the archer fell. The courtyard fell silent as he held his gun against their captain's temple. It wouldn't kill the male, but he'd surely wish he were dead.

"I'm just pissed enough to fire my weapon whether you put yours down or not." He said mildly.

Fallon tossed the soldier he'd been fighting over the edge of the palace's pod. The male's scream got progressively quieter as he fell.

His brother peeked over the edge. "Damn shame. It's gonna suck for him when he finally hits the bottom."

Leo shook his head. "Now. Are we going to have any other problems?"

The remaining soldiers dropped their weapons. Leo glanced up into the tower, his finger flexing. More weapons were tossed from the tower and three pairs of hands were held up, out of the openings.

"Well, all right then." He pushed the captain from him and motioned for Liliana to join him.

She shuddered as she reached his side. "If they're fighting this hard at the door. Imagine how hard they'll fight once they realize why we're here."

Leo nodded grimly. "Stick close to me, please."

"Gladly."

No one else barred their way through the rest of the palace and before long, they stood at the heavy golden doors of the receiving room. Leo sighed. He'd been mated in this same room, less than a week ago. How fast the world changed around him. He reached for Liliana's hand and squeezed tight. Her fury and grief broadcasted loud and clear, her magic wild and wafting around her. He briefly wondered what all that energy was doing to his son.

He wanted to put a pause on what they were doing and take care of both his mate and his son. Maybe soothe the rough edges and calm Lily a little before dealing with the heaviness they were about to go through. His face tightened in anger and regret. He had a job to do, so he pushed aside those thoughts and focused on what was ahead.

"What are we waiting for to go inside?" Lily's touch prodded him from his thoughts.

"That would be me," Xavier said from behind him.

Leo lifted his eyebrows at the sight of his father next to him. "Why are you here?"

"Support." Ranolph left it at that.

They opened the door and entered the room together. The king and queen were on their thrones in full regalia, clearly expecting trouble. Kedric stood next to his mother, leaning on her throne, chin in his hand, his pose insolent. Liliana stiffened next to Leo, her anger ratcheting up a few notches.

"What is the purpose of this?" Queen Kaylin was the first to speak.

Xavier stepped in front of them all. "I've come in an official capacity." He pulled out a small box.

The room was silent as Xavier played the Oras they'd all earlier seen from the point of Kita struggling. The prince's face blanched, his skin paling. Queen Kaylin gasped as the video played out. When it was done King Leander broke the silence.

"All I see, at most, is an ethical violation. Kedric's only crime was in leaving her to die. He's not guilty of murder."

Liliana growled. Leo tightened his grip on her hand.

"We're not here for the prince." Xavier shut down the Oras.

"The hell we aren't." Lily snarled.

Xavier shot her a quelling look before pulling up another video. This one showed Liliana's maid Bea. Leo pulled his mate closer to him.

"What's going on?" Liliana whispered.

He shrugged. Hell if he knew. He didn't think it would bode well though.

Chapter 25

LILIANA SWAYED AT XAVIER'S DECLARATION. She stared at the image of Bea floating in the air between them and the royal family. She was confused. She looked at Leo, who studied his brother. He squeezed her hand again, and she clutched him like a lifeline. Grief was ripping her heart at having to watch the video of her sister's death again.

"See, I went to the Eminzu to ask what could be done to a prince who didn't have the decency to call for a shaman when his mate lay dying. Imagine my surprise when Rugaba himself informed me that the maid he had in custody had stories to tell." Xavier pointed at the wavering image of Bea.

Queen Kaylin choked and squirmed in her chair. Liliana's gaze volleyed between Xavier and the queen.

Xavier turned to Liliana. "Bea packed Kita's bags for every trip to Adro, correct?"

She nodded, a cold wave started from her fingertips, taking over her body.

"She packed it all. Clothes, sex toys, everything Kita needed for her monthly foray into the sadistic world she and her betrothed loved. You had her pack a little something extra this time though, didn't you?"

Dread pooled in Liliana's stomach, her legs shaking and going weak. "My God."

"Mother, you wouldn't." Kedric moaned.

"She dragged you down into her sick and sordid world. She wasn't good enough for you." Kaylin hissed.

"It's the prince who is sick!" Lily shouted in defense of her sister. "Kita only did it because she loved that twisted animal you call your son."

"Careful how you speak about my son." Kaylin's icy rebuke sent a spike of fear through her.

"She was my mate, mother." Kedric moved from his mother's side, shock and grief twisting his features.

"No way would I allow that stupid whore to run my kingdom." Kaylin was unrepentant. She adjusted the skirts of her dress.

"It is not yours to run." Leander spoke up next to her, "And now, in light of this I cannot even allow Kedric the kingdom."

"What?" Kaylin screeched.

"Who do you imagine taught our son all he knows, Kaylin? Surely not me." Leander gripped the sides of his chair. His jaw clenched in his fury.

"You can't be serious, father?" Kedric whipped around to face the king, anger mottling his cheeks.

Kaylin stood and advanced to the end of the dais. "You should've been dead!" She pointed at Liliana. "You're lucky the stupid Dziva I hired failed."

"Who did you hire?" Leo's deadly voice sent chills down her spine.

To say her mate was furious was an understatement. His magic sent sparks and sharp stings across her skin as he gripped her hand tighter. Kaylin turned her head refusing to answer.

"What could you have possibly gained from killing Liliana?" Fallon's baffled question distracted them.

"My son will rule Legba. I couldn't let her get pregnant." Kaylin speared Liliana with a death glare.

"You're too late." She snatched her hand out of Leo's and caressed her stomach. "I have an heir and he will be a better king than anyone from your poisonous tree."

"Your son won't see the light of day."

Liliana reeled back from the queen's angry hiss. "*When* my son takes the throne, if you are alive to see it, that is, I'll be sure to have my husband release you from prison long enough to watch him be crowned." Magic filled her, a yellow glow covered her skin as she made her proclamation.

Leo growled next to her, his pride in her words evident.

"Kedric will rule!" Kaylin shouted, spittle leaving her mouth.

"No one from your line will sit a day on my throne, Kaylin." Leander's quiet voice sliced through their argument.

"Father." Kedric protested.

"You allowed your mate to die, without so much as a whimper of help. The kingdom will never stand for you as their leader." Leander's voice rose with every word. "Hopefully with my grandson, I will get it right."

"You will take this kingdom from my son over my dead body," Kaylin whispered, shaken.

Xavier smiled sinisterly. "I'm glad you said that because that has been arranged."

Right before their eyes, Kaylin disappeared from the dais.

Liliana's hand covered her mouth, surprise leaching away her anger. "Shit."

"Mother?" Kedric's reached for the empty space where his mother disappeared.

"I can't punish you for your proclivities, nor your part in Lady Marcolev's death, Prince Kedric, but understand this, you are no longer welcome in the Atlanta Haven. As my sister now resides there, I want you nowhere near her or my growing nephew. It's decreed and should you disobey the order I will banish you."

Kedric paled. "You can't do that."

"I have done that," Xavier announced. He nodded to Lily.

She bobbed her head in acknowledgment of his effort. It wasn't the punishment she was hoping for, but she knew he'd tried. No other Haven reached the power level the Atlanta Haven achieved. The prince would have to settle for the lesser havens to feed and she would have to be content with that punishment. At least she wouldn't run into Kedric while she was at her new home, and that was a blessing.

Leander sighed in defeat as Kedric stormed from the room. He wiped a hand over his face. "The child will need to spend time here to learn his place." He glanced down at her stomach.

Liliana put a restraining hand on her mate as he growled in protest. "We will have him here every summer as soon as he reaches his eighth year."

"He will not be alone," Leo said through gritted teeth.

Leander cleared his throat but was unable to hide his growing excitement at the prospect of the child. "Of course. Whatever you decide."

"We have further business before the night is done." Xavier addressed Leo.

Leo pulled her into a hug and kissed her cheek softly. "Fallon and my father will see that you get home. I don't know how long this will take, but I want you to rest, okay?"

She nodded. She pulled him to her for another kiss. "If it's in you to do, I want her to regret messing with our family."

His eyes lit, the silver encompassing his pupils. "I swear it, my love."

He walked from the room in long strides, his retreating energy leaving her cold. She hugged herself and shuddered. With him gone, her mind cleared and she realized she'd never asked what Bea had told Xavier. She would find out herself.

"I need to visit my father." She announced.

Fallon acquiesced, guiding her back to the lift station. She wasn't leaving Legba until she got answers.

***

Leo stopped as Xavier halted just outside the receiving room doors. His eyes opened in surprise as his brother opened a portal directly to the Eminzu council room. He himself had the power to open a portal anywhere, he'd forgotten Xavier had the same power. They stepped into the bright light in the hallway, coming out into the dim room of the Eminzu. The council of elders was gathered at a long table on a raised dais, their gazes grim as he and X entered. Rugaba sat at the head of the table, the Eldest member of the council on the other end. He released his base form, knowing already why the god summoned him there. The burning of his body changing felt good, his Cagyn beast stretching, relishing the upcoming trip.

His mate had asked him to make sure the queen was punished and anticipation flowed through him. He took note of the fear entering Queen Kaylin's eyes. Grimly he observed the resignation in Bea's eyes. Her presence in the room didn't bode well for the maid. Liliana would be devastated, as she thought of the woman as a mother figure.

Rugaba's voice filled the cavern. "Between the Eminzu and the head of the Amanda, punishment has been decreed. You will both suffer the eternal death and be sent to Azreal."

The queen fainted and Bea moaned in fear as he stalked to them. Rugaba nodded to him and Leo rolled his shoulders, loosening his body for the long trip.

He clapped his hands once and drew out the spell for Azreal. The portal opened and he grabbed Bea's hands as she tried to move away from him.

"I have information you can use. Please, don't kill me." Bea pleaded.

Used to the pleading, Leo turned a deaf ear to it.

"My brother will have fun getting the information from you. Do not worry that it will die with you." Rugaba assured her.

Bea went limp in his arms, her breathing erratic. Shaking his head, Leo shifted her weight and reached for the queen. He slapped Kaylin to wake her. Her eyes widened and she screamed as Leo dragged both her and Bea through the portal.

Chapter 26

HER SHOCK QOUTA HAD BEEN reached for the day. Or at least that's what Liliana thought as they landed at her family's airlift pod. Her father's possessions littered the lawn, her mother's shrill voice reaching them outside.

"Gods in heaven, can this day not end." She muttered, using Fallon's hand for help out of the lift.

She rushed up to the keypad, hastily typing in the code to extend the walkway. She growled in impatience as it slowly crept towards the house. She'd thought coming to her father's house would be soothing. She'd get answers from Bea, wallow in the comfort of her father's hug and go home.

Now?

Who knew what she was getting into? She sighed in aggravation and pushed through the front door. All four of her aunts crowded her parent's common room, their expressions varying from anger to pity. They were packing away some of the sculptures that had graced the tabletops in her parent's home for years. They each swung their heads around to Liliana as she walked in.

"What's going on?" She was hesitant to ask.

Her oldest aunt rushed over to quickly answer. "Your mother is finally being rid of your deceitful father."

She reared back. "Excuse you?" No one talked about her father, especially not the women who'd never liked him.

"You heard her. I'm kicking your father out, and I want you to leave behind him." Her mother stormed past them in the foyer, opening the front door to toss out more of her father's luggage. She barely missed hitting Leo's father, who'd come up behind them on the walk.

"Papa!" Liliana called, pushing past her other aunts. She raced up the stairs and found him carefully packing his art into a crate.

He glanced up at her entering his room and sighed. "Lily."

"Why is mother kicking you out? What is happening?" She touched his shoulder.

They both turned at the heavy steps stomping up the stairs. Her mother rushed in, out of breath, her eyes manic.

"The Eminzu granted me release from my mating," Arian answered her question.

Liliana paled and sat on the edge of the bed. "What will you do, father?"

"I don't care where he goes, so long as it's not here. I'm no longer forced to look at your cheating face and that of your whore." Arian spat.

"Whore?" Lily turned to her father. "Is this true, father?"

"Tell her! Tell your favorite daughter how you cheated on me with our maid. Tell her all about the women you parade in that apartment you thought you were keeping a secret from me."

Her father slammed the drawer he'd been cleaning closed. "There has been no one since Bea! You will not continue to lie on me, Arian."

Magic swelled in the room as her parents squared off. Getting between them didn't even occur to her. She was still fighting to decipher their words.

"It's not slander if it's true." Arian's hair lit with her anger.

"It was once! Once, gods damn you and it was your fault besides." He argued.

Arian laughed bitterly. "It was not my fault you slept with her."

"You had her change her form into yours. I spent the entire weekend with a person I thought was my mate. You didn't want to spend time with your mate, so you sent your maid in your place. Don't act all saintly because your pride was hurt. You were punished because of your part in the farce."

Liliana's breath caught, her gasp breaking into their argument. Arian turned her attention to her, her eyes narrowing.

"Yes, well no longer. I no longer have to claim that bitch's child as my own."

Evan's hand moved before either she or her mother could react. The slap on Arian's cheek rang in the tense silence. "I will no longer have to stand aside while you disrespect *my* daughter."

"Father," Liliana whispered. Shock at both her mother's words and her father's actions froze her in place.

"Where was the outrage for our daughter when your whore had her murdered?" Arian hissed.

Evan turned his back on them. She remembered the video of Bea Xavier had displayed at the palace.

"The queen forced her to help." Tears clogged her throat. She didn't know that for sure, but it was impossible for her to think of Bea having anything to do with her sister's death.

Arian drew a shaky breath, tears cresting her eyes. "Forced her? They were in on it together." Arian's acerbic laugh chilled her. "His whore, your mother, helped the queen kill my daughter. All so she could put you in her place.”

“No.” Liliana backed away, her hand out warding away her mother’s words. “My mother? What are you saying? She would never.”

Evan put his head in his hands.

“Papa?” She had to be lying. Bea was her mother? She walked up to her father and shook his shoulder. “She’s lying, right? Bea would never do something like that. You wouldn’t lie to me about something as big as who my mother was. Tell me you wouldn’t, father.”

“I’m sorry, baby.” Evan tried to pull her into a hug.

“No!” She pushed at his hands. “She’s lying.” She whipped around to face her mother. “You’re lying to hurt me.”

Arian crossed her arms over her chest. “I don’t lie and I’ve never lied to you, outside of claiming you as my child. Your father and I have known for years that Kita was dead. But we weren’t told the circumstances of her death until now. And now Beatrice will pay for what she’s done with her life.”

“Papa, tell me it’s not true.” Liliana expected tears, but none broke through her numbness. Her body was cold, her hands shaking as she pushed her hair out of her face. “Please.” She whispered.

“Do you think I would allow you to take something which belonged to my daughter? Kita deserved to be queen. Not some servant’s bastard.” Arian waved a hand towards her.

“That.is.enough.Arian.” Her father growled, his power saturating the room. He took a step towards his now-former mate.

“What, are you going to hit me again?”

“You’re disgusting,” he whispered.

“And you’re weak.

Lily braced her hand on the wall for balance. She needed to leave. She told her legs that, but they stayed rooted to the spot as though cemented.

Fallon cleared his throat from the door of the room. "Liliana, are you okay?"

Her head lifted, her eyes meeting his. Compassion and worry swirled in his eyes. She didn't know how to answer him. No, she wasn't okay.

"No one invited you into this conversation." Arian put her hands on her hips.

"Your volume invited the entire house, madam. Never mind the spectacle you've created on your front lawn." Fallon mimicked Arian's pose. "If you don't want anyone to know your business, I would suggest lowering your voice."

"Don't, Fallon," Liliana whispered. "Don't engage her. She's like an Abiku demon, feeding off the misery of others." Determination flooded her and straightened her spine. This woman was not her mother. She no longer felt obligated to take her shit.

"How dare you?"

"How dare I? How dare *you* talk to me as though I were nothing? How dare you sit over there self-righteous about a mistake you orchestrated? This house was bought with my father's money. If anyone should leave it should be you."

Arian gasped.

"It should be your shit on the lawn, not his. It was your punishment to raise me?" Lily scoffed. "Not hardly. I lived with you berating me daily, talking down to me, and slapping me around. It was I who suffered the punishment. So you know what? Thank you. Thank you for releasing me from any sentimentality towards you. Congratulations on being released from your mating to my father. Good luck moving around society without his money to back you." Her chest heaved as she sucked in air.

"Get out!" Arian shouted.

"Gladly." Lily swept from the room and out of the house. Fallon and his father were on her heels. The airlift they'd taken to the house was still there. She breathed out a sigh of relief. At least she didn't have to sit on her parent's—no her father's— pod waiting on a ride out of this miserable situation.

They were all silent on the way back to the portal station. She was hollowed out. In the span of a day, she'd found out her sister was murdered, her mother was not her mom, and the woman who was had helped kill her sister. How did a person react to all of that? How was she supposed to go back to life as though it were normal? She lowered her head into her lap. Fallon's palm warmed her skin through her shirt as he rubbed her back in soothing motions.

"I'm truly sorry for what you're going through right now, sister."

The tears that had been trapped behind her numbness leaked from her eyes, soaking her jeans. She choked on them, not wanting to completely break down in front of them.

"You've got a right to grieve, lass. Don't hold back on our account." Ranolph's voice was gentle as he added his hand to her back as well.

Strangers had shown her more compassion than the woman who'd raised her and didn't that just sum up her life. The warmth of their touch sank into her skin and eased the cold knot of anger and confusion. While comforting, it made her wish for Leo. She wanted to curl into his strong body and be sheltered from the bad things happening. In the weeks they were together she'd come to rely on him, on his steady presence. Her communicator on her hip rang. She sat up and wiped her face. It was her father. Her breathing hitched.

"Yes, papa."

"I…I wanted to check on you. I'm sorry, Lily, I don't know how to fix this."

She sniffed. "It's not…" She couldn't even finish the sentence. She wanted to tell him it wasn't her business, but she desperately wanted to know, to understand.

He sighed, understanding what she needed. "I wanted a weekend out with your mother. We hadn't been out alone since Kita was born and I thought we could use a weekend to reconnect. It intersected with a huge social event your mother wouldn't miss. Cagyns can transform into any form, your mother convinced Bea to take hers. Long story short, we spent a weekend together and a month later Bea confessed she was pregnant. I went to the Eminzu, furious. We were all punished, for lack of a better word."

"So Bea really is my mother." She put a hand to her forehead, an ache forming behind her eyes.

"Yes." He didn't elaborate.

"And the rest?"

"You should talk with your brother-in-law. Perhaps he can better explain."

She nodded, though he couldn't see it. The lump in her throat prevented her from saying anything else.

"Can you forgive me for my part?"

"Papa." She sighed, she couldn't answer that yet. "Where will you go?"

"Well, your mother was right about the condo I have. It's near the market square and makes it easy to manage all of my properties. There have been no women though. I swear it."

"Why does she get the house?" It was petty, but she hated to think Arian would get the house she'd grown up in.

"Because she gets nothing else, Liliana. She'll be able to keep up appearances and I will be free of her and her sisters. Trust me, I got the better deal." His small chuckle lightened her heart. "Will you visit?"

"Of course." She whispered. "You're all I have left." She ended the call, pocketing her communicator.

Arian's words about Bea being put to death hurt her. She didn't want to think the woman she'd grown up loving had been complicit in something so heinous. The way Kita had died was cruel. No one had helped her. She'd died alone, probably confused and scared.

Fallon touched her shoulder to get her attention. "We're here. Let's get you home."

She nodded and followed them through the portal station, her head down, avoiding eye contact. Had the news spread yet? She didn't want to see the pitying glances or smug smiles, so she kept her gaze on the floor. Fallon guided her through the station and into a portal, his hand never leaving her back. Ranolph parted ways with them once they reached Haven. Fallon walked her all the way to the front door of the apartment she shared with Leo. She looked up when someone cleared their throat. Paul and Roy stood like sentinels at her door.

"Are you here to watch me?"

Paul shook his head. "We're here to say thank you. You saved our lives." He pulled a bouquet of flowers from behind him.

She took the flowers with shaking hands. "I'm touched. Thank you."

Roy saluted her and pulled a tray of pastries from behind his back. "I had Marta make them. I'm told only one other person in all seven realms knows how to make them."

Tears gathered in her eyes. "Thank you, Roy." She whispered.

He nodded and opened the door for her. Fallon took the tray from him and waved them off. They each touched her shoulder and left. Fallon took the flowers and tray of pastries into their small kitchen. He manifested a glass vase and filled it with water. She marveled at the finely etched vase he'd wrought. That someone so big could make magic so delicate. She smiled.

"It's beautiful, thank you."

He cleared his throat. "Leo is…he had to take the queen to Azreal. Time moves differently when he's 'traveling', so it could be hours, or it could be days."

"I understand." It was a part of his job. She'd better get used to it. While Rugaba had banned him from hunting, he would still be…traveling. It was the life of an Amanda soldier. No time like the present to start learning how to deal.

"If you need anything, and I mean anything, Lily, both Xavier and I are a phone call away, okay?"

She nodded. "For now, I need some alone time."

"Right." He kissed her forehead and left her in peace.

Once the front door closed, the adrenaline holding her together faded and with it her strength. She sank to the floor sobbing, her grief a living, and breathing monster on her back. Everything she'd thought she knew about her life was a lie. Would she ever get back her sense of normalcy?

Chapter 27

BRIGHT LIGHT FILLED THE SPACE AS FAR as the eye could see. The first level of Azreal was the easiest to cross, but nonetheless, his skin heated, burning with the intensity of the realm. Bea's wail of pain and the queen's screams were the only noise in this light realm. And even still, the sound of their caterwauling was muffled as though there was cotton in his ears. Leo released them in order to open the second gate. Both women tried to run, and Leo shook his head as he went through the intricate spell. Once the portal opened he turned his attention to his prisoners. Both fought through the dense atmosphere to run, getting no farther than an arm's length from him.

If he could laugh he would, but no sound would leave his mouth once he entered death's realm. He was as good as a ghost, intangible, mute. It had taken him a while to get used to that. Using the power bestowed to him by Azreal, he lifted the women with his magic and pushed them through the next portal. If the heat from the first one was bad, the cold of this one stung. Like blades flaying off the skin, the punishing temperature stole the air from his prisoner's lungs, their eyes wide and darting with panic.

Dropping them again, Leo went through the pattern for the third and final portal. This time slower, not because of the intricate nature of the spell, no, the power of Azreal was strong, slowing his movements, trying its hardest trap him here in this hell where it could feed off his soul. Many candidates for Death's messengers were lost here. As he went through the spell he could see them in his peripheral beckoning to him, beseeching him to help them.

Only he in centuries had been able to get through this final gate. The cold was getting to him though, stiffening his fingers as he fought to complete the spell. The women didn't try to escape, their bodies wouldn't allow it. They stood stiffly at his side, each second it took him to finish the spell, curling their bodies as pain dragged them down. He knew the discomfort he felt was amplified by one hundred for them. He breathed a sigh of relief once the spell was finished and the final portal opened. He stepped through first, using his magic to drag the others behind. Remembering his promise to Liliana, he pulled Bea through first, letting the queen linger a bit in the punishing cold. Her body had nearly folded in on itself by the time he pulled her through.

Azra's servants stood at the gates of Azreal, both nodding to him in greeting. The screams of his victims renewed as they realized this was the last leg of their journey. Silently each guardian approached the women. Leo hated this part, but couldn't leave until the deed was done. He watched as the guardians grabbed each female by the throat, their dark nails piercing their skin. They forced the women's mouths open, closed their jaws over their mouths and inhaled, deeply. Leo saw the moment their souls left their bodies. Their corporal forms went limp. The guardians dropped the bodies and they immediately turned to dust. They pivoted towards the gates, and blew out their breaths, releasing the souls into Azreal.

Once done, they turned back to Leo. He arched his brow in surprise as one of the guardians stepped to him. He held out his wooden staff, a necklace on a leather thong draped from the end. A small black stone dangled from the leather.

'You're to wear this from now on when traveling the portals.' The voice came from his head, the guardian's mouth did not move.

Nodding his understanding, he grabbed the necklace and put it on. The guardian stepped back into his place. They spun their staffs simultaneously until the symbols for the Eminzu glowed. This was the only realm where he could not open a portal. There was no escape from

Azreal unless these two beings allowed it. He tensed and stepped between the two staffs, expecting the pain that normally accompanied his travel through the guardians' portal. There was none and he was surprised. He landed on his knees, his energy all but sapped. He stayed in the kneeling position to regain his senses and catch his breath.

Xavier cursed and slid on the floor next to him, grabbing his shoulders. "Are you alright?"

Leo didn't answer. He was busy relearning to breathe. It was one of the reasons he never let his brothers know where he would be when he hunted. He knew the shape in which he returned to Earth and he knew they would worry. He was always sent back to exactly where he opened a portal and he never wanted his brothers waiting for him.

"I'm fine." He was able to finally croak out.

"I'm taking you home." Xavier grabbed his arms intending to help him stand.

"Give me a minute." He gasped as the air he breathed continued to burn through his lungs. Getting back was always a bitch. Again, the pain was less than he normally experienced, but coming back to the Eminzu's realm and not the oxygen-rich Adro was probably the reason why.

He swallowed after a few more shallow breaths. A small drop of blood dripped from his nose. "Lily can't see me like this."

"Is this why? Why you never gave us an extraction point for you, why you never told me…" Xavier stopped speaking as worry and fear for his brother overwhelmed him.

"It's my job, brother," Leo whispered.

Xavier shook his head and helped him to his feet. "You can recover in my office, Lily won't see you there."

He opened a portal and they walked through it and into Xavier's office. X put him on the sofa and left. He came back a moment later with a glass of water. He nodded his thanks and grabbed the glass from his brother. A sensation much like what divers called the bends overtook his body as he breathed in the air from Adro. His joints ached, his skin crawled and dizziness had the room spinning as he clutched the cold glass. Three deep breaths in and out and his body fought to regulate and accustom itself to the Earth's atmosphere. He sipped from his cup, knowing from experience not to gulp down the chilled water. He peeked up at his brother, noting the frown marring his face.

"I'm fine, X. It just takes a minute."

"Every time?"

He nodded.

"You're a bastard for hiding this, Leo."

"I know," Leo said quietly. He didn't bother explaining it further.

Xavier wouldn't want to hear it anyway. He would never understand Leo sparing him the stress of knowing the details of his job.

Xavier sighed and left him on the sofa breathing hard.

No, his brother wouldn't understand the lengths he and Fallon went to take some of the harsher parts of their existence from his plate. He lay flat on the sofa to wait on his body to recover. He briefly wondered how long he'd been gone this time as time on Adro moved much faster than both Death's realm and the ancestors' realm. Hopefully, Liliana wouldn't be too worried. Thinking of her, brought a smile to his face. He closed his eyes, he couldn't wait to see his mate.

He opened them as a shadow covered him. Ranolph was shuffling side to side, looking uncharacteristically nervous.

"I'm exhausted, *baba*. What do you need?" He sat up on the sofa, groaning as his muscles protested.

"I can't figure out where to start." Ranolph avoided his gaze.

"Can it not wait?" He crossed his arms over his chest, curious despite his exhaustion.

His father shook his head no. "I'll likely not have the courage to do this another time. I've been waiting nearly a week since you've been hunting."

Leo's eyebrows winged. His father did not have the courage for something? Now he was truly intrigued.

"I ran into your mother."

Leo grimaced.

Ranolph held up his hand to stem his argument. "I need to fix this thing between the two of you, somehow."

"There's nothing to be done, *baba*." Tired of discussing Sharine, Leo stood up and moved to go around his father.

Ranolph stepped in front of him blocking his passage. "I need to tell you this, son."

"Your mate slept with the Eshu king, I am their bastard. Neither of them stepped up to parent me, you did. The end. I don't understand the need you have to discuss this." Leo brushed an impatient hand over his head caught off guard to feel the longer strands instead of the buzz cut he normally wore. He looked down at his hands. His human skin was wavering, his exhaustion making it difficult for him to maintain the power needed to keep up the appearance.

His father cleared his throat. "It didn't exactly go down that way." He sighed, fidgeting with his shirt.

"Spit it out, father. I am tired and I wish to see my mate. Say what you need to say and let's be done with the subject." Leo reigned in the impatience in his voice.

Despite his age, he was still a son, wary of his father's discipline. His tone bordered on disrespectful, and he cringed, expecting his father to lash out. He and his brothers learned quickly that it was one of Ranolph's hot buttons. When his father's usual retort about his tone didn't come, Leo narrowed his eyes.

Ranolph sighed and lowered his hands to his side. "You know Leander and I were…are, we are really close friends. He came to me when Kaylin was unable to conceive. After nearly two hundred years of waiting, he was desperate. I offered to help him."

"There were better ways to help him without your mate having to sleep with him." Leo's dry tone was not lost on his father.

"It had to be done the natural way. According to Eshu laws, the monarch can only be conceived naturally. The rules around royal births are very strict."

"But not strict enough to prevent a bastard."

Ranolph sighed. "Leander's family has ruled Legba since the beginning of time. As long as the bastard is his, it's still legal."

"So you felt sorry enough for your best friend to pimp out your wife. This is supposed to make me feel better, why?" It certainly didn't change his mind about the whole screwed up situation that was his birth.

"There were more reasons."

Leo's laugh held no amusement.

Ranolph growled. "You don't understand. I had access to a prophecy. It was foretold that the Kokoro souls would be reborn, triggering the release of Ofeeree. The prophecy predicted a king, a strong king who would unite the seven realms together in order to defeat him."

"So, because your best friend needed an heir, one who would make a powerful king, the two of you decided to use my mother?" Anger was starting to build within him. What had made Sharine agree to sleep with King Leander? "Why are you telling me this now?"

"Sharine…she wants to be in the babe's life." He sighed. "I never meant for the two of you to have such an acrimonious relationship. I hadn't realized you would use it against her."

"My whole life you made it seem as though my mother had an affair with your best friend. Who did you think I would blame? I thought you were the victim of a cheating mate." Guilt, frustration, and shame warmed his blood and darkened his vision.

Ranolph hung his head. "I'm sorry. I could've been clearer about the circumstances surrounding your birth."

"You could've been less of an ass to my mother also. I took my cue from you."

When he thought back on the indifference with which he treated his mother…no wonder she made herself scarce. The only crime she'd committed, had been at the order of her mate. And then same said mate turned around and blamed her for it. Gods, why had he treated his mother with such contempt?

"I'm ashamed of my actions. And I'm ashamed to say, that once the deed was done, my jealousy wouldn't let me past it. It drove my beast crazy to know she'd laid with someone else."

"You sent her to him!" Leo reached and braced his hand against the wall, using it to keep him balanced. Already drained from traveling, the anger coursing through his body was quickly sapping his energy.

He knew more than anyone how persuasive his father was. He imagined it took nothing to convince a woman in love to do as her mate asked. Ranolph did it easily to the soldiers he'd led when he was in charge of the Amanda.

"Watch your tone with me. I am still your father."

Leo blinked at Ranolph's sharp tone. "But you aren't, not really. Not technically." Grief tightened his chest, bringing a lump to his throat. Sharine's absence when he was a kid took on more meaning. Perhaps she'd been avoiding his father and not him.

"I've been mad at her all these years." He whispered.

"I'm sorry about that, Leonalph. I was stupid and jealous, and Leander thought if we told you it would affect the outcome of the prophecy."

"I don't give a damn about a prophecy. You ruined my mother's life so you and the king would have someone powerful to control."

Leo had studied his father for years. He knew how Ranolph's mind worked, and he had always been motivated by power. Even as a boy he knew his father craved and hoarded power. It had been a source of pride for Leo, but how had he not seen the dirty work behind the scenes? He'd fallen for his father's ruse completely. He hadn't realized being head of the Amanda hadn't been enough for him.

"That's not true, Leo." Ranolph reached out and placed his hand on Leo's shoulder. "From the moment you gripped my finger as a baby, I've loved you. Yes, it started with the prophecy, but I wouldn't trade you for anything."

"I guess you were disappointed to learn that your grandchild would be king, and not I."

His father once again lowered his eyes, but not before Leo saw the gleam of anticipation. Even now he was plotting. Damn, why had he never seen the lengths Ranolph would go for power?

"Why didn't she tell me?" He whispered, rendered mute by the onslaught of realizations.

Ranolph rubbed his hands across his face and sighed. "After all the things I've said about your mother. Would you have believed her?"

A tear escaped and rolled down Leo's face, making him mad. Damn the man, he was right. He'd have never believed his mother over Ranolph. His world had revolved around his father and the Amanda. Loyalty for both ran deep.

"Well, we'll see how your plan pans out. With Queen Kaylin dead, it leaves the king free to mate again. Perhaps this will all be moot."

"You are still firstborn." Ranolph's stubborn confidence pissed him off. His father stepped forward and Leo swatted his hands.

"Don't touch me. And pray I get over being pissed at you before your grandson is old enough to move out on his own."

"No, Leo." Ranolph attempted to grab his arm.

Leo sidestepped him and rushed from the room.

***

Rugaba paced his atrium, his ceremonial robes billowing behind him as he turned to change directions. His brother had contacted him an hour or so ago his time to say the soul had arrived. Knowing his brother's technique, impatience wouldn't let him relax. Not many withstood Azra's torture and he imagined the scorned female he'd sent to death would be no different. The first few hours of a Demi's arrival to Azreal was the best time to question the soul. They would be still in denial, trying to bargain their way out of hell. He wanted the names of her compatriots and he would make a trip there himself to obtain them if he needed to.

"Luckily that won't be necessary." Azra loped into his atrium.

"Stay out of my head, brother." He snapped half-heartedly. "What did you find out?"

Azra held out a black stone, a white cloud of magic swirling inside.

"We're still working on her. I haven't been able to get anything, save a few names. I'm giving her a little more time to savor my methods."

Rue held up the stone and smiled grimly. "You will get to meet these names, presently."

"She mentioned the death of the Mina who inhabited the elder tree."

Rugaba reared back in surprise. "What did she say?"

Azra crossed his arms over his chest. "Remember the shit I gave you about prophecy? She was killed so she could be replaced with someone a little less helpful with regards to handing out prophecies. The new inhabitant supposedly can be persuaded to give out false prophecies."

"What?" He reeled. More than one governing body used prophecy to make decisions that impacted their realm. To know deliberate misinformation could be given out…how deep did this conspiracy go? He would talk to Eminzu about replacing who so ever occupied the Elder tree. He didn't want to risk them being corrupt. He nodded in thanks to his brother for the information.

Giving him a jaunty salute, Azra disappeared. Rue unlocked his brother's stone and lay it on a sheet of parchment. A tendril of smoke wafted up as the names were burned onto the page. Rolling up the sheet and discarding the stone, Rugaba opened a portal into Haven.

He found Leo as he was leaving Xavier's office. He was happy he didn't have to hunt him down. He tapped him on the shoulder. Leo jerked to attention, his eyes dazed for a moment. He blinked at Rugaba and cleared his throat.

Sympathy for the male made him cringe. Exhaustion was clearly written across Leonalph's face, but he needed these people found. He tossed the parchment and Leo snatched it from the air.

"I have one last job before you can rest."

Leo scanned the names on the list and nodded. "Your will be done."

***

The silence was the hardest part. Not the hard bench in her cell, or the relentless cold, no. It was how eerily quiet the Amanda holding cells were. Verity shuffled for a more comfortable position cursing as her elbow knocked the wall. She wondered, not for the first time, how long she would be required to stay in the cells. She'd been picked up trying to sneak back into the surveillance room. She needed information on both the shaman and the Cagyn's disappearance, and she had hoped her contacts there would be a lot more forthcoming.

The members of the guild were antsy when they realized Beatrice was missing. Even more so, once gossip reached them that she'd been picked up by the Eminzu. Speculation had run wildly as to why she was missing. Most centered on the death of the eldest Marcolev daughter as the reason. Arian Marcolev was making the social rounds, telling anyone who'd listen how her maid had been responsible for her daughter's tragic death. If it were true, then Beatrice was not just missing, she was dead. The guild had wanted to be certain, so she'd been sent back to Haven to find out.

And promptly sold out by her contact.

She wasn't too worried. The most they could have on her was some form of trespassing, maybe bribery. She'd slid a few gold coins to ensure her entrance into their surveillance room. At the most, she'd probably be in the cells for a few more hours until she was sent to Xavier for her punishment. While she wasn't looking forward to what he doled out, she was confident she could handle whatever it was. She'd most likely be suspended from the Atlanta Haven for a few years. She rolled her head, shrugging her shoulders. No big deal.

A sound broke through the oppressive silence and she perked up. A key turned in the lock on the outer doors and she strained her ears listening for the footfalls of a guard.

Nothing.

She frowned, knowing she'd heard the jingle of a key at the door upfront. Laying her head back against the wall, she closed her eyes.

"Hello, Verity." Leo's deep voice startled her.

A questioning smile tilted her lips. She'd not expected Xavier to send his brother. "Mated only a couple of weeks, and already you're reduced to menial tasks."

He chuckled, the dark sound grim. "No, I'm here to do the job I've had these last centuries.

Her heart started thumping. If that were the case…

"You're here for me?" She whispered. "On what charges?"

"Not my concern in the end. You helped Prince Kedric get rid of Lady Marcolev, for that alone, you deserve to die."

She waved away his words. "That's not a death offense. I didn't do anything to the girl."

He pursed his lips and shrugged. "Well, there were plenty of crimes on the Oras that Sergio was helpful in supplying to choose from."

Her head swam with the implications. Damn Sergio. Dead some days, she wished she could go back and make his death all the more painful. Though, from his screams, the spell they'd used was plenty painful. Now she would meet his same fate.

His hands started working in what she could tell was a portal spell. She swallowed hard, closing her eyes when a bright light flashed and swallowed her. She blinked rapidly when her knees landed on a hard surface. Wriggling her hands, she found them bound behind her back in lead-lined ropes. She panicked and looked around, her stomach plunging in dread as the Eminzu council room came into focus. Her sick feeling multiplied as she spotted members of her guild kneeling with their hands bound. Her heart pounded, fear acrid and boiling in her throat. She turned to look at the council, the robed figures hazy and out of focus no matter how she squinted. Rugaba sat at the head of the table, his energy haloing around him in a light too bright for her to look at for too long.

She knew what was next.

Her thoughts went to her family. Yes, she would pay for her crimes, but her family would as well. Regret for that was a bitter taste. She thought briefly of begging for her life, she didn't want to die yet. Rugaba's voice filled the chamber as he listed their crimes individually and she knew then asking for leniency was out of the question. She snuck a final glance at her partners wondering if any of them would attempt to fight. Their sentences were announced…death. She lowered her head as once again, in a flash of light a portal was opened. This one into a realm from which she'd not return.

Chapter 28

APPROACHING ON SILENT FEET, Rugaba watched Oya as she stood over her scrying well. The sharp pang of longing that stabbed through his heart shouldn't have surprised him, but he was shocked by its intensity. She was no longer his, but the passing centuries still offered no solace from the need. Too many arguments and harshly spoken words lingered between them. Enough perhaps to keep reconciliation an impossible dream. He dreamed of it nonetheless.

Her shoulders slumped and she turned to him, a resigned look on her face. They stared, their gazes locked, and as usual, a battle of wills commenced. He sighed.

"I've not come to cause trouble." He held out his hands, showing her the stones Azra recently brought to him.

"Your presence has heralded bad news lately." She clasped her hands in front of her.

The corner of his lip lifted in a smile that held no amusement. "War has been stalled."

"At least for now." Was her quick reply.

He nodded. She was right, it was only stalled for now. Where one group disappeared, another would take its place. It was the way it went.

"I have some information for you."

She eyed the stones. "From Azra?"

"Do you want it or…"

She growled and held out her hand. She was so dramatic. He chuckled, dropping the stones into her palm.

"There has been activity in and around the place where your village used to dwell." He said offhand.

"I'm aware. The Ajo you allowed to live have been actively searching for my old temple."

"We both know why." He debated his next words, unsure of how she would take them.

An offer of help to anyone else would've been met with gratitude. Oya's mood changed like the winds she controlled, so there was no way to know what she'd say. He settled with a passive…

"If you need me for anything…"

Her look of scorn amused him. One of those days then. He waved and left her realm. He'd done what he needed to do, delivered the information he felt she'd find useful. It was up to her what she did with it. Arriving on his realm, he chucked his ceremonial robes and decided rest was in order. For now, the crisis was averted. One couldn't ask for much more than that. Until the next disaster, he'd take the reprieve and use the time to prepare for the next.

****

A full week had gone by.

A week.

His brothers had not seemed worried. In fact, during what Xavier called her 'debriefing' his tone had been all business. Liliana chewed on the hangnail on her thumb, her feet curled beneath her on the sofa in their living room. She was going out of her mind with worry, and all Xavier wanted to do was wrap up Kita's case. The details were no prettier now than when they'd happened. She'd lost both Kita and Bea to Queen Kaylin's scheming. She hoped the woman died a miserable and painful death. While shocked by Bea's betrayal, a part of her missed her. Xavier had played the video of Bea confessing her part in Kita's death, and even after seeing it, she still couldn't find hate for the woman. According to Bea, the guild had found out about her part in Kita's death and blackmailed her into working with them. She knew Bea wasn't evil at heart, but her confession still hurt. Watching Bea admit to the things she'd done didn't impact her in the way it would've had Arian not already told her.

The malicious way in which her mother had imparted the news still made her nauseous. So many things about her childhood were answered by Arian's hateful words. Bea being her biological mother explained much about how the woman had treated her. She'd always felt closer to Bea than her own mother.

Liliana sighed.

Perhaps the first step in healing would be to stop thinking of Arian as her mother. Clearly, the woman didn't want the title. She pulled the blanket Bea had knitted her when she was a child tighter around her. She jerked to a sitting position as the keypad at the door beeped. Leo was home. Scrambling to stand, she fought to get her legs out of the blanket. Part of her wanted to rush into his arms, the other part wanted to play it cool. Once he came through the door, all thoughts of downplaying his arrival flew from her head. He looked exhausted and defeated. She raced to his side.

"Are you okay?" She touched his arm lightly.

He stared into their living room, not moving from the door.

"Leo?"

He blinked and looked down at her. "I'm fine."

She nodded, unsure of his mood. Clearly, something was wrong. She could nag it out of him, but instead, opted to wait. It had been a week since she'd last seen him. Starting their first evening together with a fight was just ludicrous. She stood on her toes and kissed his cheek. The hum of his energy she usually felt along their connection was quieted. He needed power for certain. She guided him into the armchair closest to them.

"Are you hungry?"

She didn't bother waiting for an answer. Keeping one eye on him, she called down to the kitchens and ordered an early dinner be brought to their room and left in the hallway. At the same time, using her magic, she started warm water in the bathtub. Coming up behind him, she wrapped her arms around him. Tension rode his shoulders.

"Let's go." She ordered, walking around the chair. She held out her hands and helped him up.

Leo passively followed her through their bedroom and into their bathroom. Pulling candles from the cabinets, she set about lighting them. She lit three, lining them at the foot of the bathtub. A low thrum started in the air, as the energy from the candles filled the space. She turned and started unbuttoning his shirt. He blinked, his gaze focusing on her hands. It was a predator's look, full of hunger. His eyes glowed, the magic around his form wavering. His human skin disappeared, and his Eshu form took over. He swayed as she removed his shirt. Alarmed, she checked their connection and realized just how low his energy was. His skin was cool to her touch as she lay her palms flat on his chest. Calling forward her magic, she pulled Leo down for a kiss. She poured power into the kiss, feeding him until his skin warmed under her hands.

He pulled back, separating their lips. "Enough, *ina*. You can't afford to give me too much."

Ignoring his concern she pulled him into another kiss. "Open for me, my mate. You're shielded too tight for me to help."

He sighed as her lips skimmed his jaw, his fingers flexing on her arms where he held her. She kissed down the column of his neck.

"The baby." He murmured, his grip tightening.

She bit down on his shoulder. "Will you trust me, please?" Her tongue circled his nipple. "Let me in, my love."

He hissed, pulling her closer. His erection bumped against her stomach as she scraped her teeth across his skin. He groaned and dropped his shields. His hurt poured into her hot on the trails of bone-deep exhaustion. Her heart ached for him. What had happened in the time when he was gone? Betrayal and confusion littered his aura. Pulling in energy from the candles she'd lit, she used her magic to amplify it and push it into her mate.

A hungry growl left his mouth right before he leaned down and devoured hers. His tongue speared between her lips dueling with hers. He nipped at her lips and lifted her body. She arched her back as they separated for air. Magic filled the room, and she funneled it to her mate, gasping as his claws ripped through her tank top. He used the sharp tips to cut through her bra. Her moan echoed around them as he plumped her breast, sucking her nipple into his mouth.

He set her body down on the sink and she wrapped her legs around his waist. Hazy smoke clouded the room, the power from the candles surrounding them, tingling across her skin. Shaking hands hindered her as she fumbled to open Leo's pants. She wanted him inside, needing to release the energy building in her body. Her hair was alit with her magic, the strands blowing and dancing around her face. He growled in frustration at her attempts and batted away her hands. He made short work of their clothes, shredding first his, then her yoga pants. He gripped her hips, careful of his claws. His skin writhed, the whorls on his marbled skin coming to life.

"Yes." She hissed as he positioned his cock at her opening. He pushed into her in a single stroke, as her body tightened around him, against the invasion.

"Gods, the feel of you." He whispered, catching her earlobe in his mouth. Her stomach tumbled at his words, warmth filling her.

"Faster." She canted her hips to take him deeper. Energy suffused her body, and she threw her head back, drunk off the power. She fed it to her mate, his magic rising up and melding with hers.

"Mine." He growled, his strokes erratic as they both neared their climax.

Her body tightened and pressure gathered in her womb as he suckled one nipple while pinching the other against the back of his claws. The edges of her vision dimmed, as an orgasm swept through her body. She exploded, power rippling across their connection. Leo growled, his release heating her womb. Their harsh breaths were the only sound in the room. She waved her hand, dousing the candles and plunging the room in dim darkness. Light from Leo's skin painted the walls, the amber light dimming with each breath he took as he reigned in his power. Her hair lay across her back in a damp curtain.

He kissed her softly, lifting her from the sink, still inside her. He walked to the tub, sinking and withdrawing within her with every step. By the time they reached the tub, he was hard again. He stepped in the bathtub and rested her back against the wall. Their lovemaking was slower this time, his strokes leisurely as he kissed her breathless. Their magic steadily climbed, the sex feeding them both energy until orgasm swept through their body.

He sighed his pleasure, his teeth raking down the column of her throat. "I love you."

"I love you too." She whispered.

He pulled out, lowering her legs from his waist. Turning her, he moved her hair to the side as they both sank into the welcoming warm water. Silence filled the bathroom, the only noise coming from their shifting in the water.

"How did you do that?" He asked moments later.

"Do what?" A yawn surprised her.

"I'm going to assume the candles." He lifted her hands and nibbled on her fingers. "Not as effective as a Haven club night, but certainly a good amount of power raised."

"Oh…that. Yeah, they're not made to replace a feeding, but they do come in handy when you're on the run, low on energy and can't get to a Haven. That's the most power I've ever raised with the candles."

"Sex helps."

She chuckled, yeah, sex definitely helped boost the power in the candles. That's something she didn't have the luxury of trying while she'd been on the run. She kissed his hand.

"I'm happy you're home. Does it always take that long when you're out?"

He snuggled her closer, water slipping over the side of the tub. "How long was I gone?"

"You don't know?"

"Time moves differently in each realm, so depending on where I pick up my charge, and the time I lose in the realms of Azreal, I can never keep up."

She shuddered. "I don't like it."

"It's part of the job, *ina*." He trailed kisses along her neck.

"I know. I still don't like it." She sighed. "I know how much you love your job. You'll have to forgive the occasional nagging about it."

He smiled against her skin. "If I can come home to this, feel free to nag as much as you see fit."

She pinched his leg. His laugh warmed her heart. Especially after the riotous feelings he'd had earlier.

"What happened, Leo? Your emotions were all over the place."

He stiffened and growled in aggravation. "I ran into my father on the way in here."

"What did he say?"

"Everything I believed about my childhood was a lie. I've treated my mother in a deplorable manner, and every excuse I'd used to justify it was a fabrication."

She could relate to the sense of betrayal something like that would cause. "Sharine is still here, there is time to repair the hurt."

He was silent, his fingers tracing absently along her skin.

She let it go. He would contact his mother when he was ready. "It seems we both have faced hard truths these past few days."

"Speaking of hard truths. Kedric was sentenced to death."

"What?" She whipped around the face him.

"He was a part of a guild that was actively working to free Ofeeree. He was named with a few other very high-ranking Demis."

Gods. She put her hand over her mouth in complete shock. "Why would he do something like that? Why choose them over running the kingdom?"

Leo brushed a hand over her shoulders. "Well, with Kita dead, he wouldn't get the kingdom. His mother nearly lost their family the crown by taking so long to reproduce. A sterile king would never be allowed to take the crown."

"Gods, I never thought of that," she whispered.

"I know we couldn't punish him for the death of your sister, hopefully, this will give you some closure."

"I don't care why he died. He's dead, I can live with that." She turned back and resettled in his lap. She ran the information around in her mind, waiting to feel something. Some kind of vindication. There was nothing. She sighed. "I can't even work up a proper reaction after everything that's happened this past week."

"What happened while I was gone?"

She sighed and told him about her visit to her father's house, and watching Bea's confession. He hugged her tight.

"I'm sorry I wasn't here for you, *ina.*"

"You're here now." She turned a little and brought his head down for a kiss. "I've spent the past week in and out of Xavier's office. I'll be happy to not step foot in there for a while."

Thinking of his brother's office made her think of the huge landscape he had behind his desk. She had an idea. "You know what? Now that the danger is past, we should go to Chuita and hang out on the beach for a week or so."

"I haven't been on the Cagyn realm in a few years. That sounds amazing."

She sat up, excited with his agreement. "We can take our bonding period there, like a human honeymoon. No comms, just us, black sand and beautiful sunsets."

"Hmm, no comms." He looked into her eyes, a small smile playing along his lips. "Let me talk to Xavier first, but I think it's a great idea.

"We can get to know each other, pretend the shitty aspects of our family don't exist." She turned around and settled into his chest. She wrapped his arm around her.

"That sounds perfect." He rubbed the top of her head with his cheek. "Have I told you how happy I am with our mating?"

Her breath hitched. "Despite my initial misgivings, I couldn't be happier."

"We'll make it work, yes? We won't be like our parents." His wistful tone brought tears to her eyes.

Unable to speak past the lump in her throat she could only nod her head.

"There's so much in this world we have no control over. We can control ourselves, though and how we treat each other." He turned her to face him, more water sloshing over the edge. "I swear to treat you with respect, to hold you and our children above all else, even my job."

She gasped at his declaration. She knew how much he loved the Amanda. She straddled his lap and cupped his cheeks. "I swear to treat you with respect and to love you and our children until the last breath leaves my body."

He closed the distance between them, sealing their vow with a gentle kiss. "I love you."

Tears flowed freely down her face. "I love you too."

Epilogue

Six months later

"IF YOU TELL ME TO BE PATIENT one more time, I'm going to choke you," Liliana growled and threw a small pillow at Leo.

He laughed and ducked the projectile. He wagged his finger. "What happened to respecting your mate?"

They were seated in the middle of their living room on pillows. Lit candles encircled them, the soothing smells, supposedly helping them concentrate. From the disgruntled look on his mate's face, he assumed it wasn't working. They'd been attempting for the last hour to bond with their son, and Lily had reached her quota for patience close to thirty minutes ago.

"Why is it easier for you to bond with him?" She pouted and threw another pillow at him. "I'm the one carrying this energy leech."

He snickered and ducked the next pillow sent flying. "What did the Kira say? He would feel your tension and run the other way."

"Being referred to as an energy leech can't possibly be helping," Fallon remarked dryly, entering their apartment without knocking. He carried a tray, no doubt from the kitchens.

Liliana adjusted to life at Haven as though she were born there. It had taken her no time to get to know the giant staff it took to run the place. She knew nearly all of their names, going out of her way to help wherever she was needed. Everyone who came into contact with Liliana loved her. A well-placed smile and his mate could get anything she wanted within the walls of Haven. He knew now how she'd survived on Adro all those years alone. Lily talked to people, all types of people, all with the respect she gave to royalty.

She still nurtured the contacts she'd made while she was on the run, much to his chagrin. Whether it be supplies, information or just a listening ear, it became known that Liliana could find it and get it. Soon there was a line outside their door of people asking her for help. She'd appointed herself their advocate and had moved into an office on the ground level of Haven. She borrowed furniture from other empty offices and hired an assistant all within a week of them getting back from their honeymoon. That she'd accomplished it all without asking Xavier's permission amused the whole complex. For the first month, they'd all held their breaths waiting for him to go off on her. Instead, he'd surprised everyone by having the personnel files sent down to her office. He took it a step further and converted the office next to her into a nursery for when his nephew was born.

She was spoiled. That was all there was to it.

Fallon set the tray full of pastries on the dining room table. "You're so impatient, Trouble." He walked over to his sister in law and touched her stomach as she stood. The barely-there mound moved under his hand.

She slapped his hand away. "I hate you guys."

"She's grumpy, Fallon. Seems our son already favors me." Leo handed her a cookie from the tray, knowing the sweet treat would improve her mood. She desperately wanted to connect with their child, but the stubborn bugger was steadily ignoring his mother's efforts.

"It's not fair," she whined, chomping on the cookie.

"*Ina,* you have time. There are still six months left of your pregnancy, you two will bond." He gathered her in his arms.

She snuggled into his chest, sighing in frustration. All was right in his world, as far as he was concerned. He and Liliana were settling into a rhythm with their mating. Sharine and he had finally sat and had a conversation. There was still a distance between them, but they were working on it. His mother and Liliana got along now that a grandchild was on the way. Where she'd been scarce during his childhood, every time he turned around he bumped into Sharine. 'Just checking on, Lily' she would say. He was glad the two of them were getting along.

Every time he thought about his father's lies he got angry. He hadn't spoken to him in months, despite his father's pleas. He needed time to work through it. Ranolph had taken residence in Haven to help Xavier with locating the remaining Kokoro soul, so he saw his father regularly. Eventually, he would forgive him…he hoped.

Liliana tapped his nose. "What's wrong?"

"Nothing. I have no complaints." He kissed her, angling his head to deepen it.

Fallon groaned. "You two are too much for me."

"No one invited you into our room." Leo quipped.

"I brought your mate sweets, and this is how you treat me?" Fallon put his palm over his heart.

Liliana shook her head at them. "I can't wait until you're mated, Fallon. I'm going to wait until you're looking deep into her eyes, and unbuttoning her blouse…then I'll bust into your room just to chat."

Leo caught the longing in his brother's eyes a moment before he hid it behind a smile. It was interesting. He hadn't realized Fallon was in the market for a mate.

"Whatever you're thinking, don't." Fallon pointed a finger at him.

He held up his hands. "I'm not thinking about anything." Except…well, he knew a few single women that may be just the right fit for Fallon.

"I'm down with whatever plan you're cooking in that mind of yours." Liliana kissed the hollow of his throat and left him to pick through the tray Fallon brought with him.

He didn't have a concrete plan as yet. He smiled at his mate, but the beginnings of an idea began to take shape in his mind. His brothers deserved the same happiness he'd found. Perhaps he would just help things along.

What could be the harm in that?

About the Author

I am a full-time photographer, and a mom of two. I've been writing my whole life, and after the birth of my first kid, I decided I couldn't very well bring up a fearless human without first trying the things that scared me. So, I wrote my first book, and then subsequently more.

I write stories that I've always wanted to read: love stories that feature brown girls like me. I love the thought of fantastical creatures and worlds where anything is possible and that's what I bring in my stories.

My website, where you can get news and sneak peeks of upcoming books: http://www.driaandersen.com/

Other titles by Dria Andersen

Destiny Series

A Destiny Awakened

A Destiny Revealed

Haven Series

Haven

Soul Bonded

Paranormal Titles

Chasing Savannah

Hers to Call

www.ingramcontent.com/pod-product-compliance
Lightning Source LLC
Chambersburg PA
CBHW021133110726

47900CB00002B/332